FLAWLESS

Michael couldn't pinpoint exactly what it was about this woman that made him want Kayla more each time he saw her. He loved the way the corners of her mouth turned up slightly, giving her the appearance of always smiling. Her soft, gentle brown eyes always seemed to invite him into her soul, even when her mouth said no. The sound of her voice excited him. In his mind, Kayla Marshall was the one.

Once they settled down to watch the movie, Kayla turned off the lights and lit scented candles that gave the room a dim, romantic glow. Michael put his arm around her shoulder and she nestled closer to him.

Suddenly Michael stood up. "I forgot something," he said. "I'll be right back."

He returned from the kitchen with the chocolate-covered strawberries and napkins. He sat down and placed one of the berries gently in Kayla's mouth. As she felt the juice run down her chin, Michael dabbed at it with a napkin.

"Mmmm, Michael, this is sooo good."

When she opened her eyes, he was staring intently at her. His piercing brown gaze penetrated down deep into her soul where she'd never allowed anyone to go. She felt exposed and uneasy. "What are you thinking, Michael? You look intense."

"Do I? It's just that I enjoy watching you. You're so unique, so very beautiful, inside and out."

He caressed her face with gentleness and longing. His touch sent electric pulses through her and she knew she had to have him. Michael was the kind of man she wanted to hold her, kiss her. And to make love to her.

Flawless

CAROLYN NEAL

ARABESQUE
BET
BOOKS

BET Publications, LLC
http://www.bet.com
http://www.arabesquebooks.com

ARABESQUE BOOKS are published by

BET Publications, LLC
c/o BET BOOKS
One BET Plaza
1900 W Place NE
Washington, DC 20018-1211

All Kensington Titles, Imprints, and Distributed Lines are available at special quantity discounts for bulk purchases for sales promotions, premiums, fund-raising, and educational or institutional use. Special book excerpts or customized printings can also be created to fit specific needs. For details, write or phone the office of the Kensington special sales manager: Kensington Publishing Corp., 850 Third Avenue, New York, NY 10022, attn: Special Sales Department, Phone: 1-800-221-2647.

First Printing: April 2004
10 9 8 7 6 5 4 3 2 1

Printed in the United States of America

For my grandmother Louella Harrison, whose legacy lives on through her daughter, grandchildren, and great-grandchildren. We love you.

ACKNOWLEDGMENTS

Thanks to my husband, Michael, for the love and support you've provided the past two decades (yes, it does get better with time). Much thanks to my son—never give up on your dreams. Be all that you want to be. You never complained about the missed meals, and the late-night pats on the back were the best. Your energy and love inspires me. To my best friend and sister, Rita, your encouragement is the root of my determination.

Last but absolutely not least, thanks so much to the wonderful staff at Arabesque. Demetria Lucas, I can't thank you enough for bringing this book to fruition.

Chapter 1

"Southwest flight four twenty-three service to Chicago is now boarding at gate . . ." the agent droned as Kayla sat waiting to board her flight. She wondered if they ever got so bored with the same recital they could scream. She could certainly recite the instructions almost verbatim as she smacked her lips dryly, thinking *I guess there are worse ways to make a living*. She, in fact, was ready to scream.

Once seated with seat belt buckled, she reflected on the comedy of errors of the past few days and her stomach did a low rumble. She and three coworkers had gone to St. Louis to pitch an ad to a large chemical company. The others had been asked to leave, while she stayed on to finalize the pitch after the VP of marketing had tired of their shenanigans.

She thought about her coworker Sally Rogers, whom Kayla had begun calling the "It Girl," for she was known to give "it" up to any- and everybody. Even during this business trip, the It Girl had unexplainably had sex with just about every decision maker on the committee. Always dressing provocatively and batting those eyes so heavily encased in mascara that when she blinked they looked as though they were waving, she guiltlessly flirted with any man who had a pulse and a hefty credit line at Neiman's, Saks, Lord & Taylor, or some other pricey retailer. "Probably looking for a father figure," Kayla had surmised on more than one occasion.

Edward Oswell, "Blue Blood Extraordinaire," had been in absentia most of the time, choosing instead to play golf, and not having enough decency or sense to be discreet about it. He did, however, make it to dinner at the four-star restaurant Tony's, which the company had hosted. His arrogance and ill manners irritated her, but the other blue bloods on the committee seemingly overlooked them, due no doubt to some influence from his rich father.

And finally her personal favorite, Thomas "Tommy Too Drunk" Cronin, the only person in the world who consistently smelled of alcohol, breath mints, and Obsession cologne, no matter what time of the day or evening he greeted you, be it 9:00 A.M. or 9:00 P.M.

She hadn't wanted to team up with the notorious three because of their reputations within the company, but when all was said and done, her protest had fallen on deaf ears. Now she wondered what lies and innuendoes about her would be circulating around the company since they'd all have to justify why they returned without her.

Once the captain gave clearance, Kayla took out her laptop and began detailing the meeting in the journal. Having missed her flight the previous evening as the presentation had gone on longer than planned, she spent another night and now would be getting home late in the afternoon with just enough time to make her friend's wedding. *Yes,* she thought, *there are worse ways to make a living,* as she sat looking out at the billowing white clouds that lulled her away to a fitful sleep.

***

"I can't believe you're doing this to me, not now, not today." Slamming the phone down in its cradle, Kayla had sworn to herself that she wouldn't allow him to keep her waiting more than a few minutes. Slumping down onto her soft, overstuffed living room sofa, she shought about the promise made just last weekend, when he'd kept her waiting over two hours for a date. Finally arriving, he came with a trite apology and the sweet, sickening smell of one of those economically priced perfumes endorsed by some famous designer or celebrity, but still smelled cheap. In her mind that was worse than plain old cheap perfume. Any woman who wore bogus perfume couldn't be trusted, she decided, nor could any man who kept company with her.

Having been ready for two hours, and having called him at least four times, she found the thought of an accident snaking through her mind like a river, without a real beginning or ending, just an unsubstantiated thought or excuse. This wasn't just any date, this was something special, and she couldn't believe he'd stood her up again.

The waiting had served one purpose, it gave her plenty of time to think about her seemingly limbo situation with Justin. Lately their relationship had become like running on a treadmill, lots of energy and effort expended running, but going absolutely nowhere. She'd begun wondering when the payoff was going to come. Three years was long enough to wait for any man to decide what a woman meant to him and to make plans based on that meaning.

When she finally decided to leave for the reception,

she wasn't in the mood to congratulate anyone. She'd already missed the wedding of two dear friends, and now she'd be late for the reception. Giving herself the once-over for the umpteenth time that afternoon, she decided the look would have to do, even if the dress was a little snug around the hips and revealing more cleavage than necessary to be flattering.

The VP of marketing at the chemical company had been impressed with her presentation and tentatively closed the advertising contract. She pondered how she could be so confident in business and have her love life in such upheaval. Kayla was on the fast track at work, and the more she accomplished, the more driven she became. In her office hung a framed saying by Harry S. Truman, that read BEING PRESIDENT IS LIKE RIDING A TIGER. A MAN HAS TO KEEP RIDING OR BE SWALLOWED. That summed up the competitive nature of the advertising game in her mind, and she savored every minute of it.

Deciding to escape the contradictions of her life once she was inside the car, she turned on the CD and sang along to its mellow sounds. It was a perfect day for a beautiful May wedding. The sky was a lovely blue, the temperature was warm, but not hot. It was typical Chicago weather for the time of year. As Kayla drove her car toward downtown she wondered if she'd ever meet a man she'd love and trust enough to marry.

Her soul was that of a romantic, but all she'd managed to do in the past few years was kiss a lot of frogs. There hadn't been one that turned into a prince. At one time she'd hoped that Justin would someday get down on one knee and lovingly plead with her to marry him, promise her a lifetime of happiness, filled with love and passion.

But then her thoughts drifted to reality; it was the song by Erykah Badu about the bag lady and she knew there was a lot of emotional baggage in her life she'd eventually have to extirpate. She had loved the song the first time she heard it and knew all too well the metaphor the artist was conveying. She was definitely a bag lady, although she hadn't determined which kind.

Inside the reception hall, the dance floor was crowded with couples slowly dancing to the soulful singing of Luther's "Here and Now," which Kayla swore had become the national anthem for wedding receptions. She thought that singing to her favorite songs in the car had mellowed her mood, but seeing the couples dancing so intimately made her think of Justin and instantly she became melancholy.

Hesitantly walking into the foyer of the room, she was looking for Debra and Kit, the newlyweds. Feeling guilty for missing the wedding, she wanted Debra to know she was there for the reception. No excuse for Justin's absence had come to mind. Her friend had been in similar situations with men and would understand. No in-depth explanation would be necessary. Quickly deciding she wasn't in the mood for such an auspicious occasion, she made her goal to find the newlyweds, congratulate them, extend her love and support, then leave.

All she wanted was to go home and curl up with a book and her favorite companions: a quart of butter pecan ice cream and some music. Maybe she could catch something on the Lifetime channel that would fit her mood more appropriately. She loved the stories inspired by actual events about women who'd triumphed over some type of adversity, even the ones with the *he done me wrong, but I not only got even, I got rich and found me a real man* theme.

But escaping into a he-done-me-wrong story was the last thing she needed. Her mind returned to the previous idea of a book, ice cream, and music. Thoughts were running rampant in her head.

Not paying attention to her slow descent down the reception hall steps, she caught her heel on a loose piece of carpeting, causing her to lose balance. Just as she veered forward, threatening to fall, two lean, hard arms reached out, grabbing her firmly but gently, saving her from imminent descent. Taking in all the air her lungs could hold, she gasped for a breath. When she turned and looked up, there were two of the most sparkling, smiling, deep-pooled brown eyes ever created. His dark, curly hair was cut short, and he smelled faintly of citrus and sandalwood.

The air rushed through her mouth as she sputtered, "My goodness, thank you so much, I can't believe I just did that. What an absolute klutz."

"No problem, you looking much too good to end up sprawled out on the floor." They both laughed an easy, comfortable laugh that sang with anticipation. He had the nerve to have two of the sexiest dimples in his cheeks she'd ever seen. His eyes had a youthful, innocent appearance that reminded her of mischievous boys before they become worldly men.

Smiling broadly she gushed, "I guess there's a compliment in there somewhere. Thanks again."

As she balanced herself and turned to walk away, he replied, "You're welcome, Miss . . ."

"He's trying to flirt with me, probably here with some obsessed female ready to chase me away right now," she mumbled in a low voice to herself. Turning around just in time to see that boyish, dimpled smile spreading, she answered, "Marshall . . . Kayla Marshall," and instantly knew he was trouble when she felt a slow, sensual humming in the pit of her stomach. Her life was complicated enough.

Find Deb and Kit, congratulate them, and get out of here raced through mind again. He extended his hand, giving her no choice but to extend hers.

"Michael James, nice to meet you, Kayla. Are you a friend of the bride or groom?" He held her hand a fraction too long, but it was a nice fraction, so she didn't remonstrate. Letting go, he then put his hands casually behind him and stood back on his heels as if gearing up for a conversation.

"Both, we all work together." Those brown eyes were making her feel comfortable and awkward at the same time. Unsure of herself, she spoke ever so politely. "Excuse me, Michael, I think I'm gonna get a drink and find a seat. Thanks again for saving me from the fall." Smiling once more, but feeling it to be inadequate, she turned to walk away, somehow knowing he'd persist.

"If you don't mind, I'd like to join you. Sometimes it's not safe for a single man to be at one of these functions unescorted."

The comfortable feeling took over her as a huge smile lit up her face. She couldn't help thinking, *Finer than any man should be with a sense of humor, and did he say single and unescorted?* His return smile was equally as broad as he took her arm gently and escorted her to a nearby table.

"What would you like to drink?" He had manners, a rare trait. She couldn't help giving Michael a warm, heartfelt smile.

"Well, considering the day I've had, a rum and Coke sounds good." She didn't have time to be pretentious, ordering something like a mimosa. Instead, she opted for something with a bite.

"I'll be right back, and please don't stop smiling." It came out sounding staged and artificial, she thought, a weak pickup line she was sure he'd probably used hundreds of times. No, she thought, as fine as he was, probably more like a million.

"What?" Her smile turned cynical, as she wondered what kind of cat-and-mouse game he was playing.

"It's just that when you came in you looked like you were on a mission, but your smile seems to light up the room."

That's it! she thought. *He may as well have said, "Do me, baby."* At least that was more direct. Not this corny, unimaginative you-light-up-the-room line. What happened to the innocent boyish charm? she wondered. Surely he could come up with something more original and creative.

Grabbing her purse and getting up, she fumed, "Listen, Michael, I really do thank you for saving me from the fall, and offering to get me a drink, but I'm not in the mood for this."

"Kayla, in the mood for what? I just sincerely complimented on your nice smile. Just let me get you that drink and I'll leave you alone." He recoiled from her, his shoulders dropping slightly, looking genuinely hurt.

Suddenly feeling guilty about making a snap judgment, she apologized. "I'm sorry, it's been an incredibly bad day, I'm just in a foul mood. I didn't mean to take it out on you. You've been nothing but charming since I walked—excuse me, make that tripped—into the room. I'm sorry." The sincere look in her soft brown eyes made her apology acceptable and inviting.

"Well, at least stay long enough to enjoy some good music and have a drink or two. It may relax you." His smiling eyes, coupled with a tempting boyish grin, were working overtime as he turned to leave. Kayla found his charm a bit disarming. She liked dealing with scoundrels—at least you knew exactly what they were. Men like Michael usually hid their flaws until you'd fallen in love. Then that huge flaw would hit you like a Texas tornado, devastating and without warning, leaving nothing but destruction and sadness in the aftermath.

His black tailored suit couldn't camouflage his solidly built body; his broad shoulders and narrow waist couldn't be hidden, or ignored. He obviously took care of himself, not overly muscular, but lean and hard, like a runner. She could still feel his big hands around her arms from when he'd broken her fall. Nice and strong, but at the same time gentle. He was just over six feet tall, and sexy beyond description, although his solid build made him appear shorter. He had a nice walk, more like a confident stride, and with a butt that made her fan and pray silently as if she were in church. She shook her head as if to clear the thoughts that were starting to form about this man and his beckoning bottom.

Glancing around, looking for familiar faces, she nodded at a few people from Lancer and Newhouse, the advertising firm where she worked. Just as she was about to cross her legs, he was there with two drinks, looking admiringly at her legs. Quickly averting his eyes, he appeared to be uncomfortable at being caught looking, but not enough to discourage him from setting the drinks down and grabbing the chair next to her. "I'd like to join you, if you don't mind," he said.

She welcomed the company. Now she wouldn't have to engage in some meaningless dialogue with phony coworkers.

Michael was immediately attracted to Kayla but from the way she'd just reacted he knew she had a history with men that wasn't favorable. He had glanced at her several times as he waited for their drinks at the bar. She was naturally beautiful with auburn hair that hung just past her shoulders. Perfectly arched eyebrows framed the most beautiful brown eyes he'd ever seen. Her figure was soft and curvy, perfect for him, he thought. He was determined to get to know this woman no matter how difficult she made it.

"Thanks again, Michael . . . right?" She hoped he wouldn't guess that she was pretending not to remember his name, because he definitely wasn't someone she'd forget. She was the first to admit to being a hypocrite, and hated when men tried to be coy; it was a woman's exclusive domain. Anyone who watched the Animal Planet channel knew that it was always the female who played hard to get, ignoring the male while he did all the posturing and preening, sending out those signals of sexual attraction.

"That's right. So, Kayla, tell me about this 'incredibly bad day' you've had. Maybe it'll help put things in perspective."

Sipping on the drink and getting lost in those deep brown, sparkling eyes, she began to feel comfortable again. "I think I've already put it into perspective," not meaning it to sound as low and suggestive as it had flowed from her lips. Somehow this man was making her forget she'd just met him. She straightened her back, and squared her shoulders as if that would somehow get her back on track. She looked away and thought, *That sounded too much like flirting.* Her eyes returned to his handsome face. He slowly delivered her such a beautiful, warm smile that if she lived to be a hundred it would be remembered. He had one of those smiles that made women go to Victoria's Secret and purchase sexy but uncomfortable underwear.

When the band started playing Maxwell's "Fortunate," one of her favorite songs, she began to sway side to side, rhythmically, in her seat. It didn't take Michael long to extend his hand and ask, "Would you like to dance?" He was past anxious to get his arms around her. If she felt as good as she looked, it would be close to impossible for him to control himself.

She muttered, "Yes," unsure why she was so quick to be in the arms of a stranger, even if they were nice, strong, comforting arms.

His being a graceful and smooth dancer and the intoxicating aroma of his citrus, sandalwood cologne all worked toward relaxing her, and after a few minutes of closed eyes, Justin was out of sight, out of mind. Men in personal situations as a rule made her nervous, but somehow this seemed right as rain. Her mood had begun to mellow, which she attributed to the rum. Her mind focused on how good and natural it felt being in Michael's arms as their bodies seemed to move in unison with the music. There seemed a familiarity, yet a newness about the way his body moved with hers. When the music stopped, she smiled and thanked him, unsure what the flood of emotions she'd experienced meant. She was feeling warm and close, a strange new feeling for her and not necessarily one she trusted. She very much liked being in control, and this man was making her lose it.

Walking slowly back to the table, Kayla felt oddly curious about where to lead the conversation when she heard Debra call her name. She turned in Debra's direction, and saw her for the first time that evening, looking so beautiful it made Kayla's eyes misty.

A woman is never more beautiful than on her wedding day, someone once said, and Debra, being no exception, looked like one of those beautiful black porcelain angels in a white, flowing, beaded wedding gown. Her hair was in an elegant French roll with ringlets at each temple. Her face glowed with serene happiness reserved for those who felt the true rapture of being in requited love. A true portrait of beauty, she could easily have been a model for a delicate, outrageously expensive miniature figurine in a Hummel gift catalog.

They'd grown to be close friends, but Kayla knew that Debra wouldn't have time for long girl talks, Saturday shopping marathons, and late-night dinners anymore. She missed her friend already, but still she was infinitely happy for her. Marrying Kit Warson, a VP at the advertising firm where they both worked, would be a dream come true for any woman. Kit, several years older than Debra and handsome to a fault, had declared himself a dedicated, die-hard bachelor. Women chased him without shame or subtlety. You could see envy and resentment in some of the women's eyes when the two announced their engagement at a company-sponsored function. The competitive nature of the business didn't usually yield good friends, but the backbiting surprised Kayla and Debra. Kit, being a VP, wasn't privy to such goings-on. Debra had decided to leave the company so that there wouldn't be any further gossiping and accusations of impropriety.

Kayla and Debra were the only two black female senior account representatives in the company, and out of necessity had formed a sisterly bond. They consulted each other daily for advice on accounts and recently had become more absorbed in each other's personal affairs as well. Although they'd only been friends a short time, Kayla had grown to respect and admire Debra, something that wasn't always easy to do in the advertising business with its overabundance of sharks and backstabbers. Debra was grounded and focused, and she was a brilliant marketing strategist. Kayla thought it was a shame that she'd decided to give it all up and start over.

Debra also understood Kayla's work schedule, her drive and ambition. She didn't seem too disappointed when Kayla was unable to participate in the wedding because of prior work commitments. She liked that about their friendship: it was absolute, each one understanding and appreciating the other. It made Kayla wonder if men ever felt that type of understanding and acceptance of a woman. Certainly none of the men she'd ever dated did. They complained constantly about her long workdays; her unyielding drive to be successful eluded them. They wanted trophy women to decorate their arm, to show off to their friends and other men they didn't know. An intelligent woman with drive and goals wasn't what they sought, even though they loved the financial remuneration she brought. It definitely was a male thing she felt she'd never understand.

"Hey, Kayla, I missed you at the wedding, what happened?" Looking around, she continued to ask, "Where's Justin?" Debra knew instantly she'd asked the wrong question, and Kayla looked away as she searched for an explanation. When she looked at Michael she could tell he was listening intently for her reply as well.

Debra quickly rebounded. "Well, I see you met Michael. Watch him, girl, he's a rascal. We go back to our days of partying in New Orleans at Xavier." Debra gave Michael a playful punch on the arm.

"Congratulations, Debra, I'm glad to see you and Kit made it legal," Michael said. He chuckled and bent down, giving her a kiss, never fully taking his attention away from Kayla.

Feeling warmed by his stare, Kayla said, "Yes, but a chivalrous rascal, he saved me from making a fool of myself." Debra noticed the twinkle in Michael's eyes and looked at Kayla, who had an uncharacteristic silly grin on her face. Feeling like a third wheel, she excused herself.

"Well, I'm glad you made it. I've got to talk to my new mother-in-law. I think she's still in the bathroom crying," Debra said. They all laughed, and the two women embraced. "I'll call you when we get back from Nassau, or do we need to talk before I leave? You know we'll be gone for two months. Kit's family is from there so we'll spend time there and traveling the islands." Debra had a sixth sense when it came to knowing when her friend needed help.

"No, girl, I'm fine. I've got some tough decisions to make, but I'll be fine. You enjoy your honeymoon and vacation, Lord knows you deserve all the happiness your heart can embrace." Lowering her head, leaning toward Debra, and in a conspiratorial whisper, she said, "Be sure to wear him out, I hear there's nothing like making love on the beach."

They both laughed wickedly, hugged once more, and said good-bye. Debra accepted a final farewell hug from Michael as well as a kiss on the cheek. Kayla felt an unexplained twinge of benign jealousy, or maybe it was envy, when he bent down to kiss Debra. She dismissed it in her mind as being an indictment of Justin's lack of affection and attention lately. Kayla decided to take a quick rest room break.

Returning to the table, she found that Michael had been cornered by a tall, rail-thin woman wearing far too much makeup, and too little clothing. Her short spandex black skirt and knit see-through crochet top were so tight and revealing, Kayla swore she could see what the woman ate for lunch. The woman was trying desperately to engage Michael, who apparently wasn't interested in conversation, but that didn't seem to discourage her. Kayla, shaking her head in disgust, definitely wasn't in the mood for a three-way conversation.

Michael turned his attention toward Kayla and loudly asked, "Are we leaving, *honey?*"

He's obviously attempting to be cute, Kayla thought. Turning away, she saw him stand, excuse himself, and walk confidently over to her.

"I thought you were coming to rescue me. I told you these things make a single man nervous. Were you going to abandon me without saying good-bye?"

He really did have an engaging sense of humor,

but she wasn't about to fall for his boyish charm or painfully cute dimples.

"You didn't look like you were suffering to me. As a matter of fact, you looked quite comfortable," she refuted and started to turn to walk away, but he stopped her.

"Kayla, wait," he said, gently grabbing her arm. "I would very much like to see you again." If it was possible to express amusement with the eyes, then he was doing just that.

Stopping to shift her balance onto one leg, as if she were dealing with an insolent child, she took a deep breath. "Michael, you seem like a very nice man, but right now my life is too complicated. I'm not in a position to see you." She knew her heart was telling her something different, but when had she ever listened to it? She dealt with tangibles, not abstracts or feelings.

Quickly glancing at her hands, he smiled and commented, "I don't see a wedding ring. Are you married?"

Kayla assumed he'd already checked her hand out, and determined she wasn't married. He casually put his hands in his pockets as though an explanation was forthcoming and he'd patiently wait for it. "No, I'm not, but I am in a situation that requires a lot from me right now," she said.

"What does that mean? A 'situation' as opposed to a relationship. If it's like that, then it's not at all complicated."

His tone and manner weren't accusatory, more like inquisitive, but Kayla was offended just the same.

"Justin is his name, huh? He must be a fool if he stood you up."

"Excuse me?" She couldn't believe he had such audacity. He was nervy, but at the same time interesting. "I will not discuss this with you, it's none of your business. I can't—no, make that don't want to—see you again."

Although she was trying to sound convincing, something in her eyes was saying just the opposite to Michael.

He stood his ground with his eyebrows arched in caution. He knew now wasn't the time to pursue her, but he *would* pursue her. He didn't know what her "situation" was with Justin, but he was confident he'd know once Debra and Kit returned from their honeymoon.

He wasn't sure if he could wait that long, but since she wasn't giving her number he would have to wait. He'd stored the fact that she worked at a competitive firm, Lancer and Newhouse, in his mental Rolodex. If he needed to contact her there, he could. Whatever her situation was, he had to see her again. Kayla Marshall was feisty and attractive to him in a way that frightened men. Those beautiful brown eyes beckoned a man to take care of her, love her, stroke her, while her mouth spewed words of independence; she was a paradox. He knew he should have run the other way, as women like her were difficult to get next to, but she stirred something in him. Meanwhile, he thought he'd better get out of the reception hall as the sharks were already circling, especially the desperate one in the short, tight spandex skirt.

"Well, at least let me walk you to your car," he offered. His eyes did that smiling thing again.

Unable to resist a man with manners, she felt her mood softening. She shifted her head to one side as if trying to figure out what species he was before finally murmuring, "Sure, why not?" She warned herself mentally about getting caught up in him. He asked her again for her telephone number when they reached her car.

"Sorry, but no, Michael. Have a good evening." She drove away and watched him in her rearview mirror as he stood watching her. There was something about him that sent electric waves through her.

As she guided her Lexus into the garage of her recently purchased ranch home, she felt overwhelmed with unanswered questions. Was this all life had in store for her, coming home to an empty house? Had she invested too much into her career, material possessions, and not enough into her personal life? The advertising business was competitive, fast-paced, and demanding. She worked late almost every night and took work home on the weekends. She never had enough time for socializing or even developing friendships outside of the industry.

She'd given up her mentoring program at the high school she'd graduated from. She no longer participated in church events, or any of the many volunteer programs sponsored by her sorority. Last year she'd visited Atlanta two different times to attend the baby showers of sorority sisters who'd moved there and were now expecting their second and third child. Nearly everyone in her college crowd was married, some even into second marriages.

She did have her situation with Justin, whom she loved, but who seemed to take her for granted lately. When they had begun dating three years ago, he showered her with dinners, dancing, flowers, and impromptu afternoon lunches. When it was good, it was really good, but now that it had turned sour, it was more like spoiled milk. She wasn't sure what the problem was. Justin wasn't showing up for dates, had stopped bringing fresh flowers, which he knew she loved receiving more than anything in the world, was always criticizing, and was usually too tired or too busy for intimacy. Whenever he was in the mood, it never lasted nearly long enough. She had debated in her mind on occasions if he was seeing someone else.

Being on the fast track to a much-deserved promotion and eventually a vice presidency position, which she was determined to have by age thirty-two, was taking its toll. She'd sacrificed time with family and friends to get to this stage in her career, and despite the temporary times of euphoria, something was missing or ajar with life. Was it Justin, or the job, or maybe was this all that life offered? Going too fast to take time to figure it out, she thought it easier to just cope for now, remaining status quo, feigning contentment like she was convinced most people did in life.

During the second year of dating, she and Justin had agreed to a monogamous relationship, making her so happy she tossed out her little black book and refused all offers of blind dates from well-meaning friends and family. The club scene and looking for "the one" had grown tedious and futile. She laughed at how women, herself included, seemed to say, "the one," as if he'd be the Messiah, whose sudden appearance would cause a star to shine brightly in the heavens over her house, hearkening his presence into her life. It hadn't happened with Justin and probably would never happen, but a woman had a right to dream.

Like so many women she was an enigma, always

needing one thing, but desiring something else, never fully understanding the difference between the two; never fully appreciating or listening to the inner voice that told her when something or someone wasn't right. She ignored it and sought that elusive love of her life, unsure what signs to look for and making it up as she went along. She and her best friend, Sandy, had spent countless hours debating on the paradigm of a good man, only to discover that the only men that could hold up to the model were their fathers, and perhaps a combination of Malcolm X, Michael Jordan, Denzel Washington, Morgan Freeman, with a smidgen of Larenz Tate thrown in. The latter was a bit young for their taste, but definitely had lots of potential, especially once they saw him without his shirt in *love jones* and cooking breakfast for a woman he'd only taken out once.

In college Justin was handsome, popular, and always surrounded by pretty, popular girls. The trophy girls, Kayla called them. The girls seemed to flock to Justin. They reminded Kayla of pigeons in the park when people threw food to them—all of them pecking at him for a treat, or attention, pushing and shoving each other trying to get at the little crumbs he threw to them. They rarely went to the same functions since they traveled in different circles, but she knew who he was; in fact everyone knew who he was. He came from an old-money Chicago family.

His father and mother had met while attending Florida A&M University and each had gone on to eastern colleges to pursue advanced degrees. His father was a doctor, his mother a lawyer. The original Huxtables, she often mused. They were on the A list,

and anybody who was anybody, or wanted to be somebody, knew the Kincaids of Chicago.

When Kayla saw Justin at a United Negro College
Fund fund-raiser four years after graduation, she
could have sworn that time stood still for a brief instant. He was standing in the middle of the large
ballroom surrounded by adoring females. "Some
things never change," Kayla had said to no one in
particular, as she sucked her teeth in disgust. Women
are always willing to make fools of themselves when it
comes to good-looking men, she thought, and
laughed when she included herself in that assess-
ment.

Justin was impeccably dressed. The navy Armani
suit with a white shirt he wore seemed to be tailored
for his slender body. Even from across the room, his
dazzling fourteen-karat smile made her palms sweat.
Kayla scanned the room looking for Sandy, who was
probably running late as usual. She needed someone
to take her mind off of Justin Kincaid. Kayla looked
around and appraised the well-dressed crowd. Some
looked as though they'd spent an entire month's
salary on their ensembles. Venturing through the
large room and over to the bar, she felt awkward and
self-conscious. She'd arrived at the bar when the bar-
tender leaned forward, gave her a warm solicitous
grin, and asked in a low, Barry White–like voice,
"What's your pleasure?" He was overtly flirting, but
she wasn't in the mood to even feign interest.

She smiled faintly and answered curtly, "I'll have a
white wine, thank you." He poured her wine, while
they engaged in small talk for a few minutes. She excused herself, turned to look for an empty table, and
began walking around the middle of the crowded

room. Kayla soon found herself standing face-to-face with Justin Kincaid.

"Kayla? Kayla Marshall? I thought that was you, how are you?"

She could only stare at his gleaming white teeth, full sensual lips, and penetrating dark brown eyes.

He moved his head from side to side as if trying to get her to recognize him. "I'm Justin Kincaid, we went to Northwestern together."

Did he dare think she didn't know who he was, and how in the hell did he remember her? She rarely had time for social events in college, working part-time, volunteering at church on several committees, mentoring at her high school alma mater. She did all that while maintaining her scholarships. Her plate was full and she liked it like that. Too busy to think about life's dance: that male, female thing that tripped so many people up. Love and courtship was the last thing on her mind in college, but now with Justin Kincaid standing in front of her the situation was different.

She managed to finally find her voice. After swallowing the large lump of straw that had magically lodged in her throat, she replied, "Hello, Justin, of course I remember you. It's been a while. I'm doing fine." What a lame reply, she thought, and if not for her feet feeling as if they were nailed in place she would've run away.

Without provocation, he gave her a hug and a sweet delicate kiss on the cheek, which made her knees weak.

Why'd he do that? her mind seemed to scream. Justin stood back and eyed her appreciatively. "You've obviously been taking great care of yourself, you look wonderful, Kayla."

"Thanks, Justin, I see you are the same shy person you were in college." They both laughed an easy laugh, like old friends.

"What have you been doing the past few years?"

"I'm an account representative with Lancer and Newhouse, an advertising firm."

The raising of his eyebrow with approval indicated he'd heard of them. "Oh, yeah, that's a great firm."

"Kayla, there you are, sorry I'm late." Sandy approached wearing a low-cut, red dress that clung to her shapely figure in all the right places, making Kayla suddenly feel like a frumpy old maid in her conservative pin-striped brown suit with a high-collar white blouse.

Kayla immediately wished she'd gone home to change, or at least freshened up her makeup. She'd opted to work late and had thought nothing of it until this moment. Seeing Sandy and all the other women who'd obviously taken time to groom themselves before attending the function, she didn't even have the benefit of a swish of mouthwash. Her desire to run away or at least magically disappear had returned. Being so distracted by him, she hadn't seen her friend approaching and felt awkward. Sandy was eyeing Justin and clearing her throat, indicating she was waiting for an introduction.

Kayla regained her composure and smiled faintly as she introduced the two. "Justin, this is a very good friend of mine, Sandra Neal. Sandra, this is Justin Kincaid. We went to college together."

Extending his hand, he greeted her pleasantly, appearing only to be mildly interested. "Nice to meet you, Sandra."

"Likewise, Justin, but please call me Sandy, all my

friends do." Her tone was sparked with interest, and Kayla instantly knew Sandy was sizing Justin up. She had a casual, easy way of flirting with men and they loved it. Sandy was an instructor of the "love dance," as Kayla had nicknamed the mating ritual. Sandy had danced it more times than Kayla could have in a lifetime and was an expert at sizing men up.

Sandy's brown, short-cropped hair was parted down the middle and rounded on each side to frame her high cheekbones. Her almond-shaped eyes were lightly dusted with a shade of bronze eye shadow that complemented the bronze lipstick and blush, which were all applied to perfection. Kayla vowed then and there she would take time for herself when attending any function where eligible men would be in attendance. She didn't like feeling inadequate in personal or professional situations.

"Let's grab a table before they fill up," Sandy purred, smiling and looking directly at Justin.

"It's getting late for me, ladies, I'll have to take a rain check. I have court early in the morning and I need to review some documents." He looked into Kayla's eyes and said, "I'd really like to see you again, Kayla, if you're still single." The smile on her face answered him adequately, because the words wouldn't come. "Well, I'll take that as a yes. May I have your number?"

Justin took a business card out of his breast pocket and handed it to her. All the while his eyes never left hers. Kayla was certain he heard her heart pounding. Her hands shook nervously as she searched her purse for a business card. When she handed it to him he held her hand ever so delicately, which sent her knees south again. "I'll call you soon, you both have a nice evening." He winked at her, smiled faintly at Sandy, and left.

Sandy looked into Kayla's lovesick eyes, "Girl, he is *way* too fine and slicker than okra. He has to be a hundred percent bonified, female-sniffing canine. Nice eye candy though."

Kayla snapped out of her daze. "You can really be crude sometimes. Just 'cause a man is fine and smooth doesn't mean he's a dog."

"*Puuhleez,* look at how he's working the room, even as he exits. He's probably getting more numbers. You are way too naive when it comes to these men, Kay, you'd better start getting that itch scratched a little more."

"Sandy!"

"What? Quit being so sensitive, Kayla, I'm just saying he's a little too smooth."

Examining her friend closer, Kayla scoffed, "My goodness, San, how'd you even get into that dress, grease yourself with butter?"

"You know, Kayla, if you were anybody else, that probably would be an insult." She dismissed it.

True to his word, Justin had called and they made plans to have lunch together. They spent more time talking and laughing than eating. Before lunch was over, Justin had her home number and a date for dinner on Saturday. She couldn't believe the warmth and consideration he extended her, opening doors and treating her like a lady. She loved that about him. They were inseparable after that. He'd surprised her with a trip to Acapulco and constantly pampered her with gifts. Justin had intimated that once their careers had taken off, they would become husband and wife, and that insinuation kept her close to him.

Three years had passed and now Justin's interest was waning. He took her for granted, canceling dates, standing her up for the wedding, and always claiming to be too busy with work. When they did get together, his thoughts and passion were obviously somewhere else. Kayla kept hoping that whatever it was driving him away from her would be brought to light.

She initially thought maybe it was the differences in their backgrounds. His parents had shelled out big bucks for four years of undergraduate studies at Northwestern as well as three years of law school at Washington University in St. Louis. Even in college, he dressed in designer clothes and drove a BMW, which he claimed was a high school graduation gift from his parents. His mother was definitely a coldhearted snob; she had on more than one occasion slighted Kayla. His father was just the opposite, earthy, warm, and friendly. His parents' marriage was definitely a case of opposites attracting. His mother's taste was more geared toward pheasant under glass while his father's was geared to plain old down-home cooking.

Kayla made sure to keep a clean house and was always meticulously groomed whenever he saw her. She did everything possible to project a good image. Whenever she and Justin spent the night together, she got up twenty minutes before the alarm went off, doing a quick ritual of washing her face in cold water to reduce any puffiness, fluffing hair, brushing teeth, and whatever else she could do to make herself look fresh and appealing. Then she'd gently ease back into bed, pretending to be asleep when the alarm sounded. Initially he complimented about how wonderful she looked in the morning, and how she made his "nature rise."

But lately there were no compliments, and the only thing rising was her resentment for his rude behavior. He'd even been insensitive enough to comment on the few extra pounds she'd put on. Once while they were out having dinner, the waitress brought over the dessert cart with a delicious array of wonderful sweets. Kayla was deciding which chocolate fantasy to order, when Justin interrupted her thoughts. "I don't think you need to order any dessert, Kay." His raised brow and the straight narrow set of his mouth indicated he was quite serious.

She couldn't believe how insensitive and rude he was, and the waitress seemed to be embarrassed for her as she slowly sank away from the table. Instead of confronting him, Kayla sank back in her chair, feeling hurt as she acquiesced, "You're probably right, I haven't had time to get to the gym or get in any walking."

Kayla sometimes battled with weight, but she was nowhere near overweight. More importantly, she didn't buy into the theory that the extra pounds meant you had other psychological issues you were hiding. She hadn't been molested as a child, nor had she been neglected, nor was she seeking perfection, none of the usual psychobabble that the talk shows claimed to cause young women to battle weight. She was the first to admit enjoying a good meal and was addicted to Baskin Robbin's butter pecan with no apologies or excuses. She exercised when she could, but her work schedule didn't always permit a consistent workout schedule, and she made no apologies for that either.

Justin finally called that night long after she'd returned from the reception, asking for forgiveness. "Come on, baby, it's not like you haven't broken dates before. I swear, I went to the office early, came home with a ferocious headache, took some Tylenol, and lay down. I fell asleep and when I woke up it was after eight. I'll make it up to you, I promise," he said, sounding sincere, but clueless.

"Justin, you can't just make up for a disappointment like that. You know how important Deb is to me. I missed her wedding waiting on you. How can you even think it's so trite that a simple apology can make it all right?"

Kayla was frustrated and after a few minutes of silence asked, "When did you become so inconsiderate?"

More silence. Finally she murmured, "I'm too frustrated and tired to deal with you now. I'll talk to you later."

"All right, Kay, but I think you're taking this too far, it's not like she's moving away and you'll never see her. I'm sure you'll see the wedding pictures." She could hear the deep sigh in his voice and knew it was futile. He'd never understand. After all, he didn't have any friends, just associates.

He was slowly becoming the king of insensitivity, and her patience was wearing thin. "The thrill is definitely gone," she mumbled to herself.

Kayla was barely out of the shower the next morning before the doorbell was ringing. She grabbed her bathrobe and wrapped her head in a towel. The bell was ringing frantically now. "Just a minute!" she yelled as she headed toward the door. She stopped and looked through the peephole to see Sandy. "Girl, what's your hurry this morning!" she said, swinging open the door and shivering from the cool air.

"I thought you were still sleeping. We need to talk. This isn't a conversation we should have over the phone." Sandy walked in quickly, closing the door behind her.

"What's wrong?"

Sandy stole a quick glance at Kayla and looked away. "Here, I brought you croissants."

Taking the bag from her, she said, "This must really be bad. Let me finish drying off. Put on some coffee for the croissants. I'll be back in two shakes. You wanna walk this morning?"

"Uh, maybe. I don't know. Hurry up, we need to talk."

Kayla looked at Sandy, who wasn't making eye contact. She knew this was very bad news.

After a quick change, Kayla returned. "Okay, let me have a cup of coffee and give it to me straight." Kayla walked toward the kitchen, eager for a croissant. She wanted to tell Sandy about her decision to leave Justin and all that had transpired over the past twenty-four hours, but her thoughts were interrupted when she noted the slight tremble of her friend's hand as she poured the coffee.

"Kayla, you know you're the dearest friend I have in the world and would never do anything to hurt you. I've agonized over this all night and have decided that straightforward is the best policy." She took a sip of her coffee as Kayla stood, munching on a croissant.

"And?" Kayla said, eyes leveling on her croissant, but burning with curiosity.

"You know I went to a fund-raiser last night. Well, I saw Justin there. And, Kayla, he wasn't alone."

"Oh." Kayla immediately looked up from the croissant she had found so interesting. She always tried to detach herself when bad news was headed her way, a sort of coping mechanism. It seemed to soften the blow. She sat down and crossed her arms as if settling in for a long conversation.

"Yeah, he was there with some tall, skinny girl. Matty, the social butterfly, was at the party and I knew he would know who this woman was. You know how he loves networking and name-dropping. So I asked if he knew her name because she looked familiar. He told me her name was Susan, and that her father was some bigwig lawyer. Evidently she is well known in the upper echelon, because her parents are well-connected old money. Well, anyway she and Justin didn't act like casual acquaintances. They were all up in each other's faces, whispering and openly flirting."

Kayla immediately thought back to a few weeks ago when she'd seen Justin out with a tall, thin woman. She was certain he'd told her that the woman's name was Susan. She was tallying this all up in her mind, wondering what to make of it. Strangely she wasn't upset, or even hurt, just oddly curious.

"Tall and thin, huh? Had that uppity look like she smelled something bad, like the kind of heifer that shops at Walgreen's for cologne, but tells her friends it's something she picked up at Lord & Taylor?" Kayla had the corners of her mouth turned down in imitation with her nose slightly elevated.

Snapping her fingers and pointing, Sandy shrieked, "That's the heifer! You know her?"

Kayla became quiet and pensive. "No, but I've seen her."

Sandy became concerned about the calm behavior. "So what's up? Are you okay? I know I've been busy, but I'm always here for you, Kay, we're family. I was almost ready to kick Justin's behind myself. He almost wet his pants when I walked over to him."

Kayla's eyes lit up. "No, you didn't! What'd you say?"

Sandy stood and began acting out the scene as she described it to Kayla. "Well, first I gave the anorexic scarecrow the evil eye; then I looked at Justin directly and said, 'I thought you and Kayla were going to Deb and Kit's wedding.' Girl, I wish you could've seen the look on his face. He looked at Ms. Scarecrow, and the man began stuttering! I—I—we." She finally took a deep breath, ready to re-create the scenario. "Now you know they're lying to you when they start stuttering. Trying to buy extra time to come up with that convincing lie."

They both giggled, as Sandy continued, "I just gave him the 'talk to the hand' sign, and said, 'I guess you had a change of plans.' Well, anyway, Ms. Scarecrow was too upset. Her uppity behind turned, swung her cheap, Diana Ross–looking weave over her shoulder, and left." With her cheeks sucked in and nose tilted high, her exaggerated enactment and the way she imitated the hair toss was hilarious.

Kayla was laughing so hard she could barely speak, but somehow managed to finally get control of herself. Wiping the tears from her eyes, she said, "I swear, Halle better be glad you weren't up for an Oscar. Even Angela Bassett could take notes from your melodramatic self."

After catching her breath and calming herself down, Sandy replied, "I can't believe you ain't upset. I fretted all night about telling you. I came over here prepared to call the Suicide Hotline number for you."

"Now you *are* being too melodramatic. They haven't invented a man worth killing myself or anybody else over."

"You know, that's right!" They high-fived each other and began laughing again. "Honestly though, Kay, are you in shock or something? You are taking this way too easy."

Kayla walked over to get a second cup of coffee. "Well, it's sorta a long story, but I feel like walking so let me finish this coffee, and get my gear on. I'll give you the real four-one-one."

Sandy's interest was truly piqued as she reared back in her chair. "Don't tell me you've been holding out on me. And here I thought we were girls." Sandy was gesturing with her fingers in the peace sign pointed toward her heart.

"All right now, you know you need to stop watching those hood videos."

Once outside, Kayla took a deep breath and began telling Sandy about the time she saw Justin and Susan together.

"A few weeks ago, Deb called me saying that she had tickets to this really nice dance, but Kit wasn't feeling well so they were going to stay home. She didn't want the tickets to go to waste, you were out of town, Justin swore he was working, so I went by myself. I got there around 9:30 and the place was deader than Abraham Lincoln but I decided to stay a few minutes and have at least one drink. Especially since I'd gotten all dressed up, I thought, well, at least let the rich and snooty entertain me for an hour."

Kayla laughed as she recounted the evening. "Girl, I should have known something when I pulled into the lot and saw nothing but Mercedeses, Infinitis,

BMWs, and expensive foreign cars. Bourgeois folk cars, and don't say a word about my Lexus," she cautioned Sandy before continuing.

"Some little Steve Urkel–looking guy asked me to dance. I mean, he seemed pretty harmless, so we danced a couple of times. The dance floor was almost empty. We talked a little bit, and then he started to act like we were going to be an item so I politely excused myself and went to the other side of the room."

Sandy said, "Why didn't you get downright rude with the man?"

Kayla's only reply was a shrug. "Anyway, the music was boring, a bunch of folks standing around passing out business cards and playing that guessing game. You know, guess where I went to college, guess where I work, guess who I know. They all read the same trade journals and newspapers so they know who's been promoted and who's working where, they just like to pretend they don't.

"As you can imagine I was pretty bored and decided to leave when all of a sudden I look over and see Justin and some tall, remarkably thin woman at a table talking. I wasn't sure if they were together or not until I walked over. I thought he was going to jump out of his shoes he jumped up so fast. Then I knew they were together; otherwise he wouldn't have been nervous."

Sandy was laughing at Kayla, who had become animated, using her hands and acting as if she were jumping. "Who's the melodramatic one now?" Sandy asked.

"No, girl, the man literally jumped a good foot off the floor! Started talking about, 'Uhh, what are you doing here?' Like I'm not allowed out without him. I swear I wanted to slap him blind."

Sandy was cracking up at the last remark. The cool and collected Kayla never lost her temper.

"I said, 'I see you finished work early, or is this business?' I pointed to the thin woman. Girlfriend was too upset! She turned all shades of red and left in a huff. And yes, she had a huge weave, so I'm assuming it's the same woman. Anyway Justin had the nerve to ask me if my comment was necessary."

Kayla stopped for a minute and took a drink of coffee, before continuing. "Can you believe his nerve? I'm not going to tell you what I told him, because you know I try not to go foul. He left with me. He spent most of the night apologizing, saying he'd finished work early but someone at his job had tickets and he came with them. He claimed Susan was just a friend who was there with someone else.

"Now, do I look like I Snow White? No, I don't, so I didn't want the man telling me any fairy tales. I knew then that I needed to end the relationship. Just been too busy."

Sandy shook her head. "Girl, I can't believe you kept all that drama from me. Now you know we need to go to that fool's office and get real loud in front of him and his lawyer comrades. Create some tension for him. I hate it when men like him think they can get away with treating you like you something from the bottom of their shoe."

"Please, Sandy. Justin isn't worth any drama. He'll get what's coming to him."

Sandy agreed. "Yeah, he will, but in the meantime I say we go pour acid on his car like Glenn Close did in that movie."

Kayla cracked up but managed to tell Sandy, "You're too crazy! No more revenge movies for you."

Sandy laughed and said, "No, not revenge movies. More like street justice movies. I love 'em."

"I hope you don't share that information with your dates," Kayla teased.

The walk with Sandy and the talk about Justin was a catharsis for Kayla as she found herself thinking clearly about what she needed to do to get her personal affairs in order.

Chapter 2

"If I don't start losing weight faster than a half pound a week, I'm going to just give up. I've been exercising for the past two months and haven't seen any appreciable results." As sweat trickled down the sides of her face, Kayla could feel her bra was damp, and her panties were starting to ride. "I need to get better foundations if I'm gonna be walking and sweating all the time." She looked over at Sandy, who wasn't winded, or sweating, and wondered how she stayed so focused and composed. Everything, even exercising, always seemed to come easy for Sandy.

"Quit your whining, you're in great shape. You're going to be in better shape when you drop that two hundred pounds of unwanted, deadweight named Justin." Sandy couldn't help smiling wickedly and giving a knowing wink at Kayla.

"Why do you always have to bring Justin into the conversation? This has nothing to do with him. Sistahs need to stop thinking that everything has something to do with a man. I want to look good for me," Kayla said, making sure the irritation was reflected in her voice.

"You are not overweight. I wish I had some of that top of yours."

Sandy looked over to Kayla and smiled. "Now you know my motives are purely sisterly. Tell that fool there are plenty of men out there who'd be drawn to you like bugs to a porch light. If I were a dude, I'd be all over you." Both let out a hearty laugh.

"Well, we know what kind of man you'd be." Smirking, Kayla rolled her eyes.

"Woman, quit trying to be nice. I'd be a dog and love every minute of it. Why should men have all the fun? Just because they have that testosterone thing happening? You know we women got what they really want." Sandy smiled wickedly again and so did Kayla. "That's why it's caused wars, men want to possess what they don't own. "

They high-fived each other and laughed heartily again.

"So tell me more about this Michael that you met at the wedding, and explain to me again why you didn't give him your number."

Kayla sighed. They'd had this conversation before. "Quit playing dumb, Sandy, I've got too much going on now to think about another relationship. They take too much time and effort. After all I *was* committed to Justin."

"Ms. Thang, what does that have to do with at least exploring other possibilities? He sounds like a nice guy. I'm surprised Deb hasn't hooked you two up. I knew all along Justin wasn't the one. He's always been too slick and way too snobby." Sandy never bit her tongue when it came to how she felt about Justin. She protected her friend and believed Kayla had no business thinking a snake wouldn't bite you even if it was a pet, or that a dog could be anything other than a dog regardless of how many tricks it knew.

Looking over at Sandy with raised brows, she continued. "Unlike some people, she's not all in my business trying to hook me up."

"Well next time, take his number, 'cause unlike some people," she said, returning the annoyed look at her friend, "I know if the right man came along you wouldn't turn him away."

"I swear you're the most aggravating woman in the world," Kayla said, smiling faintly at having a good friend who would always look out for her, and be honest, even when it was difficult. She didn't have many friends, but the ones she had were the best.

"Let's do another ten minutes and cool down. I've got a hot date tonight," Sandy said.

"When haven't you had a 'hot' date even on a Sunday night?" Kayla tried to sound annoyed, but knew she wanted to hear the details on Monday.

Monday morning found Kayla in good spirits as she turned on her computer, ready to begin working on the presentation. She was working on a new marketing campaign for a large computer company that had three segments. One involved an elderly couple declaring how simple the computer was to use as they received photos from their grandchildren. The second had a college student doing research on the computer. The third included a musician using the computer to produce music. All were using the same computer with different enhancements to meet their customized needs. The hook would be the economical price because customers would only pay for what they wanted or what they would actually use. As their interest or needs changed, they could add enhancements at a discounted price.

This presentation would put a huge bonus in her pocket, as well as put her a step closer to the much-wanted promotion she so desperately sought. Her thoughts were suddenly interrupted by Edward Oswell. "Hey, Kay, you're here awfully early, aren't you?"

When Kayla had returned from her St. Louis business trip, the rumors weren't as bad as she thought. They'd all evidently agreed that she'd been asked to stay because she was kissing the behind of everyone on the committee. It had absolutely nothing to do with the fact that she was the only one from the group who did exactly what she was sent to do, and did it expertly, spending weeks preparing her portion of the presentation, researching the company thoroughly. It just seemed easier for them to think that she wasn't any more competent than they, rather she'd just done a better job of kissing ass. The rumor didn't bother her much because she knew others who'd worked with her would know better.

It did annoy her that people who weren't willing to do their share would be allowed to prosper in their jobs because the powers-that-be overlooked the inadequacies. Sally was the company trollop, and the other two men played golf with the top brass. Kayla had worked twice as hard as all three of them, brought the company more revenue than all three of them collectively, yet when it came time for promotions and raises they were right there with her. She admittedly hated the "good old boy" network that was alive and kicking at Lancer and Newhouse, but knew it was the way of corporate America.

Turning from her computer with just a bit of atti-

tude, she refuted, "Well, Ed, not everybody has a rich
daddy, with rich friends. Some of us actually have to
work for a living. And my name is Kayla." *Only my
friends call me Kay,* she felt like saying, but knew it was
inappropriate. Edward turned a slight crimson shade
and looked away, but remained in her doorway. Feeling a twinge of guilt for reacting so saltily, she asked,
"Did you want something?" After all, his rich daddy
yielded a lot of power, always helping him get big,
rich clients. Edward wasn't well liked in the office.
Everyone knew he'd never worked for anything in his
life, but no one challenged him. It was rumored even
his job was a gift. Someone at Lancer and Newhouse
owed his father a favor.

"No, I just wanted to know if you needed any help
with the Johnson account." Kayla stared at him in disbelief. He'd never offered to help anyone do
anything before. She thought back to St. Louis and
how absolutely useless he was. Only a privileged white
male could put in so few hours and effort, yet continue to keep his job, and swear *she* was there because
of affirmative action.

She'd walked in on a conversation with white male
coworkers, who'd suddenly stopped their animated
discussion when they saw her. They didn't know she'd
heard them discussing how they were losing out because of affirmative action. It made her want to
scream at them to look around their current company, and any other Fortune 500 company, and point
out their losses. There were very few jobs at the top
that were occupied by blacks or any other so-called
minority. But she knew a debate would be useless.
She'd learned a long time ago you couldn't change
people's perceptions.

Ed's selfishness and backstabbing were the joke of many lunch conversations at Lancer and Newhouse. That was one thing on which blacks and whites agreed on. An uneasy, queasy feeling grasped her. She could feel a knot forming in the back of her throat as she struggled to answer.

"Thanks, Ed, but I think I've got it under control. Are you okay? You don't look well." She noticed beads of perspiration on his forehead. His usually cocky posture wasn't present, nor his usual air of importance. He stood leaning against the frame of her door, hands in pockets, shoulders drooped, with a blank expression that Kayla couldn't read. Even his blond hair, which usually looked as though it'd just been styled at one of those fancy, cappuccino-serving, expensive salons, was dull with telltale tracks from a wide-tooth comb. He'd obviously just combed it. His expensive tailored suit, which was in need of a dry-cleaning, also revealed something was amiss.

"No, Kay—sorry, Kayla—I'm fine. Thanks for asking. Well, I've got a presentation to prepare myself so maybe I'll see you later. Let's do lunch this week." All the time his eyes kept darting around, giving him the appearance of a frightened deer. It was not at all like the barracuda his personality was more comparable to.

The pleading in his distant, icy blue eyes made her affirm, "Sure, Ed." To her knowledge, he'd never gone to lunch with any of their coworkers, only the president and cofounder Samuel Newhouse, so it wasn't the thought of lunch with him that made her curious, it was the invitation that caused her concern.

Margaret, her secretary, stuck her head in after a few minutes. "Was that Edward Oswell I just saw leaving here?"

"Yes, it was," Kayla responded, never looking away from her computer. She was thinking about what the visit could mean, but was unwilling to share her thoughts.

Margaret walked slowly and cautiously into the office. "What's going on, what did he want?"

"I'm not sure. He asked if he could help with the Johnson account."

Margaret leaned back, her glasses low on her nose, and peered at Kayla, like an old school marm. "No, he didn't, that man has never helped anyone. He must be up to something really insidious."

Kayla, slightly amused by Margaret's uncharacteristic informal conversing, knew he was up to something, but would keep her poker face until she found out what was on Ed's mind. She turned away from her computer, giving Margaret her full attention. "Well, now, Margaret, we don't know that. I'd prefer to give him the benefit of the doubt."

Kayla tried to sound convincing as she continued, "Maybe the gossip about him isn't true. He's gotten a bad reputation because people are envious when you have something they don't."

Margaret's neck recoiled, reminding Kayla of a cobra ready to attack. "What could that be? The man's never had to work for anything in his life. That's not gossip, I know that's the truth."

"Money, pure and simple—people who don't have it envy those that do. His family has plenty, which comes with an altogether different set of problems."

Kayla had already said far more than she'd intended on the subject. "I need those PowerPoint slides for my presentation by this afternoon. Are they completed?" She knew the slides weren't complete, but felt uncomfortable with the direction of the conversation. Changing the subject hopefully would change the cloud of concern that had begun to encircle her.

"No, Ms. Marshall, but I'll get right on them." Margaret gave a slight smile and turned to leave. This sounded more like the secretary Kayla had come to know and respect over the years.

"Thanks, Margaret. Hold my calls for about an hour. And please close the door when you leave."

"Sure." Grabbing the handle, she pulled the door shut. Her raised brows and thin lined mouth revealed her concern.

Kayla pondered whom she could call internally to inquire about Edward Oswell, cursing herself for not being more sociable at work. She'd been invited to lunch and drinks after work by her coworkers, but wasn't interested, or had other plans. She thought of John in the mail room. He'd had a crush on her and flirted constantly. Instead of calling, she decided to pay him a visit. Checking her makeup, she reapplied lipstick, fluffed her hair, and headed out. "Margaret, I'll be back in about twenty minutes." Approaching the mail room, she loosened her shoulders and slowed her walk, putting a little more swing in her hips than normal.

Disappointed John wasn't there, she walked over to her mail slot, removing a large interoffice envelope. She was unwrapping the string when a familiar voice greeted her.

"Well, if it ain't the fine Ms. Marshall. Girl, when you gonna let me buy you a drink?"

Despite his casual air with her, John never allowed anyone to overhear him flirting with her. Knowing what it took for a black woman to survive in advertising, he admired her.

"Hello, John, long time no see. How you doing?" Kayla had entertained the thought of going out with John some years before, but knew if it ended badly it could cause problems at work. She didn't want an office romance sidelining her career. John continued to occasionally ask her out, but she always said no.

He entered and sat on a low counter near where she'd taken the envelope, casually tucking one leg loosely under the other. They were only inches apart. "I think you just made my day—no, my week. Girl, you looking better every time I see you. When are you gonna break down and let me take you out? We could just go out for a drink, no strings attached. We are friends, you know. Although none of my other friends are quite as fine as you."

Kayla was happy that her cinnamon coloring wouldn't reveal the warm blush she felt spreading over her face and throat. "You certainly are great for my ego, John." Tilting her head to one side, narrowing her eyes, she began eyeing him up and down, uncharacteristically flirting. "Maybe if you're a good boy, I'll let you buy me that drink real soon."

"Yeah, right, Kayla, you've been telling me that for too many years, so stop teasing me, girl." Both of them laughed good-naturedly.

Clearing her throat and folding her arms in front of her, she geared up for the real purpose of her visit. "John, you know a lot of what goes on around here. I had something curious happen recently and I'm wondering what it means. Do you think you can help me?"

Playfully flipping her chin with his forefinger, he said, "Sure, baby girl, you know I got juice." His solicitous grin told her she had him in the palm of her hand.

Taking a deep breath and slowly releasing the air, she asked, "Is the gossip true about Edward Oswell? They say he's sneaky. I've heard some pretty bad things about him. Stealing accounts, taking credit for other people's work, things like that."

John's smile disappeared and he became rigid. "Why, did that punk do something to you? You know I'll—"

Interrupting him before he got overly excited, she quickly replied, "Oh, no, it's nothing like that, I was just curious," deciding this wasn't the place or the time to discuss Oswell.

She was smiling at his display of male bravado, his willingness to protect her. Feeling uncomfortable about manipulating him, she threw him the bone he'd been asking for. "John, if I agreed to have a drink with you, can you accept it as a friendly gesture, one coworker having a drink with another?"

His smile returned, which pleased her. "Sure, Kayla, you know I'd like to take you out, but if you don't feel the same that's okay. I can enjoy your company for a drink. I know you'll let me know when you ready to get your groove back."

"Listen to you trying to be charming." She smiled and tried to look coy, but something in his posture told her he knew she was teasing him. "So how about getting that drink tonight?"

It was John's turn to play now. He winked his eye at her and she noticed for the first time just how sexy his eyes were, and his lips had that pouty look that women paid money to get. His dreads looked well maintained, and the few scars on his smooth mocha-colored face gave him a roughneck kind of hand-some quality. He looked ruggedly exotic, like he could carry a woman off to some island and make wild passionate love to her day after day. She was certain John was the kind of bad boy your mother warned you to stay away from, but you were drawn to like college kids to beer.

His muscles rippled through the clingy long-sleeve shirt with every arm movement, and his narrow waist only made her predatory lust run further amok. He seemed to sense the effect he was having on her as he leaned forward, oozing more sexiness than anyone should be allowed in public. He mused, "What, no plans with that uptown lawyer boyfriend of yours?"

He smiled that solicitous grin again, the one Kayla was certain had landed many young girls and women in trouble before they knew how their panties had suddenly melted away. "You ain't too much older than me, girl, we could be real good together."

The thought of Justin snapped her back and erased the erotic thoughts that were billowing in her head. "Be nice. I'll meet you at the bar downstairs right after work, say around 6:30."

He settled back and folded his arms. "Kayla, you work late, not me. After work to me is 4:30." She turned up her nose at drinking before 6:00.

"Well, I can't get there before 5:30, why don't you start without me?"

"Sure, why not? My girlfriend tells me the same thing."

She chortled. "You are crazy, I'll see you at 5:30."

Turning to leave, she could feel his eyes on her back, feeling uncomfortable at the thought of him checking out her behind. Putting up her finger, moving it from side to side while continuing to walk, she warned, "I know what you're thinking. Cut that out."

"Kayla, it's all true," he called out. She turned to find that his serious look had returned. "Stay away from Ed, he's as wrong as two left shoes. Sneaky as hell."

Returning to her office, she began working feverishly on her presentation, but couldn't get rid of the uneasy feeling that bad news was headed her way in the form of blond, blue-eyed, blue blood Edward Oswell.

At precisely 5:30 Kayla turned off her computer and headed toward the bar to meet John. Once she arrived her eyes slowly adjusted to the dim lighting, but before she could single him out, he stood and waved her over. She walked to the table and slid into the brown leather booth. The place reminded her of the bar on *Cheers,* where everybody knows your name. It was the preferred watering hole of many workers in the building who'd decided to stop for a drink before hitting the snarling Chicago traffic. The place served the best hot wings in the world, she thought as her mouth began to water.

She took a deep breath and smiled slightly as she looked into John's eyes.

He began to speak. "I didn't think you'd show up." His slightly slurred speech and slumped posture told her he'd had a couple of drinks already and information would be easy to extract from him.

"Why would you think that? I told you to start without me and I see you're a man who listens." She couldn't help chuckling as he squinted at her and she guessed he was completely oblivious of what she was talking about. After less than forty-five minutes she knew more than she had ever wanted to know about

Edward Oswell. If a third of what she'd heard was true, then he definitely was the slithering, sneaky snake everybody accused him of being, and all she could wonder was what nefarious dealings he was trying to involve her in.

Chapter 3

It was Saturday and Kayla was meeting Sandy for one of their marathon shopping sessions. This was one of their favorite weekend activities. They both loved to shop at flea markets, boutiques, and particularly the high-fashion shops. Both swore Chicago had the best shopping in America and were pleased that so many of the shops were owned by black entrepreneurs. Kayla also enjoyed the many art galleries and museums all over Chicago.

Weekends were important to Kayla because her mantra was if you worked as hard as she did, you'd better play hard, or you were at risk of burnout. She spared no expense when it came to her fun time.

They started this Saturday with a brisk early morning walk in Kayla's Hyde Park neighborhood and afterward shopping. The area was known to feature homes by the famous architect Frank Lloyd Wright. It was a lakefront community noted for its racial and economic diversity. The area was anchored by the University of Chicago, and many determined it to be the intellectual oasis of the city.

Kayla had chosen this community because of its picturesque lakefront beauty and charm. She was only a few miles from her parents, who lived in

Chatham. Both Kayla and Sandy enjoyed the spon-
taneity of going wherever the day took them. They
shopped for books, clothes, household goods, and
whatever else came across their path. They called it
their "scouting day." Kayla loved the fact that it could
all be done in her own neighborhood and she always
had a wonderful view of the lake.

Sandy excitedly told Kayla about her role in her
company's new marketing plan while they cooled
down from their walk. There were men who were
pensively playing chess and talking trash. The usual
lot of older men playing chess weren't around but instead there were hoards of younger ones playing
chess and walking about. Sandy and Kayla got more
than their share of admiring glances and several whis-
tles. Even a few of the older men that were there
smiled appreciatively as they walked by. True to form,
they each accused the other of getting the attention.

After hours of shopping and browsing they returned to Kayla's house for a quick change of clothes.
Lunch was next and they had worked up quite an appetite. Sandy suggested the new soul food restaurant,
Southern Kitchen. It was nearby and had gotten rave
reviews. This was the only soul food restaurant in all
of Chicago Kayla swore she hadn't tried, and she enthusiastically gave Sandra the thumbs-up on the
suggestion. She did feel somewhat guilty, thinking
about the extra pounds that stubbornly clung to her
like wet paint.

As Sandy pulled into a parking space, Kayla said, "I
think I'm going to join a gym or something. I'm approaching thirty and the pounds are getting harder
to fight off. Seems like lately everything that goes into
my mouth ends up right on my hips and butt."

Sandy sucked her teeth, took a deep sigh, and said, "Maybe so, but it's all in the right places."

Getting out of the car, Sandy said, "You've got the classic hourglass figure. You're just obsessing because you know Justin likes really skinny women. He can be so shallow."

Kayla chuckled because there was some truth to Sandy's comment. She looked at her friend and said, "That sounds real legit coming from a sister who won't even date men that don't wear designer digs, clock at least six figures, and have a ride with buttery soft leather seats contoured for her behind."

Feeling no shame about being assessed correctly, Sandy rolled her eyes and huffed. "You're right, because I believe I deserve that kind of man.

"And why you stayed with his commitment-phobic behind as long as you did is beyond me anyway. You deserve much more; besides you know that kind of brother loves them bony anorexic-looking women. It goes along with the image."

Rather than get into another endless debate with Sandy about this issue, Kayla chose to ignore her and gave her the "forget you" look they each understood and respected. "Okay, okay, but don't come crying to me when his pseudo love kicks you in the butt again," Sandy retorted.

"Believe me, hard-hearted Hannah, I won't. I'd just as soon call psychic friends or one of those 'I'll tell you what you wanna hear for three dollars a minute' numbers. Heaven forbid if you would show some emotions other than skepticism and doubt. Besides, I'm not seeing him anymore, I just haven't officially broken if off. I told you I've been too busy with other things."

Sandy took her friend by the arm. "Come on and

let's go, I'm starving. Is that an emotion?" They eyed
each other with slight amusement and headed toward the restaurant.

Once inside, they were greeted with a beautifully
framed montage of timeless black entertainers, including Billie Holiday, Louis Armstrong and Sarah
Vaughn, with a few contemporary music artists included. Beautifully framed black artwork could be
seen throughout. Kayla recognized many of the artis-
tic works and knew the restaurant had paid lavishly
for the paintings and prints. The owners didn't
scrimp on other parts of the restaurant either, as a
huge assortment of fresh flowers in a handsomely
crafted large clay vase adorned the foyer.

Each table was covered with a white linen table-
cloth and small crystal vases with fresh, single white
or yellow roses in them. The light fixtures were an
ivory sandstone texture, giving the place a warm
glow. The booths were beautifully crafted dark wood
with black leather seats.

Kayla noticed all the young, well-groomed people,
wearing an assortment of trendy sportswear. Most of
the women looked as though they'd just stepped out
of the salon, with their hair and nails done to perfection and well-applied makeup adorning their
faces. Although dimly lit, the atmosphere was light
and friendly. This was definitely a place Justin would
enjoy, Kayla thought. Hating to admit it, even to herself, he was very image conscious. To some extent,
she was as well, but he was far more obsessive about it
than she would ever be.

As the waitress escorted them to their table, someone called out Kayla's name. Kayla looked around and
saw Barbara Parker, whom she'd known since elemen-

tary school. Barbara's family had moved across the street from Kayla's parents' home in the third grade, and for years they were dedicated blood sisters. Each had punctured her own finger with a pin, rubbing the bloody fingers together while reciting an oath of everlasting friendship. Barbara now worked for a competitive advertising firm. Though they'd known each other forever, they rarely called one another.

Barbara and Kayla occasionally ran into each other and made promises to call one another but never did. She was well respected for her creative campaigns, and enjoyed a fine reputation among her peers in the industry. "Barb, you look great, I hear you are really creating a name for yourself at Brooks and Walsh."

Barbara smiled at the compliment as she embraced her old friend. "I'm trying to keep up with you, I heard you got a fat promotion. Congratulations."

As the two stood looking and quietly appearing to be reminiscing in their thoughts, Sandy interrupted, "I wish you two would listen to yourselves. You've known each other since you made mud pies, and you're getting all your news secondhand." Sandy stood with her sister stance, hands on hips and plenty of attitude.

"I'm here with some friends from work. Why don't you two join us?" Barbara pointed toward their booth.

"I'd love to, Barb, but I've got some work at home that's calling my name, so I'm going to eat and run." She hated lying, but she didn't feel like shop talk, which was always the dominating conversation whenever people in the industry got together.

Kayla looked over at Sandy for support. "Yeah, I'm going out of town in a few days, and I've got to plan for my trip."

"Working on a Saturday? No wonder you got that fat promotion. Well, let's get together next week."

Kayla wished she'd had a dollar for every time they'd agreed to get together, but rather than pursue the issue, she gave Barb a hug and a promise to call the following week.

After Kayla and Sandy settled down to their table they were only a few feet from Barb and her friends, who seemed to be having a lively conversation. Sandy was busy reading the menu while Kayla was trying to see who was with Barb. She craned her neck slightly up, looking like a turtle poking out of a shell. Kayla recognized two of the female representatives and when she glanced at the lone male in the group, she saw the same smiling eyes and cute charming dimples from the wedding. Even from a distance, Kayla got a warm feeling. The same feeling you get curling up in front of a fireplace ablaze with a cozy warm fire on a cold snowy winter day. Her heart did that humming thing again and she whispered "Michael" so low that she wasn't even sure if it had come from her.

"Are you ladies ready to order?" The waitress seemed to appear from nowhere and brought Kayla back to her senses.

Kayla and Sandy placed their orders. They were in conversation when Sandy's eyes lit up and a smile spread across her face. "Well, well, look at that fine specimen."

Kayla turned to look in the direction that had captured Sandy's attention and saw Michael coming to their table.

"It's Michael, the guy from the wedding. Please don't embarrass me." Kayla laughed nervously and lightly fanned as if trying to cool off.

"Me? Look at you. You're the one fanning, trying to cool down. You look like you're ready to jump the man and he hasn't even made it over here yet." Sandy couldn't help being amused by Kayla's unusual nervousness.

"Hello, Kayla, it's good to see you again," Michael said as he extended his hand.

Trying her best not to smile from ear to ear, Kayla shook his hand. "Hi, Michael. It's good to see you too." The slight smell of citrus and sandalwood and the firm touch of his hand made her relax. She cleared her throat and introduced Michael and Sandy. As he shook Sandy's hand, Kayla took in the sexy dimples, smooth skin, and lips that begged to be kissed.

"Nice to meet you, Sandy." He extended his hand to shake hers.

"It's really good to meet you too, Michael," Sandy said enthusiastically.

He turned his attention back to Kayla and said, "Well, I've got to rejoin my party. I saw you over here and thought perhaps you two could join us."

"No, thank you, Michael. We've got to eat and run," Kayla said reluctantly. She was intrigued by this handsome man, but knew she had other things to do.

"Well, may I call you?" Michael inquired as he looked deeply into Kayla's eyes. The warmth of his stare made her nervous as she searched for an answer. Kayla looked over at Sandy, who had a knowing smile on her face and a look of "yes" in her eyes.

"I'm sorry, Michael, but like I told you at the wedding, I'm involved with someone." Kayla's reply wasn't convincing and sounded weak. Her heart said yes, but she didn't listen to it.

He was obviously disappointed as he let out a

barely audible "Hmmm." One could tell by the determined set of his eyes that it would not be the last time he'd ask to call her.

Sandy cleared her throat and extended her hand to Michael. "It was certainly nice to meet you. I'm sure we'll meet again. Have a nice evening." Michael gave a polite nod and left.

"Why'd you tell him that, Sandy?" Kayla tried to sound upset, but was amused at the implication her friend was making.

"Because he's obviously smitten with you, and he seems very nice." She took a drink of water and added, "And about as fine a man as I've ever seen." She smiled and fanned herself with a napkin.

Kayla laughed and said, "Girl, you too much."

Chapter 4

Another workweek was ending, Friday had finally arrived, and Kayla was anxious about the weekend. She had a date with Justin Saturday night. She hadn't been able to end the relationship over the phone and now that the time had come she was anxious. She had a big presentation planned for the following week, but for whatever reasons couldn't focus on it. Kayla had always been meticulous about her presentations. Even Margaret, her secretary, had asked how the presentation was going when she noticed Kayla just couldn't get it together. Kayla decided to finish working on it over the weekend and have everything ready by Monday morning.

She got home late Friday, and found herself stalemated on the presentation; her usual concentration wasn't to be had. "Give it up, girl," she muttered while picking up the television remote and the take-out dinner she'd picked up from the nearby restaurant.

Kayla had decided to buy a new dress several weeks before, thinking it might spark some interest in Justin. It was a beautiful, understated black Donna Karan number that looked as though it was designed for her. The dress accentuated the best of her figure.

Sandy commented when she saw it, "Of course you

know I will have to borrow that, Ms. Girl. It's a bit conservative for my taste, but it sure is classy looking. Need I ask who you had in mind when you bought it?" Kayla hated it when Sandy was right, which was most of the time.

Kayla began her Saturday with an early morning walk, all the while searching for the right words to end the three-year relationship. Even though she suspected Justin was cheating on her and he'd been disinterested lately, they'd had some good times together. She wanted to end the relationship gracefully over dinner. Kayla knew that Justin was very into his image and would never behave badly in a restaurant.

At 7:45 Kayla was looking at herself approvingly in the mirror, and as she turned sideways she said aloud, "I really do look good." She'd always gotten nice compliments on her eyes, which she agreed to be her best asset. They were big, dark brown, and expressive, and she liked playing them up with just the right amount of eye shadow, liner, and mascara. Kayla had learned very early how to apply makeup properly, loving how it made her look. She didn't wear much during the week, but on the weekends she became more daring. Justin had insisted she not wear any makeup, claiming she was such a natural beauty; plus he didn't like it getting on his clothes.

The doorbell interrupted her thoughts. Looking at the clock on her nightstand, she grinned. "Seven fifty-five. Well, at least he's still prompt." Kayla opened the door like Vanna White, very grand and animated.

Justin was obviously impressed. "Wow! You look magnificent! You look like the old Kayla."

Kayla was instantly devastated. She felt like a balloon that had been suddenly punctured with a pin. "What the hell does that mean?"

"Kayla, you know I don't like it when you use offensive language. It's so inappropriate for someone with your education and intelligence."

Kayla's glare was so intense she knew Justin would have to back down, and tell her what he meant.

After a few seconds he asked, "Are you ready to leave?"

She couldn't believe he had the audacity to say something so callous and expect her not to call him on it.

"As soon as you tell me what you meant by that comment, we *might* leave." Her emphasis on the *might* didn't seem to get a rise out of him. Determined to clarify what he said, Kayla did not realize until that instant what a doormat she'd allowed herself to become. She stood, arms folded, waiting. The mundane look on his face told her he actually thought an explanation was unwarranted and if she didn't press the issue none would come.

"Kayla, you are blowing this way out of proportion. I just meant that you'd put on so much weight lately and—and—now you look like you've lost some. You look like you did when we first started dating."

Her face felt as if it were on fire she was so angry. "And speaking of dating, I understand you were out with Susan again the night of Deb's wedding. You know, the night you told me you were working." Her voice dripped with sarcasm.

"Did Sandy tell you she saw me?" he asked dryly.

Kayla stood with her arms folded, her eyes burning with anger.

"Well, did she tell you?"

"You know, Justin, I thought you were asking a rhetorical question. I can't believe you expect me to play cat and mouse with you. Of course she told me she saw you out."

"Kayla, please let me explain."

She held up her hand to stop him. "No, please don't! Whatever your reason for lying to me about what you were doing that night, just save it for Susan. I don't want to hear it." Kayla looked at him and took a deep breath.

"Justin, I've been waiting to tell you this, but there's no need to postpone this any longer. You are truly the most self-centered, manipulative man I've ever met. I've managed to overlook it because I thought we had something special, but that's not true."

He stepped toward her with his arms outstretched, but Kayla stopped him. "Please don't. Just leave. I never want to see or talk to you again. My intentions were for us to end this as friends, but too much has happened." She walked over to the door. "I could never be friends with a liar and a cheat. Bye, Justin."

This experience was new for Justin and his reluctance in leaving had nothing to do with his feelings for Kayla. He couldn't believe she was asking him to leave. In his mind he'd be the one to tell her when it was over. "Look, we can work—"

Kayla stopped him by shouting, "Leave!"

Justin refused to accept this kind of rejection. He knew Kayla found him irresistible, even when he had been as wrong as two left shoes. He always managed to find the right words to say, or the right gift to sway her back to him. For now, he thought she needed time to cool down. He'd never seen her so angry. When he looked at her, she gave him a defiant glare that told him it was time to leave. He strolled away with his hands in his pockets like he didn't have a care in the world.

"How could I have ever been so wrong?" It was more of a declarative statement than a question. It was finally over and she was very upset, but he had merely walked away as if he'd been told his dry-cleaning was ready.

Kayla spent the remainder of the weekend trying to concentrate on the presentation she had scheduled on Monday, and avoiding Justin's calls. He had apologized a thousand times on her voice mail. Her usual ability to focus was gone. Her mind drifted to the breakup with Justin, the attraction she felt for Michael, the immense amount of time she was putting into her job. She felt overwhelmed for the first time in her life.

Kayla set her alarm to wake up Monday morning at 5:00 to prepare for her presentation and by 6:30 she was still diligently working, hurrying around the house and chastising herself for being so negligent. "I can't believe I've waited this late to get this presentation together. Luckily Mr. Johnson and his group won't be in until 10:00."

She got to work before her secretary, which should have been the first omen of what was ahead. By 9:00 she was a wreck. Everything that could go wrong did. Margaret called in sick, which was something she hadn't done in all the time Kayla had been there. Her PowerPoint slides hadn't come out the way she wanted, and most importantly she hadn't taken the proper amount of time necessary to prepare a good presentation. Her energy level was low, which was highly unusual for her. She knew ad-libbing wasn't her strongest asset because her most successful presentations had always taken hours of preparation and research.

The Johnson Group was a medium-sized accounting firm looking to expand its customer base. They were committed to a marketing plan that would span several years. If she acquired the account it would yield a huge profit for the company, and no doubt put a feather in her cap. Her mentor, Sam Newhouse, had hired Kayla straight out of college and had been openly grooming her for a vice presidency slot. This was another step to getting closer to the goal. "I can do this, yes, I can," she was constantly repeating to herself hurrying around the office, as if positive affirmations were all she needed to successfully acquire the account. She knew that everything she did was viewed under a microscope, so she always pushed herself hard. Kayla realized that she was now feeling the self-imposed pressure.

The presentation dragged on forever. Mr. Johnson didn't appear as interested as during the previous meeting; Kayla knew she was losing ground. She skipped over so many important details constantly backtracking, and delivered a lackluster presentation, not at all her style. *I will never let this happen again* played over and over in her head like a ritornello from a song. She thanked the group for their time and attentiveness and promised to get back with them on the missing information they needed to make their decision.

On her returning to the office, several voice mail messages were waiting, three from Justin, apologizing profusely for being such a thoughtless fool. She felt so inept about the presentation, Justin, and herself in general that for the first time since elementary school she didn't feel in control of her life. Taking the rest of the day off and retreating to her bed was all she felt like doing.

After a few hours of sleep and a hot shower, she was feeling slightly better. Barely out of the shower, she heard the doorbell ring. When she got to the door and looked out to see Sandy, her heart sank like the *Titanic.*

"Let me in, Kayla, I know you're in there. What's going on?"

Kayla opened the door in time to see Sandy squinting slightly, one of the few facial expressions she openly displayed when concerned. "What's wrong? You look terrible," Sandy asked.

"Well, hello to you too," Kayla muttered blandly. She'd been avoiding Sandy all weekend too.

"I'm sorry for being so abrupt, Kayla, but I've left messages for you in the past two days and haven't heard a word from you. I thought maybe something had happened to you. Even your mother called and asked me if I'd heard from you."

Kayla immediately felt guilty. "Did she sound real worried?" She continued to towel-dry her hair as Sandy walked to the fridge, scouting for something to drink.

"No, I covered for you. I told her you had an important presentation that was keeping you busy, and I was sure you'd be calling her soon."

Watching Sandy as she popped open a Coke, Kayla thought of her parents, who had been married for over thirty-two years, and were still very much in love. Openly affectionate with each other, they kissed, held hands, and even joked about "getting busy." You could see the love in their eyes and how they softened when they looked at each other. Kayla wondered if anybody would ever look at her like that. She gently sat on the sofa as though it were an egg that she might crack if she sat too hard.

Taking a long swallow of her soda, Sandy waited patiently for a reply. After a few minutes she walked over to Kayla sitting on the sofa. "Well, what's wrong?"

She told Sandy about the comment Justin made, how she'd spent the weekend upset, and her disastrous presentation. True to form, Sandy was a good friend, knowing when to listen, and when to be quiet and let her friend decipher the dilemma on her own.

Sandy went to the kitchen and got a glass of water for her friend. She handed Kayla the glass and said, "You know I'll do whatever I can to help you salvage the account. And I'm glad you finally handled that insanity with Justin. It may hurt a little now, but you know you had to do it."

"Yes, I did. I waited too long to do it too. I should have moved on before now." Kayla took a drink of water and looked at Sandy. Raising the glass in a mock celebration, she said, "Cheers. Now please help with the Johnson account."

Kayla knew her friend was full of creative ideas, and as director of marketing for a cosmetic company, always created unique ideas to market and promote the company she represented. She'd been successful in directly targeting her market, creating imaginative campaigns and promotions that netted the company millions of dollars. Sandy was definitely on top of her game. She had an amazing ability of knowing where to go with ideas, developing them to their fullest potential and then executing them.

"Why don't you get some rest tonight, and tomorrow night let's get together and strategize how we can salvage this account for you? It's probably not as bad as you think, and by all means call your mother." Kayla gave her friend a hug and thanked her. "Now, Ms. Girl, you know I don't go for all that mushy stuff. You just have your butt home by 6:00 tomorrow evening and we are going to turn the Johnson Group out. They're gonna beg to let you represent them."

Kayla was dressed and out of the house by 6:00 A.M. Tuesday, ready to take control of her life once more. Margaret called in sick again, and Kayla worked feverishly the entire day trying to get caught up with phone calls, her next presentation, which was scheduled in two weeks, and various other tasks that required her attention. Just as she'd turned off her computer, her phone rang. Initially she just looked at it, her gut telling her it was trouble calling.

Reluctantly she picked up the phone and tried to sound more optimistic than she felt. "Hello, this is Kayla Marshall."

"Hello, Kayla, how are you?" She could hear her stomach start to rumble like an old car on a too-cold Chicago morning.

"I'm fine, Mr. Newhouse, what can I do for you?" she asked with a bit more attitude than she planned, not being in the mood for small talk.

"Kayla, that's one of the things that this firm needs, more team spirit. You're always willing to lend a hand. Actually, I have an enormous favor to ask of you. It appears that one of our brightest senior account executives is having a difficult time with closing business. Probably just needs a little push, he seems to be in a slump. I understand you have one pending, the Johnson Group. I'd like for you to bring him in on that if you can."

Swallowing hard, she feared she wouldn't be able to answer if she couldn't get rid of the huge lump that had formed in her throat. "Sure, Mr. Newhouse, who is it?"

An uncomfortable silence, then, "Mr. Edward Oswell."

She guessed from the formal way he said the name that it was more of a command than a request. After all, you could decline a request.

"Give Mr. Oswell a call tomorrow and bring him up to speed on the particulars. He will be there to assist, observe, whatever capacity you feel most comfortable with. And more importantly, Kayla, would you let me know what your thoughts are on Ed and how he conducts himself?"

"Sure, Mr. Newhouse, I'll give him a call. Anything else?"

"No, that's it for now, thanks for your help, Kayla."

His last statement sounded perfunctory. The day had worn her out too much to wonder what the real deal was, so she shrugged the conversation off, packed up, and headed home.

Chapter 5

Once home, she telephoned her mother, apologizing for not returning her calls and promising to make more time for family. Her younger brother, Terrance, was a senior at Morris Brown. She tried to call him at least once a month and sent money monthly to help her parents with his expenses. Kayla knew Terrance probably spent more time checking out the females at Spelman. He had declared himself a "babe magnet" when he was sixteen. He was tall like their father, with hazel eyes that drove the girls crazy. Voted "Most Popular" in his high school class, as well as "Most Likely to Succeed," Terrance was smart and athletic, which always seemed a marvel to Kayla since most of the jocks she'd met limited their conversation to sports and seemed to be under the misimpression that she enjoyed watching them simonizing their cars.

She'd dated a few jocks in high school who were all so insipid their names now escaped her, with the exception of one. Carl Vaughan was the subject of many girls' reveries at her high school. It seemed no girl was immune to his squared, well-defined jawline that models were paid good money for. He was café au lait–colored, with full, sensual lips that were only emphasized by his habit of running his fingers along each side of his moustache and licking his lips, which absolutely drove the girls to fits of fantasy. The real kicker was his smoldering dark eyes that seemed to melt all that dared to look directly into them. Handsome to a fault, he had a rock-solid body that drew collective sighs from all the females, including a few teachers, whenever he walked down the hall.

More importantly he was the epitome of a jock, captain of the football team, played varsity basketball, even soccer. The boy was a master at sports, but flunked every class in high school except physical education. He graduated a year behind his class. He carried a football on their dates and constantly talked about sports or professional athletes.

Eventually Kayla got tired of having to explain everything she said to him—not that he was moronic, just that his priorities and interests were different. The boy couldn't tell you that H_2O was water, but constantly quoted sports statistics. Formal education held no importance to him. No, Kayla had one jock and she'd never have another one. She went more for the cerebral type, even though they were usually not as well built as the jocks. She swore you could bounce a quarter off of Carl's butt and it would make change.

Her sister, Janae, was happily married to her high school sweetheart, with a beautiful little girl, and a big house in the burbs. Kayla and Janae weren't as close as when they were younger, both being so busy and now talking less than once a week. Kayla couldn't remember when they'd stopped spending hours on the phone. There was a time when she had enough time for family, but lately there wasn't enough for herself, let alone family.

Kayla felt a little jealous that her sister was so happily married. She knew it sounded cliché to admit to anyone, herself included, but she wanted it all, the great job, coupled with a loving, supportive man, and children. She loved her job and knew that she had a bright future with the company, but there was something missing, or more accurately, someone. Initially, she thought that someone was Justin, but now she wasn't sure.

She'd grown up in a close, loving family, and despite the fact that everyone was busy now with school, their own families, and work, she wanted very much to have a family like the one she grew up in. At some point she knew it would be time to get off the roller coaster and figure out what direction she wanted her life to take and more importantly how she was going to take it there.

Sandy arrived promptly at 6:00 and they began working immediately on the presentation. Kayla ordered pizza and for the first few hours the work was so intense she wondered if they'd remain friends afterward. They disagreed on several points, but came to make compromises. Finally, after hours of work they had a presentation they believed would induce the Johnson Group to sign on the dotted line. Kayla hoped she'd be able to schedule another meeting. Sam Newhouse had questioned her about the project and an expected close date. Kayla had managed to skirt the issue, but knew the man could detect a delay tactic when he heard one.

After finalizing the presentation on her computer, they strategized on reasons to call a third meeting. Kayla wished she had Sandy's sense of style and her ability to finesse anybody whenever she wanted.

"Okay, I'm beat, Kay, let's go for a quick nightcap and unwind a little."

"I'm too tired to go anywhere. I have some Moet chilling in the fridge, we can pop that, put on some music, and unwind. As a matter of fact, why don't you spend the night?" Sandy moved her head to one side, not looking at all convinced. "Come on, Sandy, it'll be fun."

Sandy stood up and began stretching her long lithe body, reminding Kayla of a cat. "Quit sounding like a twelve-year-old, and what do you propose I wear to work in the morning?"

"You know I have plenty of work clothes for you to choose from, and we can just throw your undies in the washer."

"Please, you know I can't wear your clothes, Ms. Conservative. You probably don't even own anything red, or anything that hangs above the knee. Have me going to work looking like Barbara Bush, pearls and all."

They both laughed good-naturedly. "Excuse me, Ms. Hoochie, but I have stylish clothes, I just don't choose to wear them to work."

"Oh, yeah, well, let's see these 'stylish' clothes. I do have a rep at work to maintain." They walked into the bedroom and opened the door to the expansive walk-in closet.

"Well, if you don't see anything you like I think that new store stays open late." Kayla knew Sandy loved to shop and was always ready to patronize any new store.

"I know you haven't been holding out on me, what new store? Where is it?"

Kayla began laughing uncontrollably. "Hoochies R Us!" She grabbed her stomach as she'd began getting a cramp from laughing so hard. Sandy looked as though she were ready to strangle her. "I'm sorry, Sandy, it was just too easy." She grabbed her friend by the hand. "Come on now, you know I got you good."

"I know you not trying to diss me with that old tired line! Maybe dumping that Justin is just what your conservative behind needs."

Having gained some of her confidence back, Kayla replied, "Please don't mention that name in my presence." Looking pensively at her friend, she continued, "You know, he had nerve enough to leave a message for me at work. I was sure he got the message. I don't know what else to say to him."

"Just think about all the stuff that he's done and said to you in the past year and, honey, you'll have plenty to say." Sandy didn't attempt to mask her dislike for Justin as the sarcasm edged her words.

"Did you ever call Barb?" Sandy inquired.

"No. I've been too busy."

"You should make time for your friends, Kayla. We're all busy. I think sometimes you find it hard to be friends with someone they view as competition."

Kayla pursed her lips in defense. "Don't even try that, Sandy, you know I have no problem being around attractive women."

"It's not the physical appearance that concerns you, Kay, it's the success, work thing that drives you away. Deep down you are the most driven, competitive person I know, and you constantly strive to be the best. You can deal with a beautiful woman like Vanessa Williams. Your problem comes from the corporate sister that is driven and successful."

Kayla began clapping her hands. "Thank you for the unsolicited analysis, Dr. Neal, but you should stop watching *Oprah* because you are totally off base. Growing up in a family that expects only the best from their oldest child is what drives me, and although I do lack confidence in my body, as most women do, I don't lack confidence in my ability. I don't have a problem with women who are as successful as I am, or more."

She looked at Sandy for understanding, but didn't believe her point was accepted so she continued. "Case in point, I am very close to Deb at work, who is also a senior account executive and brings in almost as much revenue as I do. And you gonna say Vanessa Williams isn't *successful* and beautiful?"

Sandy looked at her and shook her head from side to side. "Kay, you miss the mark entirely. I'm too tired to explain it to you. Just pay more attention to your actions and feelings when you're around competitive sisters and we'll talk. And furthermore, Oprah always takes the high road, she doesn't do shows on impertinent subject matter."

"Well, if it's so impertinent, why are you calling me on it?" Kayla was starting to feel challenged.

"It may be impertinent to Oprah, but it's very pertinent to you, since you are the one that needs to address the issue."

"Okay, Sandy, now you're sounding like some low-budget talk show host."

"Whatever, girlfriend, just mind my observation. Notice how competitive you are when it comes—"

Kayla held up her hand. "Sandy, please, now really, you know how competitive the advertising game is. You can't tell me that you don't go after the jugular of your competition, be they female or male."

"All right, Kayla, I'll give you that, only because I'm

too tired to debate you, and I know how you are when you make your mind up about something or get on a roll. I'll just say one more thing, and that is you need to make more time for yourself and quit spending all your time working." Sandy looked tired as she stretched and yawned. "You happy now? 'Cause you've won this one only because I'm tired."

Kayla smiled victoriously. She always enjoyed a lively conversation, especially when she could wear her opponent down. She knew Sandy was right about her spending more time away from work—she was too driven and as a result had slighted herself and her family.

The next morning went amazingly smooth, Kayla thought. She had to share a bathroom with her sister growing up, and mornings were peppered with yelling and lots of name-calling. She and Janae had constantly fought over clothes, bathroom time, makeup, curlers, and everything else.

Sandy prepared a light breakfast of bagels, cream cheese, orange juice, and coffee. Turning on the radio, she said, "You know I have a huge crush on him."

Kayla looked at her with a mouthful of bagel and asked, "Him who?"

"J. Anthony Brown from the *Tom Joyner Show.*"

"Girl, get out of here! Have you ever seen him? I think he has children your age!" Kayla laughed uncontrollably, covering her mouth, trying to keep the bagel in.

Sandy was serious, as she put her hands on her hips. "Girlfriend, you know I like a man with some experience. And no, I've never seen him, but I love his sense of humor. I . . . I just think he's creative and talented. He got what they used to say in the seventies, 'soul.'"

"I like a lot of men's sense of humor and wit, but that doesn't mean I want to get with them. You are so out there. He doesn't fit your profile of the kind of men you like. He's old and on the hefty side, definitely not your kind of eye candy."

"Yeah, you're right." Then looking Kayla in the eye, she mused, "Where do you think he hangs out when he comes to Chicago?"

Kayla responded loudly, "KFC!" They both bowled over with laughter.

"Besides," Kayla continued after the laughter died down, "Myra J., Sybil, and Ms. Dupree are the real stars of that show. They just let Tom and Jay act like they running things, like most of us sisters do." They both burst into more laughter.

After sharing a few minutes more of small talk, Sandy was grabbing her purse and briefcase, heading toward the door, telling her friend, "You make it a good day, Kayla, I'll call you later. Good luck, although I know you won't need it. You're going to be fierce."

"Thanks for always being there for me, Sandy, you're the best. If I can pull this Johnson account out of the fire, we'll paint the town."

"Not if, when, and you're on."

When Kayla walked in at 7:15 Margaret was already hard at work. "Good morning, Margaret, and welcome back. Hope you're feeling better."

"Thanks, Ms. Marshall, I'm feeling much better. How'd the Johnson Group presentation go?"

"Don't ask, but it's about to improve. As a matter of fact Mr. Johnson is usually in his office by 8:00 so please get him on the phone for me promptly at 8:05. We want him to have that first morning cup of java." Kayla was all business this morning, determined more than ever to salvage the account.

"Sure thing. Anything else?"

"Not right now, Margaret. Thanks."

Kayla spent the next half hour rehearsing her presentation and thinking about what she would say to Mr. Johnson. At 8:05, she took a deep breath and picked up the phone.

From the moment she said hello, Mr. Johnson was putty in her hands. He confided in her that the other members of the group weren't impressed with her presentation and had sought out another firm to market the project. Kayla convinced him to give her another chance and told him she was prepared to meet with the group at lunchtime and would provide the lunch.

"Well, we've got another company coming in at 2:30 today."

"I'll be there at 12:00 with a catered lunch, make my presentation without interrupting your afternoon plans, and be out by 1:30." Looking like she did when she was twelve and wishing for a new cassette player, with her eyes closed and fingers crossed, she prayed in her mind. She wanted him to say yes.

"This group never turns down a free lunch, we'll see you in our office at noon. Kayla, I have a lot of faith in you, but you'd better be prepared this time, or there won't be anything else I can do for you."

Feeling bad for letting him down, she softened her voice. "Thanks for this opportunity, Mr. Johnson, I'm certain you'll be very pleased." She couldn't remember what she'd promised her parents she'd do if they got her that cassette player, but she knew what she had to do for the Johnson Group to warrant the trust he'd put in her.

Kayla jumped from her chair with both hands raised. She could almost smell victory. She pressed her intercom button and directed, "Margaret, call the caterers and arrange to have an assortment of sandwiches, beverages, and dessert sent over to the Johnson Group at 12:00 today. Select whatever you think is appropriate from the menu, there will be five us including myself."

"I'll take care of it right away, Ms. Marshall, I have the owner's home number on my computer as well as the menu. If the shop's not open, I'll call him at home. You know, I think he has a little crush on me." Kayla had never thought of Margaret having a social life. She was probably in her early fifties, although looking much younger, divorced, attractive, and very capable. Kayla made a mental note to get closer to her more-than-efficient secretary. If all went according to plan, Margaret would accompany her to that VP slot, which would mean a substantial raise for both of them.

"Well, you talk sweetly to him because this lunch is vital to our future, and we need all the help we can get."

Margaret nodded to herself and was about to tackle the task with full steam when Kayla said, "Also call Ed Oswell and tell him he can observe the presentation. Give him the time and location, I'll meet him there."

If Margaret had any concerns she kept them to herself as she replied, "Sure thing, Ms. Marshall."

The group was obviously more impressed with her second presentation. Positive affirmation appeared on their faces and in their body language as they nodded approvingly during her presentation. All questions were answered before they were asked. Kayla had anticipated their objections and handled them skillfully. After a brief talk amongst themselves while she had gone to the ladies' room, Mr. Johnson stood up when she returned and pushed the telephone intercom button. "Ms. Baker, call my 2:30 appointment and tell him we will not be meeting with him this afternoon. We've selected someone to represent us. Thank him for his time and effort."

Kayla was so excited she couldn't help grinning while her mind shouted *Yes!* She turned her attention to the group. "Thank you so much for your business. We at Lancer and Newhouse will continue to do all we can to warrant your trust and business." Each member of the group took the time to shake Kayla's hand and express faith in her. They even joked about the superb lunch being the real deal maker. Kayla looked at her watch and wondered briefly what had detained Ed.

Kayla was walking to her car when she heard a voice call her name. She turned in the direction of the voice and saw Michael James wave and run toward her.

"Hey, Kayla, what a coincidence. I was just thinking about you." She barely had time to collect her thoughts when he asked, "What are you doing here?"

"Uh, I'm here on business." She tried on purpose to sound vague as she now knew that Michael was the person coming to see the Johnson Group at 2:30. Had he mentioned he was in advertising? She wasn't going to tell him that she had already nailed the account. Kayla looked at her watch and said, "I've got to run, I'm late for an appointment. See you." She felt bad about not telling Michael the truth. It wasn't her style to lie or not to be up front and honest about business matters. She knew it would haunt her, but she didn't know what to say to him.

When she returned to her office she was eagerly greeted by Margaret, who had several messages for her, including an urgent one from Mr. Newhouse. Margaret was elated to hear that the presentation was a success. "I knew if it could be saved, you'd do it. Congratulations, Ms. Marshall. Is there anything you need me to do? I'm taking a late lunch, I wanted to be here in case you needed me during your presentation."

Kayla thanked her for her contribution and told her to enjoy a long lunch.

"Actually I have a lunch date with the caterer."

Kayla smiled and said, "Be sure to tell him the lunch was a success, and I'm sure he'll get business from the Johnson Group. Thanks again, Margaret, for a job well done as usual. I hope you know how valuable you are to me. Have a wonderful lunch." She gave Margaret a sly wink and they both smiled. Kayla could have sworn she saw a mysterious gleam in Margaret's eyes as the corners of her mouth turned up into an ever-so-slight smile. "She really is an outstanding secretary. Tonight I'm gonna stop and get her a little something special. Meanwhile I guess I'll have to face the music and call Mr. Newhouse," Kayla said out loud and looked around to see if anybody heard or noticed her one-way conversation.

She tied up all her loose ends before calling Mr. Newhouse just in case he'd ask about the status of the

Johnson Group. She took the time to call the art department and thank them for their cooperation in helping her with the presentation board and slides on such short notice. She thought about calling Michael, but decided against it because she wasn't sure what she'd say. "This is Kayla Marshall returning Mr. Newhouse's call."

"One moment, Ms. Marshall."

Kayla leaned back in her chair and thought about her fat commission check and all she'd do with it when her thoughts were interrupted. "Kayla, what the hell happened with the Johnson Group? I just spoke with Henderson Brooks, who informed me that one of his sharpest account managers has an appointment with the Johnson Group this afternoon."

It amazed her that the suits were always out of the loop of current events. Despite their fat salaries and plush offices, they never knew what was going on with the bottom feeders. They usually got their news secondhand and late. They were out of touch with the front line. It seemed their sole purpose was to fraternize with clients from time to time. Kayla thought they had the easy jobs, entertaining clients over extended, expensive lunches or dinners, trying to entice them to do business. Occasionally they'd provide really big clients with exotic trips as an endorsement to sign, instead of presenting the client with the best campaign possible. Sometimes all the creative presentations she'd developed and slaved over for clients were overshadowed by a promise of a trip to Hawaii for two. It all seemed unethical, and didn't always go down easy, but she was a realist and knew that it was all part of their game.

"Mr. Newhouse, I can assure you that this account

is in the bag. As a matter of fact our legal department is drawing up the contract now and will messenger it over to them in the morning."

"I like being kept informed as to what's going on with major accounts, and you've been somewhat cagey the past few days. Is there something going on the boss should know?"

Kayla had to laugh to herself. Mr. Newhouse was never one to appear nervous or anxious. This was the first time he'd ever given one of his people carte blanche with such a major account. He had absolutely no input, and it was driving him crazy. "Mr. Newhouse, just know that we are going to enjoy a mutually beneficial partnership with the Johnson Group for a long time." She could hear the heavy sigh he expelled and almost chuckled at him over the phone. She knew it was more difficult to get big clients to sign without all the hobnobbing the suits did, but it was her preferred method: pure persuasion skills.

"Kayla, thanks for being such a good team player. Keep up the good work, and you'll be the youngest VP this company has ever had. And did young Mr. Oswell make any contributions?"

Refusing to make the man look bad, figuring he'd do that on his own, she responded, "Well, I didn't have enough time to bring him in on this one. I've reserved the big Visor presentation for him."

"That sounds fair to me. Congratulations again, Kayla, on a job well done. We've grown to expect nothing less from you."

Kayla could feel her chest and head swelling. It was a great feeling and she wanted this high more often. She called Ed's office, got no answer, and left a message for him. She turned to her computer and went forth planning her next project, which if done properly could yield as much revenue as the Johnson Group, if not more.

Kayla worked until almost seven o'clock before remembering she wanted to stop and get something for Margaret. She tied up a few loose ends and headed for the mall, trying to figure what neat little trinket she could purchase to show her appreciation.

After locating a beautiful ethnic-print scarf for Margaret that looked classy, having it gift wrapped, and making her exit, she walked right into Barbara. "Hey, Barb, Sandy and I were just talking about you."

"Hello, Kayla. As a matter of fact I was tempted to call you today for a late lunch, but I sort of had a conflict of interest going on." Just as Kayla was about to ask her for an explanation, he turned around. It was Michael, the handsome man from the wedding, the restaurant, earlier in the day, and now here at the mall. Kayla didn't know why but the humming in her stomach started again. He was so profoundly beguiling, he literally took her breath away. She felt herself consciously holding her breath, not knowing why, unable to describe the attraction in words. Her eyes gave her away. Barbara turned around to see what had gotten the attention.

"Oh, I'm sorry, Kayla, this is—"

Kayla interrupted the introduction.

"Michael, nice to see you again," she said, a warm smile forming on her face.

"Kayla, it's nice to see you too."

Kayla felt that same calm she had experienced at the wedding. This was unusual because she always felt nervous around men she found attractive.

Michael explained to Barb that they'd met a few

weeks earlier at a wedding, and had run into each other briefly at a restaurant and earlier that day. His deep dimples were so sexy she just knew he had women all over Chicago and the surrounding cities sighing his name into their pillow at night. Kayla turned back to Barb. "What'd you mean when you said you had a conflict of interest today?"

"Oh, never mind, I'll call you later this week," she said, waving her hand as if to clear her thoughts.

Kayla was wondering if Barb and Michael were dating, or what the nature of their relationship was when he asked, "We're about to go for a drink, would you like to join us?"

"I would love to, but I've had a full day, and I'm ready for my bed. Thanks for the invitation, Michael. Maybe next time?" Kayla looked into his pool of brown eyes as though she could detect sincerity if she looked deep or long enough. Instead all she did was get lost in those beautiful, soulful eyes.

"Well, I hope next time is real soon. Too much rejection isn't good for my ego." His voice was low and sensual, flirty. Michael's gaze was intense and Kayla felt warm under it. She figured she'd be sighing his name into her pillow tonight.

Barbara glanced from Michael to Kayla with a perplexed look on her face. Then recognizing the attraction, she mused, "Do you two want to be alone or what?"

Michael and Kayla managed to look away from each other and at Barb. They saw that she meant the comment good-naturedly. It didn't take a Rhodes scholar to figure out they were obviously absorbed in each other. They all laughed and bade good night to one another, promising to get together soon.

Kayla didn't want to think about Michael, but she did. She pondered if he was as wonderful as he seemed. She thought back to the many flawed men she'd met during her early dating years. One such flawed man had the audacity to ask another woman for her phone number while Kayla was in the ladies' room. When Kayla caught him, he came up with some lame excuse about this woman being an old friend of his cousin who had to move suddenly and lost touch with her friend.

He had a wandering eye the entire night; it was surprising he hadn't gotten whiplash from the constant rubbernecking, trying to get a look at every woman in the place. She appropriately named him "Rover." After she'd had enough of his disrespect, she told him she was going outside for a minute to cool down. Being the fool that he was, he made no offer to join her outside where she hailed a cab and went home.

When Kayla finally returned home from the mall, she took time to call her parents, and then Sandy, who wasn't home. She showered and fell asleep across her bed reading an *Essence* magazine. Her dream was so vivid she could hear her own labored breathing. She and Michael were making slow, burning, passionate love. She woke up at 2:30 drenched with sweat, heart racing, dry mouth, and horny. She got a glass of milk and returned to bed. Kayla was up before her alarm went off and was out the door before 7:00. She was determined to seize the day.

She was on a roll and felt there was no time to be complacent. Margaret was obviously pleased when Kayla presented her with the scarf she'd purchased at the mall. "Thank you so much, you really didn't have to do that."

Kayla enjoyed making people happy and knew when she made that climb upstairs Margaret would be joining her if she chose to. "As a matter of fact, if you don't have lunch plans with your caterer I'd like to treat you to lunch."

"Oh, Ms. Marshall, you don't have to do that."

Kayla retorted, "Oh, yes, I do, I don't want you to feel taken for granted and get snatched away. You're a valued asset to this company and especially to me. I can't imagine doing this job without you."

Margaret was touched as a smile lit up her face. They agreed to lunch at Maxine's Diner, which was known for its authentic jerk chicken.

Kayla spent most of the morning researching and planning her next presentation. Margaret interrupted her at 11:45 with a call from Justin.

She cleared her throat as she prepared to speak to him for the first time in several days. "Hello, Mr. Kincaid," she greeted him professionally. She didn't want him to get the impression he could slither his way back into her life.

"Hello, Kay, it's good to hear your voice, baby, I've missed you."

She countered, "What do you want, Justin? I'm very busy." There was a pause and she could picture him sitting there rubbing his forehead as he always did whenever trying to get into her good graces again. Making sure he'd say the right thing, he carefully selected his words. If only he'd be so careful at other times.

"I first want to apologize for upsetting you Saturday, and make it right by coming over tonight, cooking dinner for you, maybe giving you a bubble bath and a deep oil massage."

"No, thank you, Justin. This is not working for me and hasn't been working for a long time." A moment of silence passed and Kayla wasn't sure if he heard her.

"What's not working for you, Kayla?"

He could be so dense sometimes, she thought. "I thought I made myself clear on Saturday. It's over. We're over. I don't know any other way to say it. You are not working for me."

"Are you still upset about the wedding? I swear you can be so singly focused sometimes."

Kayla's temperature rose three degrees as she got angry. "I was trying to end this amicably, but I see you want to take it further. Well, let me tell you this, Justin." She got up to close her door because she knew that the conversation was going to end badly and she didn't want her business all over the office.

"I may be singly focused at times, but at least I'm warm and considerate, which is a lot more than I can say about you. And we won't bother to discuss your other shortcomings." She had to smile at the pun she'd just made.

He sighed as though bored and then he asked, "What shortcomings do I have, Kayla?"

The tone of his question indicated that he obviously wasn't interested in what she had to say.

"Justin, it's over."

"How can it be over, Kay? You don't fall out of love just like that."

He didn't sound at all convincing, which made Kayla wonder why she'd never seen it before.

"Justin, I've never really been in love with you, I liked the idea of being in love with you. I thought you were the kind of man I wanted, but you're not. You never loved me."

"You're just still upset about the wedding. How about we go—"

Kayla stopped him before he could continue. "Did I mention the fact that you don't listen? Justin, you don't satisfy me emotionally or physically. There's nothing left to say but good-bye." She gently laid the phone in the cradle as he continued to talk.

Within seconds Margaret buzzed Kayla and indicated she had a call. Preparing to let Justin have it, Kayla picked up. "This is Kayla Marshall."

"Hello, Kayla, this is Michael James. I just wanted to congratulate you on getting the Johnson Group. You could have told me when we ran into each other. You obviously knew why I was there. It seems I misjudged you. I didn't think you were a petty person." His voice was firm and spoke of his disappointment.

Still upset from her conversation with Justin, Kayla understood what it felt like to have misjudged someone. "I'm really sorry, Michael. I just felt awkward and didn't know what to say. Sometimes in this business you never know how people are going to react. I don't know you and just assumed the worst."

Michael thought about it and knew she was right. He liked this woman for all the things she was and all the things she said. Kayla was smart and handled herself very well. He liked her honesty and the way she accepted responsibility for her behavior.

"Apology accepted." The smile in his voice could be heard over the telephone.

Kayla relaxed and could feel comfort enveloping her.

Michael continued after a brief silence. "Well, I've been trying to get to know you since we met a few weeks ago at the wedding. My friends can vouch for me. It seems we have a few in common."

Kayla smiled at the thought. "So I've discovered. How about I give you my home phone number and you call me tonight?"

Michael replied with an enthusiastic "Yes, that'll be great."

She recited her home phone number and they said their good-byes.

Margaret walked into Kayla's office, just in time to see her smiling at the phone. "You ready for lunch?"

Kayla smiled broadly. She grabbed her purse and said, "Sure, let's go."

"Ms. Marshall, you are glowing, you really look happy. Does it have anything to do with the nice young man that called you earlier?"

"You are an absolutely amazing woman, Margaret, or am I that transparent?"

Once at the elevator, Margaret pushed the down button. "No, not at all, it's just there are some things a woman instinctively knows." Both of them smiled.

They were seated at Maxine's, one of the best Jamaican restaurants around. Kayla knew she should have the salad, but she wasn't going to sit in a Jamaican restaurant and nibble on lettuce, so she ordered the jerk chicken. She and Margaret seemed able to talk about everything, family, friends, hobbies, and of course that subject all women love to discuss whenever they get together: men.

Margaret had gone out with the caterer, Thomas. He was widowed, with a married son that lived in Atlanta. Margaret had no children, and confided in

Kayla that she'd always wanted children, but her ex-husband never wanted any, and after almost twenty years of marriage, decided he didn't want her either.

"Margaret, I know you've always had a formal relationship with your past managers, but I would appreciate it if you would please call me Kayla."

Margaret seemed to beam with delight as she lifted her fork toward her lips. "It may take some getting used to, but I think I can manage that, Kayla." They both chuckled and continued to enjoy lunch. After a sinful chocolate dessert, Margaret thanked Kayla for the wonderful lunch. When they returned to the office each went about her own tasks, knowing they'd grown closer and had gained new respect for one another.

Kayla was surprised when Ed Oswell hadn't returned her call. Dialing his extension again, she got his secretary. "I left a message for him yesterday and haven't heard from him," she said.

"I'm sorry, Ms. Marshall, but he's out ill today. You want me to transfer you into his voice mail, or leave another message for him? I expect him back tomorrow."

How curious, Kayla thought. He'd obviously gone to Mr. Newhouse and asked to be teamed with her, and now he was out ill. She thought back to the last time she'd seen him. He looked frightened, but maybe he was sick. She decided not to waste any more time trying to determine his agenda. He could try to climb his way to the top, but it wouldn't be on her back. She decided then not to call him again, she'd sit and wait for him to call and make the next move.

Shortly before lunch, Ed Oswell stormed into Kayla's office. The calm temperament of the previous meeting had been replaced by a blatant, hateful stare that sent a chill down her spine. "Well, it's good to see you've returned to the land of the living," she said.

Through clenched teeth and with balled fists he sneered, "Cut the crap, Kayla, why'd you give the wrong time for the presentation with the Johnson Group?"

Refusing to be intimidated, Kayla slowly rose as she returned the glare and sneer. "I don't know what your problem is, but I had my assistant call. You weren't there and she left a message."

"She clearly is incompetent then, because the voice mail said to meet you there at 3:00 P.M. When I got there you'd left."

She took a deep breath to calm herself down. Kayla was determined not to allow him to cause her to lose her professionalism.

Gathering her professional demeanor, she suggested, "We can clear this up momentarily. Margaret just went to make copies, she'll be back shortly. Have a seat. Would you like something to drink?"

His creased forehead began to relax and some of the red had diminished from his face. "Uh, no, thanks. Look, I think I know what happened." The anger had been replaced by nervousness as he sat down and began biting at his cuticle. His movements were quick as he peered from Kayla to the outer office. When he saw Margaret coming, he leaped from the chair and ran to meet her. Kayla came from behind her desk, unsure what he was planning to do or say.

Beads of perspiration popping off of his forehead, he grabbed Margaret by the arm. "Margaret, when you called my office and left a message regarding the Johnson presentation, are you sure you left the correct time?"

Margaret appeared startled by his appearance and quickly replied, "I'm certain. There was no question of the time. I asked you to call me if the time posed a conflict for you." She was withdrawing from his grasp and looking at him as though he were a leper. "Now please let go of my arm."

"Come to think about it, that wasn't your voice. They're trying to make me look bad." Ed stormed away as suddenly as he came.

By the time Kayla had gotten to Margaret, Ed was nowhere in sight.

"What on earth is wrong with him?" Margaret's professional demeanor was gone, the homegirl attitude was front and center as she stood with hands on hips ready to finish whatever Ed was starting.

Kayla's eyes were twice their normal size. "I don't know, he's all upset saying he was given the wrong time for the meeting, which is a lie. The correct time and place for the meeting was left on his voice mail."

Kayla patted Margaret on the back, knowing that whatever happened, Margaret was not at fault. "He's probably still a bit under the weather. Don't concern yourself with it. I'm sure he'll figure out the misunderstanding."

"He said something about somebody trying to make him look bad."

The rest of the workday flew by like a weird dream. After a brief meeting with the art department in preparation for her next presentation, Kayla felt great. She decided to leave work early and stop by Jewel's grocery store to pick up something for dinner. She would cook herself a nice meal and maybe curl up to watch television.

When Kayla returned home she was looking forward

to Michael's call. At exactly seven o'clock, the phone
rang and she instantly knew it was him. "Hello."

"Hi, Kayla, it's Michael. How was your day?"

"It was great. I'm just about to settle down to a little television. Would you like to join me?"

It was an invitation he'd waited for weeks to re-
ceive. "I'd like that very much. Give me your address
and I can be there in an hour."

Kayla gave her address and directions.

"Can I bring anything?" he asked in a low voice
that seemed to go right through her.

"I don't do much during the week. If you like we
could maybe rent a movie. Thought we could have
time to talk a little, get to know each other."

"Sounds good to me. I'll pick up a movie and a few
snacks. Anything in particular you'd like to see?"

She couldn't get over how thoughtful and considerate he was. She knew she'd never be able to settle
for less again. "Whatever you select will be fine, but
I've got snacks here."

"I'll be there in about an hour."

Michael arrived with two of her favorite movies, a
bottle of wine, a single red rose, fresh strawberries
dipped in chocolate, and a smile Kayla swore was
heaven-sent. "Are the movies okay?" he asked with a
concerned look on his face.

"They're two of my favorites. I don't know how you
do it, but you seem to instinctively know what I like."

Michael leaned over and planted a sweet, solicitous
kiss on her lips. The citrus and sandalwood aroma of
his cologne coupled with the soft touch of his inviting lips made her want to pull him closer to her, and
she did. She planted a steamy kiss on his lips that invited him to wrap his arms around her, and he did.

As they slowly parted, she continued to taste the sweetness of his kiss. "I think we'd better watch the movie before we get into trouble."

He smiled at her, dimples looking deeper and sexier than ever.

Michael couldn't pinpoint exactly what it was about this woman that made him want her more each time he saw her. He loved the way the corners of her mouth turned up slightly, giving her the appearance of always smiling. Her soft, gentle brown eyes always seemed to invite him into her soul, even when her mouth said no. Kayla was compassionate and understanding. The sound of her voice excited him. Yes, in his mind, Kayla Marshall was the one. He had been mesmerized by her since the first time she'd landed in his arms at the wedding.

Once they settled down to watch the movie, Kayla turned off the lights and lit several scented candles that gave the room a dim romantic glow. Kayla looked even more inviting by candlelight, Michael thought, and was determined that one day he'd even share such an intimate thought with her. They stole glances at each other, each of them wondering what the other was thinking. Michael put his arm around her shoulder and she nestled closer to him. They held hands, and felt the flow of electricity being exchanged.

By late evening they were seated on the floor Indian style listening to music, laughing, and talking. Kayla couldn't remember feeling so totally relaxed with a man before. They sipped glasses of wine, traded childhood experiences and stories. Michael suddenly stood up. "I forgot something, I'll be right back."

He returned from the kitchen with the chocolate-covered strawberries and napkins. He sat down and took one of the strawberries out and placed it gently in Kayla's mouth. She could feel the juice from the strawberry start to run down her chin. Michael dabbed at it with one of the napkins he'd brought from the kitchen. She closed her eyes and savored the sweetness of the chocolate and slightly tart taste of the strawberry mingling in her mouth.

"Mmmm, Michael, this is sooo good."

He had to chuckle at her delightful satisfaction with simple things. "I'm glad you're enjoying them."

When she opened her eyes, he was staring intently at her. His piercing brown eyes seemed to penetrate down deep into her soul where she'd never allowed anyone to go. His glare was removing the layers she'd planted there to try and protect herself from deep hurt. She felt exposed and uneasy. "What are you thinking, Michael? You look intense."

"Do I? It's just that I enjoy watching you. You're so unique, so very beautiful inside and out. I can't imagine any place I'd rather be, Kayla, than with you." He reached out and caressed her face with such gentleness and longing, she could feel the heat where he had touched her all the way to her feet. His touch sent electric pulses through her and she knew she had to have him. He was the kind of man she wanted to hold her, kiss her, and make love to her.

Michael could feel the heat too and leaned over and held her delicately in his arms. They were both silent for several minutes, but they knew it was a beginning foundation for their relationship. It was quiet and unspoken, but they both knew where they wanted the relationship to go.

He had penetrated her soul as no man had ever done. They spent several minutes in a warm embrace, listening to music and enjoying the flow of love that they knew had engulfed them both.

Kayla refused to answer the phone when it rang, she was far too comfortable in Michael's arms. She let the voice mail pick it up.

When it was time to leave, Michael was hesitant. "I've enjoyed my evening. You've got work tomorrow and so do I, but let's do this again real soon." He leaned over and kissed her lips gently at first, but followed with a second kiss that was more demanding. She inched closer to him and put her arms around his neck, pulled him closer, and kissed him so passionately that afterward they both reeled back.

"Yes, soon," she said, her voice barely above a whisper.

Checking her voice mail the next morning, Kayla discovered Ed was the one who'd called when she and Michael were together. He'd left her a message asking her to call him at home and to please not leave any messages for him at work, mumbling something about someone trying to make him look bad. The message sounded ominous and made her feel uncomfortable, but not uncomfortable enough not to return the call. He wasn't home, and she didn't leave him a message, finding it all too clandestine.

Kayla decided to be more daring in her work attire that morning. She had found a striking red leather pantsuit at one of the designer shops, and when she tried it on, Sandy told her she had to have it. It accentuated all of her best features, it hugged her hips just enough to be flattering, and the color made her face glow. Looking in the mirror at it on her now, she had to admit it was a good choice.

Kayla grabbed her keys and was going to the

garage when her doorbell rang. She wondered who would be calling on her so early. Her answer came quickly when she opened the door and found Justin standing there.

"Where are you going in that getup?"

"I'm going to work. Friday is casual day at the office and even though this isn't really casual I felt like wearing something different." She stopped herself as she thought, *Why am I explaining this to you?*

"Well, it's definitely different. Don't you think that's a little inappropriate for the office?"

She looked at his navy designer suit and matching tie with an immaculate white shirt and shook her head.

"It looks more like, like . . . clubbing gear, something you'd wear out tonight rather than to an office."

"Justin, what do you want? I made it clear that I didn't want to see you anymore."

"I didn't mean the outfit was inappropriate, I just don't think it looks professional enough to be worn to the office." He tried to gently push past her to get inside the house.

Kayla blocked him. "Well, maybe it's not appropriate to wear to your office, but we don't have stiff lawyers dictating what we can and can't wear in our office. That's one of the things I like about Lancer and Newhouse, we celebrate our uniqueness. It's one of the reasons for our success, we encourage people to step outside the normal realm of thinking and go for the unique ideas and presentations."

Justin shrugged his shoulders, peeking inside the house. "Well, whatever. Do you have any of the Jamaican coffee I like?"

Kayla raised her hand to stop him. "I don't know why we're having this conversation. You're not listening to me, Justin. It's over, no more Jamaican coffee for you here, or anything else for that matter."

Justin smiled devilishly and said, "Come on, Kay, you know you miss me. Girl, we could get in a quickie before work."

She returned the smile and said, "That was your other shortcoming. You need to purchase some Kama Sutra books, tapes, or something. Women want more than a quickie, Justin."

The comment threw him off guard and he retaliated. "You can be so crass sometimes. I should have known I could never put lipstick on a pig. My mother warned me."

Kayla gave him an icy stare and a cold smile. "I guess I'm supposed to be insulted, huh? Well, you and your arrogant mama can be happy now. I never want to see you again."

She pointed toward his car. "Leave. And before you get involved with another woman, I suggest you research what it takes to please a woman. Especially what it takes to please a woman in bed, because you certainly fall short there, Uncle Ben."

He looked curiously at her. "You've lost your mind. Who is Uncle Ben?"

"You are, minute man." With that she stood back and slammed the door, turned the lock, and headed toward the garage.

Kayla couldn't wait to get to her office and call Sandy to tell her about the incident.

"Now that's what Oprah calls closure, girl! Did you really call him Uncle Ben?"

"Yep, I sure did, and it felt really good. Really, really good!" They both laughed.

"You know, he told me a long time ago that he'd never been dumped by a woman. I think that's why it's been difficult for him to accept it, but he won't be showing up on my doorstep again."

"Well, let me know if you want to key his fancy car or have his electricity disconnected. You know, any of the fun stuff we used to do back in the day to let a man know we meant business. I'm game."

Kayla grinned. "No, thank you. He's immature enough. The sad thing is I can't believe I walked around for three years thinking he was what I wanted. Sandy, I don't know where my head was all that time and it frightens me. How could I have been so blind and stupid?" Kayla sat back in her chair, her arched eyebrows knitted together, displaying her beleaguered state.

"Oh, Kay, don't go beating yourself up. People stay in relationships for a lot of reasons. I do believe you got what you needed from Justin at the time. I honestly believe at the time he was what you needed to show you what you didn't really want. Does that make sense?"

Kayla thought about it. "Sandy, that's almost profound! It's funny, but now that I really think about it, you're right. At one time I thought Justin was exactly the kind of man I wanted. He was successful and smart with a bright future. But what I realize now is that he doesn't have any of the important things I want, like compassion and warmth."

"You think Michael has what you want?"

"I know he does," Kayla purred.

"Sounds good to me. I've got to run, Kayla.

They're calling for my plane to board. Call me on my cell phone if you need me."

"Have a good trip."

"I will, bye."

After putting the finishing touches on her latest project, Kayla decided to call her friend Barb and invite her out to lunch. She felt guilty about not staying in touch with Barb. Even though they didn't talk very often she knew that they would always be friends.

She couldn't help reminiscing about how she and Barb had said when they grew up they were going to buy houses next door to each other that would have a long hallway connecting their houses so they could visit without having to step outside.

The stuff kids come up with. She laughed just thinking about their conversations. They both had wanted to get married by the time they were twenty and have four children, two boys and two girls. They fantasized about their handsome husbands, who would bring flowers home every day when returning from work. Barb always said she wanted a husband who was light-skinned with red hair and freckles, which used to crack Kayla up because Barb was so dark with jet-black long hair.

Even as a child Barb was beautiful. Her medium-brown, almond-shaped eyes seemed to leap out of her dark face. Her lips reminded one of a perfectly shaped heart. Her round face suggested the look of eternal youth. She resembled one of those exotic island beauties in a Gauguin painting. When Barb answered the phone, she sounded delighted that

Kayla was calling to invite her out to lunch. They agreed to meet at a nearby deli at 12:30.

Kayla got to the deli a few minutes early and scoped the place out for a booth so they could talk privately. She was looking forward to dishing with Barb, discovering what was going on with her competitive company. She had just gotten comfortable in the booth when she saw her friend enter the deli. Kayla stood and waved to Barbara, who headed toward the table with a smile. Barbara was stunning in a form-fitting, brown and black ethnic-print dress. Her makeup was done to perfection, just enough foundation to flatter her flawless complexion, and the brown eye shadow, expertly applied, gave her almond-shaped eyes even more expression and depth. Her lips were lined with a shade darker brown pencil than her lipstick. The entire look was totally pulled together. She could easily have been mistaken for an *Essence* cover girl.

After exchanging hellos, Barbara said, "I was so happy you called and invited me to lunch. You look fabulous in that leather!" Barb was talking so fast as she slid into the booth, Kayla hardly had time to respond. "I wish I could wear something like that, Kay. You've always had such a great figure."

Kayla leaned forward. "Barb, you must be joking. Now I know you're trying to be modest, 'cause you are wearing that dress, girl."

Barbara blushed slightly. "Thanks, but I've put on weight. I've got clothes I can't even wear anymore. Every time I open my closet, my size-eight Fubu jeans hang there laughing at me. I paid too much money for them to just hang in the closet 'cause I can't turn down a good meal."

"I know what you mean, I'm thinking about joining a gym or something. I need to lose a few vanity pounds. Eat less fat and exercise more is the only formula that works for me."

Barbara waved her hand as if dismissing the comment. "Kayla, you look great, you look like you did in high school."

"I wish." Each woman picked up a menu to decide on lunch.

"Let me know if you join a gym, I need to do something myself. We could work out together. I miss kicking it with you."

"Well, let's get what we want today and worry about dieting tomorrow." They nodded in agreement. When the waitress came and set their water down, Kayla ordered a pastrami sandwich on wheat bread with chips on the side and an iced tea.

"Same for me," Barbara said to the waitress.

"So how's everything going at Brooks and Walsh?"

"It's going very well for me, I was going to call you a few days ago. Michael was rather perturbed about the way you slighted him."

Barbara waited for a response, but Kayla only gave a tight smile. "I know, we've talked about it."

"Oh." Barbara leaned over the table. "He didn't tell me that." She smiled broadly. Despite the fact that she and her childhood best friend had gone their separate ways, Barbara understood the body language and the look Kayla had when she spoke of a man who'd sparked her interest.

"So what's going on with you two?"

Kayla told her about the chance encounters and

the night he had come over. They both agreed he was a good man. "I'm happy for you. He'd asked me a few times for your telephone number, but I wouldn't give it to him without your permission." Barbara sat back in her chair, looking satisfied.

The waitress brought the iced tea and Kayla watched as Barbara put two packs of sugar substitute in her tea. Kayla preferred just lemon in her tea. As she gently squeezed her lemon and began stirring, she asked, "Now since you want to get all into my business, tell me, who are you seeing?"

As if being slapped with a subpoena, Barbara slumped her shoulders and shifted in her chair. She'd obviously been asked this question before, Kayla thought.

The waitress interrupted their conversation as she set their lunch on the table. "Can I get you ladies anything else?"

"No, thank you," they said at the same time and giggled like the two little girls they had been the last time they shared a meal.

"Kayla, I've been so busy, I don't have a social life, you know how it is. I'm surprised you got time for a man. I thought I had met Mr. Right, but he turned out to be Mr. Totally Unsatisfactory. But I must confess Michael has a brother that's a year younger than him, named Trent, that I would love to hook up with."

Before biting into her sandwich, Kayla curiously asked, "So what's the holdup?"

"No holdup, I just can't seem to accidentally run into him. It seems we don't go to the same places or know any of the same people."

"Well, how do you know you want to hook up with him?"

"Michael brought him to our company picnic a few months ago. We were having a nice conversation until these women kept coming over interrupting. I couldn't believe the way some of these chicks were acting. I see them at work every day and they're so professional and poised. Girl, when that man came around, all that went out the window. You should have seen the way they were throwing themselves at him." That eyebrow went up again, and the corners of her mouth tilted slighting downward, showing her dissatisfaction.

Kayla was sitting straight up, listening with interest. She knew exactly what Barbara was talking about, she'd dealt with women trying to hit on Justin in her presence, totally disrespecting her. Nodding in agreement, she said, "Barb, you don't have to tell me, one woman even had the nerve to have a waiter pass her phone number to Justin in a restaurant while I went to the ladies' room. This wasn't some rib carry-out joint, it was a four-star restaurant, and this heifer was hitting on a man who was there with another woman. I wanted to go and slap her silly, but I figured she'd embarrassed herself enough."

They both agreed that reports on the shortage of men, particularly black men, had driven some women to desperate measures. After enjoying a few bites of their meal, Kayla asked, "Why not have Michael fix you up with Trent?"

Barbara swallowed her food and took a drink of her tea. "Mainly because I don't want to appear as desperate as some of those women trying to hit on him at the picnic. And I'm not sure how it will affect my friendship with Michael if things don't work out with Trent."

They both nodded in mutual understanding. "You know, Barbara, I don't get it, you're a beautiful, intelligent woman, with a good job. What's the deal? There is no way you should be out here without a good man to appreciate you."

"Kay, I can find a good man. I'm looking for the one that makes me see stars, makes my palms sweat, heart skip a beat, makes my knees weak. I'm looking for that kind of enthusiasm from a man that makes you sing in the morning, passion, kismet, whatever you wanna call it. I'm not sure if there's really a name that can accurately describe it, but that's what I want."

Kayla knew exactly what she was talking about, it was a boundless, unconditional, *let's grow old and continue to have passion* kind of love. "I know what you mean. Do you think Michael's brother is interested in you?" Kayla couldn't think of too many men who wouldn't be interested.

"Well, we definitely had some chemistry going on, but I haven't heard from him and it's been a few months."

"Has Michael said anything?"

"No, not really. I haven't talked to him about it. He's been so busy asking me about you, I'm sure the last thing he wants to talk about is my having a crush on his brother."

"I think you should ask him. After all, Michael has me."

"Hmmm. Well, okay, maybe I will ask him about Trent." Barbara pursed her lips. "Yeah, if he can put a look on my face like the one that's on yours when you say Michael's name, we definitely need to hook up."

After a few minutes of silence, Barbara took a drink of her tea and said, "You know, Kayla, what's so exceptional about the two of them, even with women throwing themselves at them all the time, they aren't affected by it. They are downright good men, they treat women with respect. Michael was really loyal to his last girlfriend."

Kayla smirked. "Now how would you know that?" She set her sandwich down and wiped her mouth with her napkin and continued, "Please, a loyal man is an oxymoron. There's no such thing, no such animal exists in the kingdom of man." She waved her hand in dismissal.

"He's honest. If he'd have cheated I'd know. He has no reason to lie to me."

"So you should ask him to introduce you to his brother again. Be honest with him and let him know you're interested in Trent."

"Like I said, Michael and I are good friends, he's like a brother. If it ends badly with Trent it could damage our friendship."

"Listen to you. If it's like that, then you'd be committing incest if you hooked up with Trent."

"Believe me, there is nothing brotherly about the way I feel about Trent," Barbara said in between bites of her sandwich, "although I don't want to be one of those women who get tired of the games, and just settle for something close to what we want." Barbara's face softened as she continued, "I've been there before."

Kayla gave her a look and a nod that indicated she had too. "Well, you'll find your dream Ken even if he doesn't have freckles or red hair."

Barbara smiled and her eyes lit up like they did in fifth grade. It was a childlike smile, full of sweetness and delight. "I can't believe you still remember that." Leaning forward and looking from side to side as if about to share a secret no one else would be allowed to hear, she said, "Guess what?"

"What?" Kayla asked, suddenly becoming light-hearted, enjoying the rouse.

"Michael's brother's got freckles and red hair." They both laughed heartily.

"Tell me you're kidding, I know you're not still looking for the same things in a man you did as a little girl." Kayla couldn't disguise her incredulous expression.

"No, I'm not, it's just a coincidence. I think." They looked at each other and began laughing again.

They finished their lunch and ordered dessert. They spent another half hour talking about work, and the difficulties of being in such stressful jobs. The deli was beginning to empty out, and the waitress, who was so courteous when they had first sat down, was now giving them the evil eye and had asked on more than a few occasions if there was anything else she could get them, with a little bit more attitude than needed. They finally decided they'd spent enough time talking and had to get back to work. They left a generous tip for the waitress, and once outside they hugged and promised to get together for dinner soon so they wouldn't be pressed for time.

Kayla felt renewed when she returned to the office. She settled into her usual afternoon of phone calls, prospecting for new business, and preparing for her upcoming presentation.

Margaret walked into her office with a huge bouquet of yellow roses in a beautiful crystal vase.

"Oh, my goodness, where did those come from?"

Margaret smiled. "They were just delivered for you.

I got some too. You think they're from the big boss, Mr. Newhouse?"

"No way. Is there a card?" Kayla asked while settling the vase on her desk. She found the card and pulled it out of the envelope. Margaret was waiting and appearing to be just as curious as Kayla. "You're not going to believe this, they're from Ed."

"You're right, I don't believe you." She turned to leave.

After a few minutes Margaret returned with her card in hand. "What do you think is going on?"

Kayla sniffed the roses. "He's apologizing for being so rude the other day."

"Hmmph, you're far more trusting than me, I still think he's up to no good."

Kayla tried calling him again, but he was out, so sent him an e-mail instead, hoping that whatever he was up to was over.

Chapter 6

It was a full week of meetings, planning, and presentations for Kayla, and by Thursday she was backlogged with work. She'd promised Michael they'd spend some time together, despite their busy work schedules. Finally they were going out after work and had sworn no matter how harried things got on Thursday they were leaving work on time. Michael was picking her up at 7:00.

When he arrived he greeted her with a single, beautiful red rose. It was perfect and was not the kind men picked up from some gas station. He'd evidently gone to a florist and purchased a single rose for her. *How unique,* she thought.

They briefly shared the events of the workweek and headed out. It was Throw Back Thursday at the skating rink and the music was jamming loudly when they walked in. The crowd was older than the usual teenyboppers that frequented the rink during nights when they played hip-hop music.

Michael helped Kayla with her skates and they went out onto the rink. After half an hour, Kayla couldn't remember the last time she had so much fun working up a sweat. She and Michael were both great skaters and each tried to outdo the other. When

"Very Special" by Debra Laws began to play, which was one of Kayla's favorite slow jams, she grabbed him by the hand and they wrapped their arms around each other and skated gracefully in unison with the music. He snuggled closer and kissed her ear. It all felt so good and so right. Once the music stopped she turned to face him, looked deeply into the brown pools of his eyes, and felt herself once again getting lost in them.

She closed her eyes, leaned forward, and kissed him like she'd never kissed any man. He responded by holding her in a close embrace and returning the kiss. She felt a rush of warmth starting from her feet, gradually working its way up her legs, and spreading throughout her body. Kayla was never one for public displays of affection, but she boldly kissed this man without a thought to what anyone might say or think. She loved feeling his arms around her and the way he looked at her, as though she were the only woman in the world. It was a sort of longing, anticipating look. It made her heart pace quicken each and every time.

Kayla had never dreamed that the evening could have been so invigorating and at the same time uniquely romantic. They shared intimate moments of touching, laughing, and talking. She felt as if Michael had learned everything there was to know about her. They left the skating rink and drove to a nearby fast-food restaurant for a quick burger and fries before heading home.

Once seated, they quietly ate their food while occasionally smiling at one another. Michael wiped his mouth, took a sip of his Coke, and said, "I've been meaning to ask you if you're busy Saturday after next."

That look again, she thought. "Uh, no. I don't have any plans, why?"

"I bought tickets to the India.Arie concert. Would you like to go?

"Are you serious? Of course I want to go! I love her music."

"Well, then, it's a date, I think the concert starts at 8:00. We can have dinner before or afterward. Your pick, of course, and maybe later we can check out the comedy club near the Regal Theatre."

"Oh, Michael, that sounds wonderful. Thank you so much. What made you get tickets?"

"For one thing you told me how much you like her music, and for another it's my way of telling you how crazy I am about you."

A warm, glowing smile lit up his face as he waited for her response. "You do the nicest things for me." She looked deep into his eyes as if searching for unknown answers to known questions. "But I'm dying to know, when does all the attention stop? When does all the thoughtfulness and consideration go away?"

The somber look on her face let him know she was serious with her inquiry. He took her hand into his and let his eyes burn into her, as if trying to burn out her bitterness. "I've been as honest and forthright with you as I can be, and it is with the upmost respect that I say this to you, Kayla. You need to stop judging all men by the few sorry men who've mistreated you in the past." His voice was soft and low, while his eyes seemed to plead with her for understanding.

"I want the same things from you that you want from me, no more, no less. I happen to believe you're someone that I have a natural affinity for. I believe I can make you happy and vice versa, but you need to let go of your skepticism and just let nature take its course."

Their eyes stayed locked in a lover's dance, as if trying to reach each other's thoughts. "Even if you're unwilling to admit it, there's more to us than casual dating, but we'll never discover what that is if you continue to keep that fortress around your heart."

Kayla knew his words were true and she was the first to look away. He took her hand in his, forcing her to look at him again.

"I'm crazy about you, Kayla, and have been since the first day I laid eyes on you. I could never hurt you."

Time froze for the two of them as they waited for her to make the next move. She collected her thoughts before speaking, because she had waited a long time for a man to make her feel the way Michael had made her feel.

"I'm confused—I guess overwhelmed is a more accurate description. I've just gotten out of a three-year relationship with a man that I cared for and you came along and, well, I feel stronger and deeper for you than I have anyone and I'm overwhelmed by these feelings I have for you. It hurts so much when it ends. No matter who ends it, it hurts. I don't know if I want to go through it again so soon."

She took a deep breath. "We're in a new millennium and relationships are as tough now as they were a thousand years ago. Sometimes it's just overwhelming and encompassing."

"Kay, it's only overwhelming if we allow it to be. There is nothing more natural and basic than a man's need for a woman and vice versa. We just make it more complicated by putting other things in the equation that don't belong there."

She shifted forward in her seat, waiting to be enlightened. "Like what?" she asked with skepticism.

"Well, things like past hurts, indiscretions, head games, and flagrant lies." Michael had a faraway look on his face. He spoke the words of a man who'd been there.

"It's almost impossible to come into a relationship without bringing your past experiences," Kayla said.

"That's true, but we fail to bring what we truly learned from the experience. Instead, we choose to dwell on the negative part of the experience. I was in a relationship with a woman for a few years, and when I decided to end it, I didn't do it very well. Even though the relationship wasn't going well at the time, and it should have ended sooner, she deserved a better ending."

He stopped and looked away as if searching for the right words. He looked at her and shook his head. "You don't want to hear this, not now. Let's have dinner at my place tomorrow night." It came out more of a command than a request.

Kayla sighed deeply as if exhausted. "Sure. I want to hear all about how you dump your women," she said, smiling sheepishly.

"If I'm telling about my past, you are going to have to come clean about the lawyer. As a matter of fact, once we have this discussion, I prefer that we not talk about either one of them again. We can have a therapeutic, dirty laundry session, and then leave it alone." The finality of his tone made her believe that he preferred to leave the past in the past. Maybe that flaw was about to make its appearance.

"Would you like me to bring anything?"

Michael leaned back in the booth, slightly licked

his lips, and smiled that man-child smile, sexy dimples and all. "Yeah, your toothbrush."

Kayla could feel herself getting aroused with the teasing. "After we air all this 'dirty laundry,' you may want to kick me out."

Those dimples emphasized his smile as he said, "That'll never happen, Kayla." When he said her name, she almost leaped over the booth to tackle him. This man had something that made her want to throw caution and convention to the wind. She managed to restrain herself. As they rose to leave, he took her hand and assisted her out of the booth. She was reminded of the wedding when he'd saved her from falling.

He seemed to always be willing to give her a hand. She liked that. "I'll bet you were something else as a little boy." Her eyes sparkled as her lips turned up in a sexy smile.

Michael couldn't help continuing the flirting as he seductively mused, "Baby, I'm still something else."

Friday morning at work was busy for Kayla. Margaret was going away for an extended weekend with her caterer friend, and they were trying to make sure everything would be ready for Kayla's presentation on Tuesday. Things had been going smoothly, which was highly unusual, but they didn't want to take any chances. By three o'clock they were completely prepared for the presentation on Tuesday.

"I can't believe we got all that done and it's only 3:00." Neither mentioned the fact that they'd been at it since 7:30 A.M. and had skipped lunch. Kayla was seated at her desk, and Margaret was sitting across from her in one of the mahogany-colored wooden chairs.

They each were eating from nonfat yogurt containers that Kayla had retrieved from her small refrigerator. "So, Margaret, tell me about this long weekend you and the caterer have planned."

Margaret divulged the plans of visiting Thomas's daughter in Atlanta. Her face lit up like a schoolgirl planning her first date. Apparently they were more serious than Kayla had thought and she was happy for Margaret.

Afterward Margaret said, "You know, Kayla, I've noticed a different gentleman's voice calling for you the last few weeks." She eyed her boss watchfully, not wanting to cross the line between being curious and nosy.

Kayla knew she'd have to share her good news with Margaret, but not today. "It's a long story, and unfortunately you haven't packed, so get on out of here."

"Are you serious? I have some work to finish and—"

"And it can wait till Tuesday. Have a wonderful weekend with your caterer."

She stood up, straightened her skirt, and winked. "You know, I plan to do just that. I've left the hotel number on your computer in case an emergency comes up. Enjoy your weekend."

Chapter 7

She could smell a blend of onions, oregano, garlic, and tomatoes when she walked to the door. *And he cooks too,* she thought to herself. She wondered again about that serious flaw of his. She couldn't guess what it was. He hadn't given her any clues yet. But as sure as heaven was up, that flaw would surface sooner or later. Michael greeted her with a warm smile that Kayla believed should have been patented and sold. After a quick kiss to her cheek he inquired, "Hey, beautiful, did you have trouble finding the house?"

"No, your directions were right on target." She looked around the living room while inhaling the wonderful aroma of what smelled like homemade spaghetti sauce. The large living room was tastefully decorated in black and gray, with lots of African art and prints. "This is a lovely house, Michael, did you decorate it yourself?"

"Well, I got a little help from my mother. She has a great eye for decorating. I have a passion for authentic African art, I just can't afford it. I went to Africa a few years ago and brought these pieces back," he said, gesturing to the hand-carved jade elephants displayed on the sofa table. "A friend of mine has an import-export business and once in a while I can get a good deal from him."

Kayla thought about how Justin always criticized her African art as being so "ethnic." When she'd questioned him as to what he was really saying, he told her that black folks needed to stop looking at Africa as their motherland because they were all born in America. That comment sparked a horrendous debate that ended with her calling him "devoid of his own ethnic sense of history and culture." She couldn't understand how any African-American could not consider his original motherland as Africa if that was his family origin. The debate had been so heated they didn't speak for several days, and as usual ended when she called and apologized. Another compromise that she should never have conceded to. Yielding, always yielding, even when she knew she was right. The thought of how he never respected her opinions or listened to them made her angry that she subjected herself to his biases.

Michael continued the tour of the house. Each room had its own personality. He'd obviously taken time to clean, and that really impressed her. The bedroom was well furnished, it contained a king-sized cherry-wood sleigh bed with a lovely antique satin gray comforter. Matching nightstands were placed on each side of the bed, with cherry-wood lamps, unlike any she'd ever seen. The entire room was done in gray and mauve with lots of candles and a beautiful abstract print. Romantic was the only word Kayla could think of. She wondered how many women had gotten the tour of the house and decided to stay in the bedroom. It was definitely inviting and instantly she felt a rush of emotion.

"Earth to Kayla." Until she heard Michael's voice, she hadn't realized how deep in thought she was.

She immediately became flushed. "I'm sorry, I was thinking about something else." She wouldn't make the mistake she'd made with Justin, she would take her time with Michael and really get to know him before she offered any part of herself to him.

"Something or someone?" He was so perceptive, she wondered how many women he had known that he could judge their moods and moments of silence so adequately.

"Actually, I left a bottle of wine in the car. I'll go get it."

Giving her a quick kiss on her forehead, he led her back toward the front door. "I hope you like pasta. I make my own sauce."

Retrieving the wine from the car, Kayla decided it didn't matter how many women had made the trip to his bedroom. He was a desirable, handsome man who obviously knew how to take care of a woman.

After dinner they went into the living room where he'd set the mood with soft music and wine. "Where'd you learn to cook like that? I'm stuffed."

Michael put his glass of wine on the cocktail table and went to the bookcase.

"I like to try different recipes from cookbooks. I got tonight's recipe from this one." He handed her an Italian cookbook. She silently flipped through the pages, occasionally stopping to read some of the recipes. As she sipped her wine she could feel his eyes inspecting her.

She looked at him. "You have such an intense glare. Sometimes it makes me feel uncomfortable. It's as though you're trying to decode me or something."

He moved closer to her. "I'm sorry, the last thing I want to do is make you feel uncomfortable. I just find you so absolutely appealing and fascinating in every way, it's hard for me not to stare. I want to know everything about you. I love watching you."

"How can you say that? You barely know me." She blurted it out and immediately wished she hadn't. The look of hurt was immediately apparent, as his eyebrows knitted together and furrows creased his forehead. He tilted his head slightly to one side like a child trying to figure out a puzzle.

"You know, Kay, we talked about this briefly last night. I'm not Justin, nor anything like him, so please stop holding me accountable for his mistakes. I have faults, I'm not perfect, but damn, baby, must you judge every man by the mistakes of one?"

Kayla knew he was right, she was judging him and waiting for the big flaw. "You're right, I don't know nearly as much about you as I'm gonna know, but what I do know, I like." Michael put his arm around her and gently kissed her forehead. His kiss then traveled to her nose and gently to her mouth. The trail of lusty kisses left her skin heated with the desire for more.

"You're gonna have to let your defenses down, Kay, if we want this to work."

He removed his arm from her, evidently to give her time to think about what he'd just said. He reached for his glass, took a sip of his wine, and leaned over to her. "What do you say? Are we going to let nature take its course, or will you continue to question my actions and motives?"

Kayla let out the deep breath she was holding. She was tapping her wineglass and watching it swirl, which she was certain was the way her insides were swirling.

"Michael, it's always in my nature to question anyone's actions and motives. I am curious by nature and have found that men I've dated don't always have my best interest at heart. I think getting hurt does that to you. It makes you cautious. Very cautious."

After taking another sip of her drink but never allowing her eyes to leave his, she added, "Yes, I'm willing to let nature take its course." She wasn't going to admit it to him, but she wanted him to the point where she almost ached. Michael stirred her down deep, but she was going to take it slow and easy. He had power she wasn't willing to let him know he had.

His dimples slowly increased as he smiled broadly at her, holding up his glass. "That's what I wanna hear. Let's toast to a new beginning."

The sound of the clinking glasses seemed to indeed signal a new beginning for them. The wine and newfound desire made Kayla giddy as a schoolgirl as her smile mirrored her wonderful feeling.

He asked, "How about a game of Scrabble? If I remember correctly you bragged that you were the champion Scrabble player of the world." He held his index finger to his chin, and said, "But you've never played me, so . . ." Michael smiled impishly, knowing she wouldn't resist a challenge.

"I know you're not challenging me! Well, let's get it on!"

"Let me get a refill first. Would you like another?"

"Yes, please."

He liked that about her, she was polite and ultra-feminine.

When he returned, Kayla was sitting on the couch with her eyes closed looking as though she were feeling the effects of the wine and music.

"Are you coming?" Michael asked.

She was embarrassed when she opened her eyes and saw him looking at her as if she were dessert. He handed her the glass of wine.

"Sure, I thought you were bringing the game in here."

"You look like you are enjoying the music. We can skip the game if you like and just listen to some music."

"I'm enjoying myself being here with you listening to the music, and now I'm going to lambaste you in Scrabble."

The effects of the wine became apparent as she struggled to get to her feet. He extended his hand to help her up. "Tough talk from someone who can't get up from the sofa." She fell into his arms as she lost her footing. With his arm around her waist he pulled her to his chest, which felt firm and comforting. When she looked up into his handsome face she could feel her knees becoming weaker, as was her resolve. She put her hands around his neck and pulled him to her and kissed his waiting lips. It was a covetous, deep, lusty kiss that made her throb with a longing unlike any she'd experienced before.

She pulled back slightly from his embrace, believing that if she didn't they'd surely melt into one. She could easily get lost in him. She wondered what it would feel like to occasionally get lost in him, to totally mesh with him, become one with him. She wanted desperately to listen to the little voice in her heart that was telling her this was right.

"Why the hesitation, Kay?" His voice was low, barely audible.

"No hesitation, Michael, I was just imagining what it would be like to be your woman in every sense of the word." She couldn't believe how naughty she was being, nor how much she was enjoying it. He looked confused at first, and that slow, boyish, grin soon lit up his face as he realized what she meant. Continuing to hold her in an embrace, he was obviously becoming aroused. She could feel his passion rising against her thigh, as she herself was becoming inflamed and began arching her back to push closer to him. Their embrace tightened as he bent down to plant another deep, passionate kiss on her waiting mouth. The kiss seemed to take her breath away when they parted.

The intensity in his eyes burned through to her soul, that yearning, burning part of her that no one was allowed to enter until now. She took his hand and led him to his bedroom. It was a liberating move for her to be so bawdy.

Once inside the bedroom, they stood for what seemed like an eternity in a thoughtful embrace that meshed the two silently. They were deciding if this was the time for them to make the love they knew would eventually be shared between the two of them.

It was their time. Michael gently lifted her and placed her on the bed as if she were a sacred, delicate flower. He smoothed her hair, and rubbed her lips with his index finger. "Are you sure you want to do this now, Kay?" It sounded more like a plea than a question. At that precise moment the only certain thing in her mind was her monumental desire for him.

"Yes" was all she could moan, as he'd begun stroking her thigh, his touch seemingly igniting her body from the inside out. Pulling him to her, she delivered another fevered kiss while slipping her hand underneath his shirt. The feel of his heartbeat while rubbing his bare chest intensified her arousal and his.

He slowly began undressing her, kissing, caressing her in places that drove her to low, guttural moans that seemed to come from somewhere too deep for her to imagine their origin. Her body was reacting in ways that were foreign, but somehow natural. With her body on fire and totally nude, he undressed himself.

The sight of his naked body sparked more hot burning flames in her. He had long limbs, but they were muscular. He obviously was no stranger to hard work. His chest had just enough hair, and his manhood was more than she could've hoped for. He took a condom from the nightstand and handed it to her. No words were spoken as she caressed him, gently easing the condom on, driving him to desire her more than he thought possible. They made love slowly at first. He made sure every part of her was caressed, licked, and stroked. Feeling totally out of control, she believed she was going insane, finding it difficult to keep the moans at a low decibel.

Her body responded to every thrust as he held her tighter and tighter. He repeatedly moaned her name so melodiously it sounded as if he were reciting poetry. No matter where this relationship was going, she would always remember the way he made her feel, and the way he called her name during the final crescendo of their lovemaking. He made sure she was satisfied before releasing himself. Kayla felt the rush of fluids throughout her body, the sudden internal rush of joy. Their bodies were drenched with sweat. He was definitely no Uncle Ben.

She realized that this was the magic that everyone spoke about, but she had never experienced. No wonder Sandy and so many of her friends claimed to have seen stars at the moment of climax, as she had surely seen stars and what appeared to be heaven. They were both spent when it was over, and lay quietly in each other's arms, inhaling the love that lingered in the air, gently exchanging wet, sweet kisses. He was indeed an ardent lover who had responded to her more passionately and genuinely than she believed possible.

He kissed her lips as he got up to go to the bathroom. "Would you like to take a shower with me?"

In the darkness of the room, all she could clearly see was the gleam of his eyes as she murmured, "Yes."

"I'll get the shower started."

She had drifted off to sleep when he returned. He bent over and whispered, "Hey, sleepyhead, the shower's ready." When he led her into the bathroom, she smiled at the scented candles he had lit for them. It was romantic and gave a serene peaceful feeling. The perfect appendage for the lovemaking they'd shared previously.

She smiled and asked, "Do you shower by candlelight often?"

Handing her a bath sponge, he replied, "This is the first time." He smiled that boyish grin that melted her resolve.

Once inside the shower he began lathering and washing her. "Do you have any idea how exquisite you are, Kay? I've wanted you since the first time you fell into my arms at the wedding. There was something in your eyes that intrigued me, and it wasn't just physical. The more I'm with you, the more I want to be with you, Kay."

She took the shower gel and began washing him.

"I want to be with you too, Michael. This is such a stretch for me, you just don't know. It's not in my nature to be so—I don't know. I'm feeling emotions that I've never felt, but I like it." She turned him around to wash his back and could feel the heat from inside her again. He turned and they embraced as the water streamed down on them, pooling down around their feet as if they were one.

After a few minutes of showering quietly, each enjoying and exploring the other's body, Michael said, "I think we'd better get outta here before we drown." He turned off the shower, stepped out, and began drying her with a towel.

"You're always a gentleman." She laughed, making reference to her teasing him earlier.

"Usually yes, but I must admit, my motives are purely selfish right now." He leaned over and gently sucked a drop of water from her breast, sending them both into passion mode once again.

"You know you are wicked, but in a good way." She cupped her hands around his buttocks, turning him around. "Let me do you. I mean dry you off." She began drying him slowly, stroking his buttocks, intentionally rubbing her breasts on his back, causing him to moan. She turned him around and was pleasantly surprised at the full erection that greeted her. "And you think I'm exquisite?" They both laughed again as he carried her back to the bed, where they made love again and again until they were consumed with exhaustion, sleep, and deep satisfaction.

Kayla couldn't remember the last time she'd slept so late on a Saturday morning. It was 10:30 as the red

digital clock numbers glared at her. She felt for
Michael, but he wasn't in the bed, and she hadn't realized how big it was until she was in it alone. She
sprawled across it and remembered the night before.
"He's too good to be true," she said aloud. "Wonder
when that flaw is going to show."

She rubbed her stomach as it began to growl, and
climbed out of bed, calling for him. Kayla grabbed
the pajama shirt he'd given her the night before to
wear, but had no need for until now. He'd left a note
on the refrigerator, saying that he was out running
and would return shortly with breakfast. The
thoughts of how many women had spent the night
there returned again, but it didn't matter.

All that mattered to her now was that she was walking around in his house with his shirt on, feeling like
she belonged, and more importantly he wanted her
there. Her thoughts were interrupted by the phone
ringing. She looked at it curiously and noted the time.
She was tempted to answer but decided to let it ring
as she walked back to the bedroom, then stopped in
her tracks as a woman's voice came on the answering
machine.

"Michael, are you there? You're probably out running, call me when you get in, baby."

She continued walking to the bathroom where she
showered and did what she could to her hair. Kayla
looked at herself critically in the mirror once dressed.
Even without makeup and a bad hair day she admittedly had a wholesome kind of attractiveness. With
any luck, she'd be gone by the time he returned. She
was afraid of what might happen if she stayed. Who
was the female on the phone that was so familiar with

him that she knew he was out running? *Here comes the flaw,* she thought as she collected her purse.

Just as she got to the door Michael was putting his key in the door.

"Good morning," he said cheerfully, leaning down to kiss her. "You can't leave yet, I brought us breakfast from the bakery." The aroma of fresh-baked bagels hit her nose invitingly as he opened the bag. "I'll put on a pot of coffee, or do you like cappuccino?"

"Coffee's fine." She followed him to the kitchen, debating whether to tell him he had a message, or just wait and see if he checked his machine while she was there. Her mood had clearly changed as demonstrated by her rigid posture.

"Did you sleep well?" He had noticed her somber mood and silence, but wasn't sure what to make of them, hoping she wasn't feeling regret about last night, or had changed her mind about seeing him.

"Yes, thank you. Your bed is a lot firmer than mine, but it's very comfortable."

He thought her reply was a bit formal and decided to lighten up her mood.

"Was it just the bed causing you to sleep well?" He smiled and winked at her, hoping to see her mood change.

"I'll never tell," she said with a hint of a smile.

"You are a mysterious one, Kay. I'm gonna jump in the shower and get some of this funk off of me. Help yourself to breakfast, I'll join you in a few minutes." He started toward the bedroom, but stopped. "Usually my mom calls me on Saturday morning, so please feel free to answer the phone and tell her I'll call her back later."

A sudden sigh of relief came over her. *It was his*

Mom. What's wrong with me? she thought. "Are you sure you want me answering your phone?"

The question caught him by surprise. He turned and walked back to her.

"Kay, I told you I'm not seriously dating anyone. I'll be the first to admit, I've tried being a player in my day, but that was all in the past when I didn't know what I wanted. Trust me, Kay, I have no intentions of being anything but good to and for you." He tilted her chin up to him and kissed her lips. He stood over her for a few minutes, stroking her hair. "You can join me in the shower if you like," he said, his voice suddenly husky and full of longing.

They spent the rest of the morning in bed talking, making love, and occasionally sleeping. "I've gotta go. I'm spending this afternoon visiting my parents." Kayla reached up and kissed Michael on the cheek.

When Kayla got home she had another message from Ed saying he needed to talk with her in confidence. She hadn't seen him at work for a few weeks, and people were speculating about his absence. She'd left a few messages for him, but she could never reach him when she returned his call.

Kayla arrived at her parents' house and as usual her father was working in the yard. He was trimming the bushes, and she could smell the scent of freshly cut grass. Her parents' house looked like a spread from *Better Homes and Gardens* magazine, complete with pink and white peonies, lilacs, and daylilies. Two large Bradford pear trees provided shade in the front. Her parents loved working in the yard and spent most of their weekends planting, pruning, seeding, and any other form of gardening they could. The backyard included a vegetable garden that was her mother's pride and joy, complete with beets, tomatoes, and an assortment of green vegetables. The side of the house had a white trellis, with beautiful red and pink roses climbing up the side.

The two-story, Tudor-style house held many fond memories for Kayla. Just as she got out of her car, she saw a new red Volvo pull up behind her. She didn't recognize the car and focused on the driver. It was her sister, Janae. She waved and walked toward the car.

As she approached the car, her sister got out. Janae was truly a remarkable woman. She was a wonderfully patient mother and wife. Janae was a great cook, could sew as well as any professional, decorate, and from all counts was somewhat of a financial wizard. She'd made some wise investments for her family without any formal training. Kayla didn't understand why Janae had opted to marry right after high school and only taken a few college courses the first year of her marriage.

They'd grown somewhat distant in the past few years, both being busy with other obligations. There was one thing that she did understand and that was her undeniable love for her three-year-old, precocious niece. Clark was a natural beauty. She seemed to have taken the best features of each of her parents. She had Janae's beautiful dark, wild, curly hair with big brown eyes that seemed to have flecks of sunshine in them. She inherited a dimple in her chin from her handsome father.

Clark ran to her aunt and grabbed her around the legs. "Aunt Kay, I didn't know you was here!"

"You sweetie pie, I didn't know you were going to be here either. How's my favorite love bug?" Clark loved it when Kayla called her that.

She replied with a giggle and said, "I fine."

Kayla swooped her up and gave her a kiss on the cheek. "Hmmm, you taste just like sugar." She strolled toward the house with Clark in her arms, then paused to wait for Janae, who wore very little makeup and had her hair pulled back in a ponytail. Janae wore a gold and white nylon warmup suit with athletic shoes. "Hey, little sister, you look so cute. How are you doing?"

"Thanks, I'm fine. How's it going with you?" Janae said.

"I'm good. My little love bug is just growing like a weed." Kayla and Clark rubbed noses, their own special way of greeting each other.

"Don't I know it? She's such a good girl too, helps me around the house already." Janae patted her little girl's head and kissed her cheek.

"Yeah, Aunt Kay, me help Mommy. Me gon be big sister."

Kayla wasn't sure if she understood what Clark was saying until she saw the expression on Janae's face.

She then understood that Janae was pregnant. Janae always had a round youthful-looking face, with a slight hint of a double chin. "Well, congratulations, Mommy," Kayla said with a broad smile. "No wonder you're glowing. How far along are you? Do Mom and Dad know yet?"

"Hold on, girl, I wasn't intending for you to find out this way. I'm only about five weeks, and no, I haven't told anyone. Ms. Clark has spilled the beans so I guess I'll tell them today." Janae looked lovingly at her daughter. "Clark, do you remember me telling you that being a big sister was a secret?" Janae held her index finger up to her lips, indicating she was to be quiet. "Let me tell Nana and Grandpa, okay?"

"Otay, Mommy. Sorry." Clark pouted and looked sad for less than a second and then began playing with Kayla's earring. The resiliency of kids, Kayla thought, they needed to bottle it and sell it to adults.

Kayla turned to her sister as they headed up the path to the house. "That Volvo is sharp. I didn't know you guys had bought a new car."

"If you called every once in a while, you'd know things like that." Janae never broke her stride or looked at Kayla.

Kayla was taken aback by her sister's sharp manner. "That goes both ways, Janae, you could call me too. I don't remember you being—"

"Look, Kay, I'm not going to debate this with you. I just want to spend a nice afternoon with Mom and Dad." Janae kept her tone friendly so that she wouldn't upset Clark, who was hugging Kayla around the neck. They resembled a mother and baby koala bear.

Kayla got the message and changed the subject. "Where's Alex?"

Janae smiled as they approached their father. "He's working today. Where's that pretentious Justin?"

"Probably under the rock he crawled from. I kicked him to the curb."

That got Janae's attention. "I'm sorry, Kay. Are you okay?" She put an around her sister's shoulder.

Kayla smiled and said, "Couldn't be better."

"Hi, Grandpa!" Clark shrieked. Kayla put her down so she could run to greet her grandpa.

"Hi, Daddy," both Kayla and Janae said at the same time. Even they had to look at each other and laugh at how they sounded like little girls themselves.

"It's good to see my two daughters getting on so well. It's nice how you two timed your arrivals."

Despite the fact that he was sixty-six, George Marshall was in great shape. He'd joined a gym and worked out a few times a week. He was tall with broad shoulders, good muscle tone and agility. Most men his age had receding hairlines, but he had a headful of mingled gray hair that complemented his walnut-colored skin. Kayla laughed at her mother telling stories about how she had to chase the "old church sisters away from my husband." His hazel eyes remained clear and always appeared full of mischief.

"Grandpa, you stinky!" Clark squealed and wrinkled her nose.

Janae's mouth dropped. "Clark, that's not a nice thing to say."

"Oh, Janae, she's okay. Just being honest." He looked at his granddaughter and said, "I know I stink, I've been working in the yard all day. I'm gonna take a shower just for you. How about that?"

Clark nodded.

"Daddy, she needs to learn she can't go around saying whatever pops into her head." Janae's youthful face was masked with motherly concern.

Kayla looked at her sister in total disbelief. "Hmmph, I wonder where she gets all that directness from."

Janae rolled her eyes and was about to speak when her father interrupted. "Janae, the baby is only three, you need to loosen up, girl."

Kayla had to chuckle. She was always in awe of her father.

"Where's Mom?" She queried her father.

George scratched his head as he wiped sweat from

his brow with a handkerchief. "She's inside doing who knows what. She busies herself all the time."

As they took seats on the porch, George looked from one daughter to the other and asked, "Where yo' menfolk?"

"Alex is working today. They started on that new office building downtown a month ago and they're already behind. He's just putting in a few hours to try and get closer to schedule." She then looked over to Kayla for her response.

"I like that boy's enthusiasm for his work. He's good with his hands, he'll always be able to put food on the table." It was true, Alex was a construction foreman, and he could build anything. He had built their home and a lot of the furniture in it. Kayla had always admired him.

George looked over at Kayla. "And what about what's-his-name?"

"Justin. We're not seeing each other anymore."

"What happened, you had to kick his uppity behind to the curb?"

Janae and Kayla laughed. George was known to have a wicked sense of humor. He bellowed for his wife to join them on the porch. "Gail, come out here, woman, the girls are here." Clark had decided to play airplane as she flew around the yard with her arms stretched out.

Their mother yelled from an upstairs window, "Man, cut out all that racket. I'll be down in a minute. Hello, girls, you both doing okay?"

"Fine, Mom," Janae yelled back.

"George, you want a glass of water?"

"Yeah, baby, bring me a glass of water when you

come out. Thanks." He wiped his face again and said, "You sure know what I need, don't you, baby?"

Kayla smiled as she'd seen her parents interact this way ever since she could remember. They were always considerate and thoughtful of one another.

Kayla asked her father. "Daddy, do you remember the precise moment you knew that you'd fallen in love with Mom?" She and Janae had taken seats on the porch swing. A soft breeze carried the fragrant smell of flowers and freshly cut grass.

"I never understood that expression. I love your mother with everything in me. When I met her she lifted me so high, my feet haven't touched down yet. Why you asking, baby girl, you think you're in love?"

Kayla looked at her father and then at Janae. "I've met someone very special and it just seems like things are moving fast."

"When it happens, you won't have to ask anybody, you'll know," Janae said softly, sounding as if she were in another place.

"You know, Janae, you've never told me how you and Alex knew that it was love. I hardly ever remember you talking about other boys in high school. It was always Alex."

Janae's face took on a softness as she looked at her daughter. "It'll always be Alex."

"Gail, you'd better get out here, I think your daughters need to talk to you," George shouted as he rose from the chair. "I'm gonna put my tools away and take a shower. The three of you can get into this conversation when I'm gone. I know when something's on your mind, Kayla." He looked at Kayla and cupped her chin. "You two sisters should spend more time talking to each other. You're the oldest. Sometimes you just have to take the lead. You're both stubborn like your mother."

"I heard that." Gail was two years younger than her husband, and despite the extra few pounds she carried on her small frame, she was a beautiful, shapely woman. Gail was only five feet, and was the color of peanut butter, with skin just as smooth. She'd had her naturally curly hair cut shorter than usual, which made her look at least ten years younger. Her stylist had expertly feathered the bangs, cut and tapered the sides, with just enough height in the crown to give her face a little lift. When she smiled, she showcased perfectly even white teeth. Kayla guessed her mother would always look a decade younger than her years.

Gail gave her husband a glass of water. He smiled and kissed her on the cheek. "Talk to your daughters. Seems one of them is asking questions about being in love, and get this, it's not with the highfalutin lawyer." George laughed and left to put away his tools.

"Kayla—" Before Gail could finish, Clark ran up onto the porch.

"Nana, Nana!" Gail sat down and lifted her granddaughter onto her lap, tickling her and giving her raspberry kisses. Clark laughed and hugged her grandmother tightly. After a few minutes Clark calmed down and sat quietly.

"So, Kayla, what's going on? Did you and Justin break up?" She looked carefully to gauge her daughter's response.

"Something like that, Mom. I think it's been over for a while. I just didn't want to admit it. Thought I'd put too much time and effort into it for it not to work. Couldn't see what was right in my face."

"Women are so used to giving of themselves and

their time until sometimes they don't know when to stop. You don't look unhappy. Have you met someone already?"

Kayla couldn't contain the smile that eased on her face. "Oh, Mom, I have. He's so wonderful, it's scary." Gail and Janae leaned forward as if not to miss a word. Even Clark's beautiful brown eyes were looking at her aunt like she understood what was being said. "I'm afraid we're moving too fast."

"Why do you think that? How slow or fast are you supposed to go?"

Kayla looked at her mother, unable to answer the question. All she could render was a smile.

Janae took her sister's hand in hers. "Enjoy it and listen to your heart, you'll know if it's love or something else." She smiled and hugged her sister. "I'm so happy for you."

Clark watched the exchange curiously at first and then giggled.

Kayla whispered to Janae, "Are you going to tell them?" She was referring to Janae being pregnant.

"No, I'm going to wait until later so Alex can be with me." She smiled at her sister.

"You know, Kayla, I knew Justin wasn't the one for you. He and his whole snobby family." Janae was trying to suppress a laugh.

"What?"

"You told me how uppity his mother was." Kayla had to laugh herself as she thought about Justin's mother, Maudeen Kincaid. The woman had the nerve to constantly brag about her direct lineage to one of the oldest, wealthiest black families in Chicago. She had on more than one occasion slighted Kayla and she wore a perpetual scowl, that look of haughty boredom reserved only for the privileged, like she was looking down her nose at everyone else.

"Tell Mom about the family picnic you went to." Janae looked at her mother. "Trust me, Mom, you'll love it."

"Janae, I can't believe you want me to amuse you with the antics of that bourgeoisie family." Kayla was laughing too.

Gail leaned forward, anticipating the story.

"Mom, first of all, the woman always looked at me like she smelled something bad. When I got to the family picnic, she had the nerve to look me up and down and say, 'My, my, Kayla, you certainly stay within your budget when you shop for clothes.' Just because I had on a T-shirt and jeans."

"No, she didn't!" Gail guffawed. "What were you supposed to wear? Was the family picnic at Carnegie Hall or something?" All three of them bowled over with laughter.

"Mom, the woman wore white linen slacks and a silk blouse! She stayed away from everybody, for fear of getting dirty, I think. But the real kicker was that she had the family picnic catered."

"Catered?" Gail asked.

"You heard me. Catered. They actually had people serving them in the park at a family picnic. There was no loud laughter, children running and playing. No loud, trash-talking card games, gossiping, and nobody got drunk and started a fight. It was like something from a science fiction movie where all the people are obedient and quiet, like they were drugged or something."

Janae interrupted Kayla when she said, "In other

words, nothing like our family picnics. Mom, they didn't even do the electric slide, no games, nothing. None of the fun stuff that make family picnics memorable."

"His mother organized the picnic and you could tell some of the family members weren't all that happy, but nobody said a word, not one complaint."

"I'm glad you broke up with him, I never liked him anyway." Janae stood up to go to the kitchen for a drink of water.

Clark jumped from her grandmother's lap, and closely followed her mother. "Me neider, Mommy."

They all laughed again, even Clark. "Well, honey, you don't sound like you miss him or his mama," Gail said teasingly.

Just as Janae and Clark returned from the kitchen with a pitcher of fresh lemonade and glasses, Alex arrived. He leaped from his truck and ran toward the house. As soon as Clark saw her father she began running to meet him, screaming, "Daddy, Daddy!"

"She is such a daddy's girl," Janae announced with pride.

"Hey, buttercup." Alex lifted his daughter up to greet her with a kiss.

She held her finger up to her mouth and said, "Me didn't tell Nana and Grandpa!"

He leaned over to kiss his wife and they exchanged a knowing look.

Gail inquired, "Tell us what?"

Chapter 8

The workweek was finally over and Kayla was excited about the India.Arie concert. Saturday morning found her shopping for a new outfit to wear on her date with Michael. She'd asked Sandy to help her as she had been unable to find anything the last few times she'd looked. "I've got to find something really special." Kayla sounded exasperated as she explained to Sandy. "This is soooo special, I just want it to be perfect. I've got a beauty shop appointment at noon."

"Are you going out to dinner before or after the concert?"

"We have reservations at Captain's Hard Time Dining before the concert. Then we plan to laugh the night away at that comedy club down the street." Kayla smiled at Sandy, then whispered, "And maybe a little private dancing at my place."

"Sounds like a good time will be had by all." Sandy's voice mirrored Kayla's whisper. She thought for a minute and added, "You know, that shop over on Cottage Grove carries designer, upscale styles. You won't have to worry about seeing someone wearing the same outfit. They limit their styles to one, maybe two sizes for any dress, pantsuit, blouse, or whatever."

"Well, let's go." Kayla was like a child on Christmas Eve—she couldn't contain her excitement. Not only was she seeing one of her favorite neo-soul artists, she was going with Michael and that meant the evening was destined to be special.

She'd been shopping for a special outfit for the past month. Nothing caught her fancy until she walked into the upscale store specializing in designer one-of-a-kind fashions. Her eyes beamed with excitement.

"Oh, Sandy, look at this!" Kayla held out a three-piece pant set. The duster was ablaze with fiery hues of a midsummer sunset, a perfect color for the September night of the concert. The button-front duster had a tulip hem. The solid orange sleeveless tank and side-zip pants had flattering, fitted styling.

"Now that is exquisite!"

Sandy walked over for a better look. "I love the tapered legs and vented side seams on the pants." She twirled the outfit around on the hanger. "You're so conservative, I'm surprised you like this." Sandy batted her eyes in mock surprise.

"I know it's not really something I'd wear, but it's just gorgeous." Kayla felt the softness of the fabric and admired the bold color.

"Kayla, I'm only kidding. You should buy it if you like it. Who says you have to buy conservative all the time?" She gave the outfit back to her friend and demanded, "Try it on."

"You think I should?"

"Yes, try it on. Those are your colors. Your coloring and eyes will set that off nicely." Sandy clicked her tongue and batted her eyes. "I mean it, Kay, try it on!"

Kayla was in the fitting room when she shrieked, "Girl, this thing is over four hundred dollars!"

Sandy laughed as she waited for her friend to get over sticker shock. "You said you wanted something special. Special does cost, and plus I see the matching shoes out here and they're . . ." Sandy faked a cough before continuing, "special also." She could hear Kayla giggle in the fitting room.

Kayla stepped out, and Sandy and the sales clerk gasped; Kayla looked stunning. The orange top revealed just a hint of cleavage, making the ensemble sexy, but earthy. The duster was fitted at the waist, revealing her shapely figure. The long sleeves flared slighted at the hand, which gave them a soft, feminine appeal. The tulip hem of the duster fluttered provocatively with each step or movement she made.

"Ma'am, I've seen only one other woman with that ensemble on, and that was when it was being modeled for buyers. I swear you make *that* model look like a *man* in that outfit. You look amazing!" The clerk snapped her fingers and high-fived Sandy, who was standing looking at Kayla with her mouth opened in silence.

"Sandy, why are you quiet? What do you think? Is it too much?" Kayla knew she looked good but wanted Sandy's brutally honest opinion.

"When Michael sees you in that, I doubt if you make it to the concert. You might have to go right to the private dancing." All three women laughed. "Whatever is beyond fabulous, that's what you look like. I have to agree with her." Sandy looked over at the clerk, who was standing with her arms folded and a look of satisfaction on her face.

"You must have it, and you must get these too." Sandy handed her a pair of iridescent bronze-tone shoes. The shoes were subtle but added the finishing touch to the ensemble.

"I actually bought those to be worn with the outfit," the clerk said with confidence as she pointed to the shoes. "If you think the price is too much, I'll give you a small discount. You'll have to tell everyone where you got it from, 'cause I know they'll ask. I couldn't buy that kind of advertising." She winked at Kayla.

"Sold! Now quick, ring me up before I change my mind."

Kayla arrived at the beauty salon with barely five minutes to spare. The place was packed with patrons getting all manner of services. She waited patiently, reading old *Essence* magazines for almost half an hour until Judy, her operator, was available. Kayla loved talking to Judy, who seemed to know everybody in Chicago and all the latest happenings. She virtually transformed every woman who sat in her chair. Kayla sometimes didn't recognize the women whom she'd seen in the waiting area once the stylist got her hands into their hair. She consulted them on makeup, waxed their brows, and gave all kinds of tips on keeping that *just stepped out of the salon* look. Judy took great pride in her work and was rewarded with a prosperous salon and loyal customers, which made the wait longer, but well worth it. Tonight would be something special for Kayla and she wanted the full services of the salon.

Michael arrived at 5:30 to pick Kayla up for dinner. When she opened the door, he stood in the doorway for several seconds before he realized he was holding his breath. He tried to speak but words didn't come out.

He was finally able to speak after Kayla began laughing. "You . . . you are stunning!" His right hand immediately covered the left side of his chest as if trying to keep his heart from spilling out. "I can't say I've ever seen anyone look more beautiful." Michael bent down and kissed her gently on the lips.

"Well, that's just about the nicest compliment I've gotten in the past hour." Kayla chuckled lightly. "Thank you, Michael."

Kayla assessed Michael, who was wearing a brownish European-cut suit with a multicolored, collarless shirt that contained hints of green, brown, a deep dark yellow, and burgundy. The matching handkerchief peeked out from the pocket of the jacket. The look was striking and he looked as if he had just stepped from a page in *GQ.* He looked virile and handsome and the unmistakable smell of citrus and sandalwood was in the air. It was hard for her not to look at him like he was the most desirable man on earth.

"You look mighty magnificent yourself."

Michael bowed slightly and extended his arm. "Madame, are we ready?" Laughing at his gallant gesture, Kayla wrapped her arm around his and they left for dinner.

The evening was all that Kayla expected and more. Michael remained a gentleman the entire night as he opened doors, pulled out her chair, asked her if she was comfortable, if he could get her anything. All the little things that men seemed to have forgotten, Michael remembered and did them naturally.

The concert reminded Kayla of the beauty and

power of live music. No matter how much technology claimed to have captured the real sound and voice of a musician, nothing beat the sound of a live concert. India.Arie wowed the audience with her soulful, earthy, mellow sounds as she belted out songs about love. She sang about love for one's self, family, and lovers. She related to the audience and they loved her girl-next-door naturalness and image.

Every once in a while Kayla would feel Michael staring at her and when she turned to look at him the attraction between the two was packed with more power than a hydrogen bomb. They would kiss and smile, then hesitantly turn their attention back to the concert. Kayla believed it was the most enchanted evening she'd ever had.

"Oh, Michael, thank you so much for the dinner and concert, it was all just too much. I had a wonderful time!" Kayla could barely contain her excitement.

Michael looked over and took her hand, kissed it, and said, "I hope that doesn't mean you're ready to go home. The night is still young and the comedy club awaits."

"I'm ready, I just can't see how tonight could get any better."

Michael murmured, "I could."

Kayla couldn't help rewarding his teasing with a quick smile.

"I don't think I've ever laughed that hard or long in my life," Kayla said. She and Michael were continuing to laugh during the drive home as they recalled the antics of the comedians at the club. "I thought I was going to die when that woman pulled off her wig, and she was a man! I thought she was an unattractive old woman! Whew, that was too much!" Kayla was holding her side as she tried to compose herself.

Michael's robust laughter filled the car. When he was finally able to speak he said, "I mean he even had the old lady voice, I couldn't believe it either. He reminded me of this little old lady that goes to my church. I had to do a double take at first. I tell you, it takes a secure man to look and act that much like a woman."

"Either that, or they pay him a basket load of money."

Michael looked over at Kayla and traded with, "There ain't that much money in the world." They both cracked up again.

"Thanks again, Michael, for the most delightful evening I've ever had. It was absolutely perfect."

He pulled her to him as they stood in her living room. His arms seemed to naturally anchor around her waist. She could feel the heat between the two of them. His smoldering gaze made her legs weak and she could feel her knees starting to give.

"You're quite welcome. I always enjoy your company and look forward to more evenings like this." He kissed her again, but it was nothing like the kiss of earlier in the evening. This kiss was filled with longing and passion. Michael withdrew slightly and touched her lips with his finger. His breathing was deep and there was no doubt that he desired her. She felt his hard desire as their lower bodies remained pressed together.

Kayla responded as she put her arm around his

neck and brought him back to her mouth. Her fiery kiss on his lips sent them plunging into a world of passion. They were the only two that existed.

Michael's hand ran fiery touches up and down her back, causing her to arch her body into his. Her body was so ingrained into his, it sent him into deep currents of longing as he held her closer and tighter. He removed her duster and then her top. He marveled at her breasts as they peeked at him from her red lacy bra. His mouth watered as he gently kissed her mounds of breast before unhooking her bra. He then hungrily took one breast and then another until Kayla was moaning loudly and calling his name.

He lifted her up and carried her into the bedroom where he continued to slowly undress her. The sight of her in nothing but a pair of red panties was more than he could bear. He couldn't get enough of her as he licked and kissed every part of her body.

Kayla couldn't remember how they got into bed or how her clothes were removed; all she thought was that if he didn't enter her body soon, she'd explode. She felt intoxicated by his arousing sexual scent. She began undressing Michael and had to catch her breath when she took in the full sight of his manly chest. She ran her fingers across his chest and around his back as she pulled him to her. Neither could speak as their deep breathing didn't allow it. When she finally removed his pants and saw him bulging out of his briefs she moaned slowly, "Ummm." It was all that she could say.

Kayla trembled with excitement, but managed to reach over to the nightstand, where she took out a condom, removed it from the package, and gently eased it on his bulging male member. The feel of her hands as she covered him caused him to moan her name, softly and more sweetly than she'd ever heard. She sat back and watched him slowly come to her. She rested on her elbows as he kissed her. She then tilted her head back and he began a trail of kisses down her neck to her toes with many lingering stops along the way. When Michael entered her she was in rhythm with him and their united thrusting took them to the stars.

Kayla finally understood love's dance and all that it meant. Michael understood what it mean to make love to a woman that he truly loved. What they had experienced did transcend the biological, it was love. The two exploded together and meshed as one in a human puddle. Michael eased out and the two just lay wrapped in each other's arms for what seemed like eternity.

He was the first to move as he looked into her face and said, "I love you."

She smiled up at him and whispered, "I know."

Kayla spotted John as soon as she walked into the building. "Hey, good looking, what's going on?" His playful eyes danced over her body as his smile tricked her into smiling back.

"It's going good. How about you?"

"I don't know, been thinking about going back to school, but it's such a commitment." John shrugged his shoulders. "I'm only about thirty hours short of my bachelor's degree."

"But, John, that's a worthwhile commitment. Why wouldn't you go back? The company will pay for it. I say do it and get it out of the way."

"Yeah, I don't want to stay in the mail room all my life, but I'm not sure if I want to deal with the suits on a daily basis either."

"What was your major?" Kayla asked curiously.

"What else? Business." John's response was dry, but that didn't discourage Kayla.

"You could always get some experience in whatever it is that you want to do and go into business for yourself. There are all kinds of ways to keep away from the suits if you really want to. Don't let that stop you from moving ahead."

He nodded before replying, "You're right. Listen, why don't you let me buy you a drink after work? I'd like to bounce some ideas off of you." Kayla looked hesitantly at John. "Come on, don't give me that look. I let you take me out and get what you wanted about Ed Oswell."

"Man, when are you going to let that rest?" Kayla asked and rolled her eyes upward.

"We'll call it even if you meet me for drinks at the bar tonight after work." John nodded toward the local bar and grill down the hall from where they stood. He continued, "You know it's not like I have a lot of people I can talk to about this. Most women just want me for my body." John narrowed his eyes in an attempt to look overtly sexy.

Kayla couldn't stifle the laugh that lingered in her throat. "Okay, but this isn't a date, we'll meet at 6:00. This time no drinking before I get there, I don't want you claiming I took advantage of you again."

John was forced to laugh this time.

He walked toward the mail room as Kayla stood waiting for the elevator, and she mumbled, "I'll bet women really do try to take advantage of that body."

John's walk was more of an unintentional swagger. Just as he passed two women in the hall, they turned around and did a double take. One of the women whispered something to the other and they slapped each other's hand and giggled. John turned around and winked at the ladies, causing them to giggle more. Kayla stepped into the elevator laughing.

Kayla called Michael's office at 5:30. Lately he'd been showing up at her house unannounced, and although it didn't really bother her she didn't want him taking for granted she'd be there. He wasn't in his office and she left him a voice mail. She tied up a few loose ends for the day.

She and John got to the bar at the same time. "Hey, there's a booth over there, let's grab it," John said and he guided Kayla to the booth with his hand on her back.

Once they were settled into the booth Kayla said, "I thought you just wanted drinks."

John rubbed his stomach. "I did until I got a whiff of the hot wings. You know they're the best in town."

Kayla replied, "I know, that does sound good. Let's get an order and split it."

"Sounds good to me."

The waitress walked over to get their order. She and John flirted back and forth as Kayla watched the exchange. John motioned for the waitress to bend down and he whispered something in her ear, which made her develop a slow sensual smile. When the waitress left, Kayla teased, "Man, you really think you got it going on, don't you?"

"No, I don't *think* I got it going on. I *know* I got it going on."

She let out a chortle.

The waitress returned quickly with their drinks and set them on the table. "That was fast service. Whatever you said to her must have been really good." Within a few minutes the two were sharing a plate of hot wings and talking about what courses John would need to complete his degree.

Kayla explained the company's commitment to furthering its employees' education and would pay for John's textbooks as well.

"What the hell's going on here, Kayla?" She turned to find Michael standing within a few feet of the booth. His handsome face was tense and his eyebrows looked like a straight line. This was definitely a look she hadn't seen on him before. His tone of voice was unrecognizable.

"Michael, this is John. John, this is Michael." Kayla was trying to hurry and chew the food in her mouth so she could swallow it. He had caught her by surprise and his manner was something new to her, almost threatening.

"I didn't ask who he was, I asked *what* was going on." His tone was forceful with a hint of meanness. Kayla didn't like the tone or implication. She wiped her mouth with a napkin while trying to control her rising temper. John's previous smile had suddenly turned sinister as she knew there would be trouble if she didn't handle the situation quickly and carefully. She knew John was a bit of a roughneck and a fight in a bar wouldn't be unusual for him.

"I'm sorry, John, but excuse me please."

John stood up but his eyes never left Michael and the two were engaged in some sort of male visual sparring ritual, which would declare the first to look away the loser. Their piercing icy glare created an air thick with threatening violence. It frightened Kayla. Michael towered over John by several inches and looked like he could take care of himself, but Kayla didn't want any punches flying, especially because it was all a misunderstanding. It wasn't like her honor was being protected as the two men continued to stare each other down.

Kayla slid out of the booth and grabbed Michael by the arm. They walked to the bathroom area where it was slightly darker than the rest of the restaurant. Kayla hoped the short walk had calmed Michael down but when she turned to look at him, anger was still etched in his face. "What is wrong with you? I'm here having dinner and drinks with a coworker—"

Before she could finish Michael interrupted. "It didn't look like coworkers having dinner to me, you were leaned forward and he was obviously looking at you like—like—like you were on the menu."

Kayla clicked her tongue in disgust. "Please don't be foolish." She had become angry all over again.

Michael continued, "The way you two were eating off the same plate looked a little more than friendly to me!"

"How dare you!" she shrieked.

"No, Kayla, how dare you! I thought we had something special. I decided to surprise you by taking you out for dinner after work and I see you in here all in some other man's plate!" Michael's tone was rancorous. She couldn't believe that the same mouth had brought her so much pleasure before.

She snapped loudly at him, "Don't you say that to me. Don't you ever talk to me like that. As a matter of fact until you can apologize, Michael James, don't talk to me at all." Kayla turned quickly and left. She was hurt and afraid.

Michael was furious as he stormed past Kayla and John and out of the restaurant. "How dare she sit in there with some man eating off his plate and tell me to apologize!" Talking loudly to himself, he got in his car and sped from the parking lot.

"I am so sorry, John. That was my boyfriend. I mean he is my boyfriend. I mean I don't know what he is after tonight."

"Don't apologize, Kayla. What happened to the up-town lawyer?" John smiled that rugged smile again and said, "Never mind, at least this one has a pulse." That made Kayla smile through her anger. Her appetite was gone and all she wanted was to go home.

"I'm going to go and freshen up, I'll be right back." Kayla returned to the area where she and Michael had stood, and became sad. She pulled open the door to the bathroom and walked in. She splashed cold water on her face, then softly dried it with a paper towel. She didn't feel any better, but she had cooled down. She reapplied her lipstick and took a deep breath before heading out.

"Listen, we can do this some other time. I have enough information to get started. Classes don't start for a few months and my application is already in." He turned and looked toward the direction of the entrance and said, "Sounds like you've got some straightening out to do." John smiled and took her hand in his. "But if you ever need to talk to me I'm here for you, Kayla. We are friends, you know."

"Thanks, John. I'll see you tomorrow." Kayla stood and turned to leave but remembered she had to pay for her share of the meal and drinks. When she re-

turned to the table John had taken out enough
money to pay the tab and left a sizable tip for the waitress.

"Where are my manners? I've got money to pay for
my—"

"Kayla, please, I invited you. You've got a lot on
your mind, let me do this for you." He leaned over
and gave her a kiss on the cheek and a slight embrace. "You gonna be okay?"

She smiled at him. "I think so." When Kayla turned
to leave she saw Michael staring in disbelief with a
look of pain on his face. He turned and stormed out
of the restaurant for the second time. "Damn" was all
Kayla could manage.

Kayla tried calling Michael when she returned
home but there was no answer. He was obviously
avoiding her. She wouldn't try to call him again. As
far as she was concerned he was the one who misunderstood what he'd seen. He was the one that
stormed into the restaurant like a child stopping
short of accusing her of cheating on him. How could
he think so lowly of her after all they'd shared? She'd
given him all she had and he repaid her with mistrust. The more she thought about it, the angrier she
became.

A week had passed before Michael decided to call
Kayla. He had erased the message she left for him the
night he caught her in the restaurant with the
"roughneck." Michael called him that even though
he heard Kayla say his name was John. He believed
Kayla had better taste than that, but he'd been fooled
before by a woman and preferred to be cautious. His

heart still ached from not seeing her, from not holding her, or hearing her voice. Somehow he thought the pain would ease as the days progressed, but instead it grew deeper.

"Hello, Kayla. This is Michael." His voice had lost the casualness that she had grown to love.

"I know your voice, Michael."

"I thought we should talk."

"We should talk, but not before you apologize." Kayla had been as close to being a doormat as she was ever going to be with Justin. No man would ever come close to walking over her, no matter how much she loved him. She had to assert herself and not back down even as she felt her heart cry out his name when she heard the sound of his voice.

"Why should I apologize? Even if he was just a coworker as you claim, I saw you flirting with him. I saw the way he was all over you and the way he looked at you." As the words tumbled from Michael's mouth they burned his throat. He never wanted any man to look at her that way. She was his and it made him crazy to see or think of her being with any other man. "I saw the way you two were laughing."

"Michael, we are friends, we work together. He's returning to school and wanted some advice."

"Save it, Kayla, maybe this wasn't such a good idea." Michael hung up the phone.

"Hello? hello?" Kayla couldn't believe he was being so unreasonable and stubborn. She picked up the phone to call him, but placed it back in the cradle when she thought about the situation. She was not going to be the loser by giving in to him. She had done nothing wrong. If they were going to be together Michael needed to control his temper. The anger in his face and voice had frightened her. Her mind wandered to that possible flaw again. Maybe that was it: his temper.

"Come on, Kayla, clearly you are in love with this man, and he's in love with you. It's just a lovers' spat. Couples do have them, you know." Janae was trying to reason with her sister.

"I know that, Janae, but it's just that I refuse to allow another man to try and take advantage of me. It seems I'm always the one who has to yield, even when I know I'm right."

Kayla had called her sister for advice and they'd arranged to meet at the park near Janae's home. They watched as Clark played with other children in the sandbox.

"I didn't say you have to 'yield,' Kay, I just said give him some space and try talking to him again. Just don't let too much time pass."

"It's already been two weeks, and if that's all it takes to give up on what I thought we had, maybe it wasn't what I thought it was."

"Huh? Quit trying to psychoanalyze everything and just call the man." Janae was rising from the bench that she and Kayla had shared. "I need to get Clark home for some lunch. You want to join us?"

"No, thanks, but I'll walk over with you and give my niece a kiss. You really think I should try and call him? You understand what I'm saying though, right?"

"Yep, I do. Don't try to make him out to be like you know who. He's nothing like that pompous fool. Michael's hurting. He thought he saw you out on a date with another man. Just think about how'd you'd feel if the shoe were on the other foot."

"I have, Janae, and I wouldn't have jumped to conclusions and not given him a chance to explain."

"That's easier said than done, big sis. Sometimes people just react without thinking through. Sometimes it hurts too much to think it through and you just react."

Once they reached the sandbox, Kayla reached down and picked up Clark. "Hey, love bug, I've gotta go. You be a good girl and I'll see you soon." Clark nodded and the two rubbed noses.

Kayla looked at her sister and reached over to give her a hug. "Thanks again for listening, Janae. I couldn't have asked for a better sister."

"Same here, but really, Kay, call him. Put your pride aside for just a minute and call him. Passion can make people do all kinds of things. This man is quite passionate when it comes to you. He's very different from any man you've had before. He's had time to think."

Michael had called Kayla and left two messages for her by the time she returned home. His messages didn't include an apology, which didn't compel her to return the calls. She picked up the phone to call a few times, but she hung up each time as she got halfway through. She couldn't bring herself to compromise her principles again, not even for passion.

Kayla continued to avoid Michael's calls. She concentrated on work and was determined not to allow the incident with Michael and John to interfere with her job. She would remain focused on work. She'd made that mistake with Justin. Michael had called, left messages for her, and had been to her home several times. She didn't want to hear what he had to say. As far as she was concerned he had said it all when he indirectly accused her of cheating.

She had presentations to prepare and new business to scout. She was in her office by 7:30 A.M. planning for her presentation, which was on Thursday. It was her biggest yet, and would surely provide her with a huge bonus check. She still owed Sandy a night out for helping her with the Johnson presentation. She was deep in thought wondering where they might go when she heard Margaret's voice. "Good morning, Kayla. You are an eager beaver this morning."

Kayla spun around in her chair. "Good morning, Margaret. Did you have a good weekend?"

Margaret's entire face seemed to light up. "Very good. And yourself?"

"Very relaxing."

"Everybody needs one of those every once in a while. But you can wait until you get to be my age to have them more often."

They both smiled. "Do you want me to bring your planner and my pad in now?"

Kayla looked at her watch and her presentation on her computer. "Give me about an hour and then come in. Thanks, Margaret."

"I'm gonna get myself a cup of coffee, would you like me to bring you one?"

"No, thanks, maybe later." Kayla turned back to her computer and began polishing up her presentation.

After about an hour Margaret stepped into Kayla's office. "Kayla, do you have a few minutes? We need to talk privately."

"Sure, Margaret," she said, turning from her computer, unsure of what Margaret's stiff posture meant.

As Margaret walked in, she closed the door, something she'd never done without being asked to. "I don't like gossip and ordinarily I don't participate in it, but I've heard something you should know." Margaret's knitted brows told Kayla it was something serious. "I've heard that Ed Oswell is about to be promoted to a VP slot."

Kayla couldn't believe her ears as all kinds of questions flooded her head. "No way, Margaret, that's just gossip. First of all, the VP slots are filled. Secondly, Ed's only major successes have been the ones commandeered by his father. Not to mention the fact that I was asked to bring him in on some of my presentations because he was having a difficult time closing clients."

"I know all of that, Kayla, but just listen to me. They haven't made an official announcement yet, but Greer Novack is leaving."

Kayla thought back to the messages Ed had left her at home, and how he hadn't returned her calls, the flowers he'd sent; it was all adding up to something insidious. Surely he wasn't sharing the good news with her. Maybe he was trying to get her approval since everyone assumed she'd be next in line for a VP slot, and even that was a few years away.

They'd only been involved in a few presentations together over the years. During those presentations his input was mediocre, and it was well known that he wasn't willing to put in the hours required of such a highly visible position. Had his family's money and position bought him a promotion? "Well, don't sweat it, Margaret, I'll find out what's going on."

Margaret sighed deeply. "Okay, but please don't think this is a rumor. I've been around a long time and know just how the boys upstairs can quickly turn." The two women had become close and knew that this promotion should have been Kayla's.

Kayla decided to call Ed's office. "Hello, Ms. Marshall, I'm sorry but Mr. Oswell's on vacation this week. Would you like to leave a message?" *Vacation, that's for people who work!* her mind yelled.

"No, just let him know I've returned his call." Hanging up the phone, she couldn't believe the politics of the advertising game. Her phone rang and she debated whether to answer it. She wasn't in the mood to talk to anyone. She picked it up, listening to Margaret announce that Mr. Oswell was on the line for her.

"Good morning, this is Kayla Marshall," she said, trying to remain professional when all she wanted to do was cuss him out for being such a sneak.

"Hello, Kayla, it's Ed. How are you?"

"I'm fine, Ed, as a matter of fact I just tried to call you. I got your message on Saturday, what's going on?"

"Well, I need to talk to you in private, but not on the company phone. Can we meet later this evening, around 8:00 in my office?"

"Ed, that's awfully late, and I do have plans for this evening."

"Please, Kayla, you're the only one I can talk to. Please. Things aren't always what they seem, but I know I can trust you. It's something you need to know before it goes public."

"All right, Ed, but if it's about the rumor regarding a promotion, I already know."

"Don't believe everything you hear. I'll see you tonight. Thanks, Kayla." His voice became low, somehow reminding her of a wounded, cornered animal—dangerous.

At four o'clock, Kayla called Sandy to confirm their dinner plans and to get her take on the events of the day. They met at a nearby restaurant at 6:00.

"Well, what do you think it could be?" Sandy put her fork down as the steak was so massive that it could easily have fed two people, and dabbed her lips with the napkin.

"I don't have a clue." Kayla's appetite had disappeared and she'd pushed her plate away shortly after receiving it.

As they sat and sipped their wine, Sandy leaned over. "Maybe he's getting a case of jungle fever," she said, smirking devilishly.

"Sandy, please, they don't get any whiter than Ed. That blue blood probably doesn't sleep on colored sheets."

"Well, it's getting time for you to meet him. Call me when you get home," Sandy said, gathering her purse in preparation to leave.

Kayla looked pleadingly at her friend. "Oh, no, don't do that, girl. Come with me."

Sandy slung her purse in her lap, a sure sign she was weakening. Kayla put the pressure on.

"Come on, San, I don't want to be alone with him. If he knows someone's waiting for me he'll make it quick. Help a sistah out, I'd do it for you." She put her hands together as if praying. "Please, San, you can go with me, meet him, and then wait in my office." Batting her eyes and looking pitiful, she continued, "I'll even pick up the dinner tab."

"All right, all right, just stop begging and looking pitiful, and don't think I've forgotten that you were picking up the tab for dinner anyway." As she pushed her seat back, she grunted. "Okay, let's see what kind of drama your boy is up to. Probably wants to give you that 'what a great team player you are, and I hope I can count on you for support,' which really means you have to work twice as hard to pick up his slack, then a fake pat on the back, while he tells you about the promotion you should've gotten." Even she was amazed at getting through the diatribe without taking a breath.

"Sounds like you've heard that one a time or two. Well, you certainly don't sound bitter." They both laughed as they left the restaurant.

After getting off the elevator Kayla looked at Sandy and in a low, cautious voice said, "I don't have a good feeling about this at all." She peered around at the semidark offices. Only a few lights were on near the exit door and a quietness that made them both uncomfortable saturated the office.

"You're just being paranoid, which in this business can be a good thing." Sandy tried sounding cavalier, but the edge in her voice was pronounced.

When they arrived at Ed's office, the door was ajar. The two women looked at each other nervously. Kayla slowly pushed the door open slightly and the acrid smell of smoke and blood wafted around their noses and floated down into the back of their throats, sending them into panic. Kayla pushed the door farther, and as Ed's desk came into full view, the two women screamed and ran toward the elevators at the sight of Ed slumped over his desk with brain matter and blood spewed everywhere, a small gun near his right hand.

They both backed away and ran toward the elevator. "Wait, wait, we should call the police. We can't just leave him there like that." Sandy was breathing hard and her words came out choppy. "He obviously killed himself, so we're not in any danger. Come on, let's go to your office and call the police."

"No, San, we don't know if he killed himself or not. We can call the police from the car. I just don't want to be here." Kayla looked around frantically as they got onto the elevator.

"You're right, something's not right about all of this," Sandy agreed.

Once they reached the car and Kayla telephoned the police on her cell phone, Sandy asked, "Why would he kill himself? More importantly, why would he kill himself and set you up to discover the body?"

Shaking her head, voice trembling, she slowly mumbled, "My God, San, I don't know. I just don't know."

Sandy put her arm around her friend for comfort. They sat quietly waiting for the police.

The police arrived and questioned the two women separately as what appeared to be hundreds of police and medical personnel went about the task of investigating the scene. After what seemed like hours of questioning in her office, Kayla was allowed to leave.

The first person she saw was Mr. Newhouse as he rushed toward her and gently wrapped his arms around her. "I'm so sorry you found him like that. Are you okay?"

Kayla could only mumble, "I'll be fine." The uncharacteristic embrace, even though brief, made her feel uncomfortable. She gently freed herself, and looked around for Sandy, who was talking to one of the detectives. The pleading in her eyes sent her friend over immediately. "Sandy, this is Mr. New-house. Mr. Newhouse, this is my friend Sandra Neal."

"Sorry to meet you under such circumstances. Are you all right, Ms. Neal?" Extending his hand to shake hers, he covered it with the other hand, a usually comforting gesture that was of no comfort to Sandy.

"I'll be okay. I'm ready to go."

"Yes, this has been an ordeal for you two. Please allow my driver to take you ladies home."

"No, thank you, Mr. Newhouse. We can drive," Sandy said and the two ladies thanked him for his consideration and left.

They'd decided to leave Sandy's car in the garage as neither wanted to be alone and during the quiet drive home both tried to make sense of the tragedy they'd seen. "I tell you, Sandy, I just don't get it."

"Didn't you say that Ed had been acting weird the last few weeks?"

"Yeah, weird, not depressed. I don't know, he acted more like he was nervous or afraid, not depressed. I don't know what to make of it all." She let out a deep long sigh.

"You've always been good at reading people. Think back, was there anything to suggest he was suicidal?"

"No, Sandy, I keep telling you the man was nervous or afraid, not depressed or hopeless."

"Well, you know he'd just done it. I could smell the cologne when we got on the elevator, and gun smoke and blood as soon as we opened his door. If I live to be a hundred, I'll never forget the sight," Sandy said, shaking her head as if trying to clear the image.

"I—I don't know, but this just doesn't seem right. That man had everything to live for. He came from money. He was about to get a big promotion," Kayla said.

"Kay, let me stop you, I know how your imagination can go astray. You never know what goes on behind closed doors. How can you say the man had everything to live for? You said yourself he was nervous or afraid. Look at all the money and legacy Gloria Vanderbilt's son had. He took a flying leap off the balcony of their very expensive town house while she was home. Hell, she probably didn't even know the boy was depressed.

"You said you rarely saw or talked to Ed. The rich have their bouts with depression just like everybody else. Money, power, status, all the material possessions someone like him deemed essential to happiness don't solve life's problems."

"I know that, San, but it just doesn't fit. I just can't imagine someone as vain as he was shooting himself in the head like that. He was more the sleeping pill type and I knew it was something." Kayla was gripping the steering wheel so hard the palms of her hands were white. Her eyes were wide and attentive despite the late hour. She was wired.

"What is it, Kay?"

"Wasn't the gun near Ed's right hand?"

"Well, yeah, and so?"

"And so, Ed was a lefty. I know it sounds elementary, and hokey, but I'm telling you he was left-handed."

"Kay, how in the hell can you say that for sure?" Her voice was dripping with skepticism.

"Any time we sat in meetings he'd tap his pen on the table with his left hand, looking totally bored. I distinctly remember at the company picnic and softball games others teased him about being a southpaw."

Sandy agreed. "I think you should call that detective tomorrow. That's some stuff they should know. I mean he could have shot himself with his right hand even if he was a lefty. Don't read anything into this, girl. If someone else shot him, surely they'd know which hand to put the gun in."

Kayla was about to protest when Sandy raised her hand to stop her. "Look, Kay, you're the most observant, analytical person I know and don't think I'm downplaying what you're saying, but right now you're—we're both still in shock. Let's get some hot tea, and go to bed. I promise in the morning if this is still troubling you I'll go to the police with you. But for now let's just talk about something else."

The two friends drove home in silence, but thoughts of Ed Oswell and the unforgettable scene played in their heads like an awful movie.

Once at Kayla's house, Sandy put on a pot of water to make hot tea. "I'm exhausted, but I don't know if I can sleep." Sandy patted her friend on the back as she made her way to the kitchen. "Maybe something warm and soothing will help our nerves."

Kicking off her shoes, and heading toward the bathroom, Kayla said, "I'm gonna take some Tylenol. My head is throbbing."

"Bring me some too."

When Kayla returned to the kitchen, Sandy was busy stirring herbal tea. "Here, I don't know if these will do any good. I just don't feel like I'll ever get over the sight of that man slumped over like that." Kayla shuddered, handing the Tylenol to Sandy.

"I don't know what could ever be so bad that I'd kill myself," Sandy said. Her faraway look suggested the vision wouldn't leave her either.

"I just don't believe it was suicide, San." Sandy looked at her friend, and before she could object, Kayla held up her hand. "I know, I know, my imagination may be running wild. But my instincts tell me there's more to this than meets the eye."

The ringing phone woke Kayla at 6:00 A.M. "Hey, baby, I just saw the local news. They said someone was found dead at your office."

"Michael?" Kayla barely recognized his voice, he was speaking so rapidly, something he rarely did. She was in a bit of fog and had to think twice about what he was saying when she realized it wasn't a bad dream. The scene from the night before played in her head again.

"Yeah, baby, it's me. Are you okay? You sound confused."

Her words came slow, as her throat felt tight and her mouth was dry. "Michael, Sandy and I found his body. It was Ed Oswell."

"What? Are you serious, Kay?"

"Yes, I have no sense of humor when it comes to finding dead bodies. We walked in just after it happened." Not even her dry wit could elevate her from the low she felt.

"Oh, my God, are you okay? Why didn't you call me? I'll be right over."

"No, Michael, I'm okay, Sandy's here with me. I'm still really tired. I'd just like to get some sleep. Can I call you later?"

"Of course."

"Bye, Michael, I'll call you later." She placed the

phone into the cradle gently and rolled back into a deep sleep.

Kayla sat staring out of the living room bay window at the crisp brown dry leaves that covered the ground. The season was changing and the morning air was now cooler and crisper. The trees were taking on their autumn colors. She watched as a male and female jogger ran past, the steam coming from their mouths, their faces slightly crimson and serious looking. She thought about all the small things people take for granted in daily living. She thought about how Ed was no longer going to enjoy waking up to a quiet, cool fall morning. He wouldn't enjoy seeing the changes of the season, or a cup of coffee while reading the paper. It was the little things in life that somehow appealed to her at the time.

Kayla knew that people killed themselves, but somehow Ed seemed to be the kind of person that enjoyed his prosperity too much to end his life so prematurely. She thought about all the times he had sat in meetings with his crisp white designer shirts and tailored suits, each strand of blond hair in place looking like the poster boy for Club Med. How quickly life's balance can shift, even for those with everything, she thought, and more importantly she wondered, *What is "everything"?*

Chapter 9

"Detective Civello, all I'm saying is that there was something going on with Ed and it wasn't depression. Sandy and I both smelled cologne when we stepped onto the elevator. I mean if the man was going to kill himself why would he bother to put on cologne?" She looked over to her friend for support, who obliged with an affirming nod. Detective Civello, a seventeen-year veteran on the force, was known to be cynical and tough, but also knew a contrived crime scene when he saw one. He wasn't sure what these two women's involvement in the murder may have been, but he'd let them keep talking.

"Also did you know Ed was left-handed?" Kayla thought she detected a slight twitch but wasn't sure. His face looked as though it were etched in granite. There was no reading this man, he gave no clues as to what could possibly be on his mind.

"No, we didn't know that, but we are checking everything out at this point. We'll take your observations under advisement and if you remember anything else please call me." Handing her a card, he stood up, indicating their time was up.

Kayla and Sandy looked at each other in agreement; they knew when they were being dismissed.

Rising slowly, Kayla picked up her purse from the floor. She wasn't going to be shooed away like some pesky insect. "You know, Detective Civello, I realize you people are overwhelmed with unsolved murder cases, but you could try to be more passionate about your work. We discovered the body of a coworker, and have been traumatized by it. We may not have the instincts of a police detective, such as yourself, but we know something foul when we smell it." She positioned her purse strap on her shoulder. Her eyes never left his. "Take that under advisement." She nodded at Sandy, indicating it was time to go.

Civello had been accused of a lot of things in his seventeen years on the force, but never had anyone so calmly and righteously put him in his place. He cleared his throat. "Miss Marshall, we investigate an overwhelming amount of murder cases, and each one is given the same attention and merit. We are looking into this as a homicide. More than likely Mr. Oswell was murdered by someone he knew intimately. Therefore everyone is a suspect until we find out otherwise. We aren't at liberty to discuss the particulars of the case with someone so close to the victim, but rest assured we are doing all that is humanly possible to solve this homicide." His etched-granite face never changed, he seemed to be repeating a speech he'd delivered hundreds of times.

Kayla, Michael, and Sandy walked into the packed church silently. Once seated Kayla whispered, "Thanks so much for coming with me."

Smiling faintly, Michael patted her hand. He had to squelch the desire to kiss her and tell her that things would be okay. He knew she was worried and had been to see the detective investigating the homicide. Michael was determined to stay close to her because he didn't know what had happened with Ed. He believed it could have been someone who worked with Kayla, and the thought of her being in contact with someone capable of murder made him put his arm around her and pull her closer to him.

Michael felt he would protect Kayla at all cost and had secretly visited the detective himself. He tried to uncover what danger was near the woman he'd fallen in love with.

Kayla looked around at the crowd and nodded at a few people from Lancer and Newhouse, thinking back to the last time she'd seen some of them in a social situation, the wedding reception of Kit and Deb, who were seated several pews in front of her and Sandy.

The thought saddened her, a happy, memorable wedding reception just four months earlier and now a sad, mournful funeral. The priest began the mass and Kayla began her closer observation of the crowd. Her eyes locked with Detective Civello's as he also turned to scan the mourners. He nodded at her slightly and continued scanning the room with his eyes, aware that whoever had killed the victim was probably attending the funeral. Kayla could almost read his mind as her thoughts were the same.

Outside the church solemn mourners prepared to depart for the burial. "It's such a shame, he was in his prime."

Kayla listened intently to Mr. Myerson talking to a large woman with the biggest, ugliest, pale-blue-print-feathered hat and matching blue-print dress Kayla had ever seen. She looked like a big blue bird. She determined the woman was probably his wife, judging from the way she'd latched on to him. Monte Myerson was a self-made successful owner of a local food chain, one of Ed's first accounts. Kayla was slowly making her way over to him, continuing to listen to his conversation with the large lady.

"He came by the office the day before the tragedy to inform me he wouldn't be handling our account any longer, wouldn't say why. Yeah, it's a real shame."

She'd made her way over to Mr. Myerson, unsure of what to say, when Mr. Lancer intercepted.

Shaking hands briskly, he said, "Thank you for coming, Monte, I'm sure the family appreciates your presence." Politely nodding at Kayla, the two men strolled down the stairs.

"Kayla Marshall, I know that look. What's going on in that steel trap you call a brain?"

Turning to look at Sandy, who'd stayed in the church to talk to a former coworker, she replied, "Oh, nothing. I don't think I can take the burial. Let's go."

Sally Rogers appeared hastily from the church wearing a black dress with a neckline so low you could almost see her navel. "Mr. Lancer, Mr. Myerson, wait a minute please. I need to speak to you." Her spike heels clicked quickly down the stone steps, loud and irritating, just like her.

All attention had turned to her obvious display of bad taste as she chased the two men down, blond hair blowing freely in the wind. Sandy looked at Kayla, shaking her head. "Let me guess, Sally Rogers, a.k.a. the 'It Girl'?"

With blatant disapproval engraved on her face, Kayla shook her head. "She's probably trying to fina-

gle that account, but judging from the look on old
lady Myerson's face, she ain't having it." They both
smiled a weary smile. Kit and Deb made their way
over to her, and they exchanged hugs and condo-
lences. Kayla knew she'd never take another sunrise
or sunset for granted. Family and friends would forever be cherished and never would she feel alone
again. She had a loving family and a network of
friends she could call on in any crisis.

Michael put his arm gently around her waist, a re-
assuring gesture that brought comfort to her. Despite
the feeling of comfort she continued to feel some
sadness because there were too many unanswered
questions. Ed's death had affected her to the ninth
power and she wouldn't rest until the answers were
known to her.

"I can't get over this feeling that Ed was trying to
tell me something. It's just not right." She continued to look straight ahead as Michael maneuvered
his way through the parking lot and finally out onto
the street.

"I know, Kay, and you've done your part, you went
to the police." Michael glanced over at her. "Most
people wouldn't have done that. You said the man
had all kinds of enemies at work. Who knows what
makes a man like that do the things he does? Suicide
isn't that far-fetched. I mean people kill themselves
for all kinds of reasons."

"Yes, they do, but usually there are signs along the
way."

"Yeah, but most people don't recognize them till
it's too late." His voice becoming low and soothing,
he said, "Just let it go, Kay."

"I can't, Michael, it was like he was trying to tell me

something, something important. He said he trusted me. And plus that detective says they were treating it as a homicide. They wouldn't have been at the funeral if they remotely thought it was suicide."

Michael pulled the car over and parked. "Where are we going?" Kayla asked as she looked confused.

"That's exactly what I want to know, Kay, you are leaving reality here. I don't know where you're headed, but you need to pull up and come on back. You've said yourself that there's no telling what he was into. Maybe he'd done something to jeopardize his promotion and couldn't face it."

Michael took a deep breath. Kayla was a very determined and driven woman. They hadn't talked about the incident with John and he had tried several times to talk to her about it. Now wasn't the time. Kayla had other things on her mind. He knew that Kayla was the kind of person who would step out on a limb to help someone, or to correct a wrong. He believed the situation presented some kind of danger for her. He didn't want her going off trying to solve the murder or asking the wrong people questions.

"Kayla, promise me you won't start snooping around this situation." He gently caressed her face and kissed her lips. "I'd lose my mind if something happened to you."

She saw the concern in his eyes and it touched her heart.

She brought his face to hers and they kissed passionately. She pulled back abruptly when she realized what she'd done. *There I go thinking with my heart again,* she thought. Where Michael was concerned it was hard for her to do otherwise, but there was a nagging issue that kept her at bay. He still had not apologized for his behavior the night he saw her and John at the restaurant.

Michael tried to pull her back to him but she resisted. He'd missed the closeness they'd shared. Previously her warmth made him want to get closer. Now she was pulling away and it was all his fault. He felt he had to take responsibility for what happened and he swore he'd make her see it was a foolish mistake. He'd give her space for now, but at some point they'd have to discuss whatever it was that drove the wedge between them. The hesitation Kayla always seemed to have with him made him wonder if she wasn't still in love with Justin.

The mere thought of her being in love with another man caused a sharp pain in his chest and a low gasp escaped his throat. He turned and looked at her.

"You okay?" she asked.

"No, I'm not." Taking a deep breath, he continued, "I know now is not the time, but we need to talk about us, Kayla."

"I know." She barely spoke above a whisper.

Chapter 10

"I missed you at the funeral." Kayla looked at John as he continued sorting mail from the huge bag that sat on the counter.

"Hey, Kayla, how ya doing?" His dreads moved with the slight tilt of his head and Kayla finally figured out who it was that he resembled. He looked like Eric Benét with a slight bad boy edge to him.

"I'm okay, I guess." A moment of silence passed. This wasn't the usual flirty John; he was quiet and solemn.

"So why didn't you make it to the funeral?"

He stopped sorting the mail and gave her a look that could stop a clock. Something close to a sneer spread across his face. "'Cause I didn't like the man." He looked around for anyone who may have been in a position to overhear him and when satisfied there wasn't anyone, he continued. "I don't think that punk had the guts to kill himself. Somebody put him out of his misery."

She was startled by the harshness of the words although she'd been thinking the same thought.

Her face and voice softened as she put her hand on his shoulder. "John, whatever did he do to you for you to continue hating him, even in death?" He'd told her about the many underhanded things he'd done to others, but didn't include himself.

Her softness made him relax as well. "Well, for starters he tried several times to get me fired."

"What!" she screeched in a decibel higher than her normal speaking voice. Looking around to see if she'd drawn attention, she then walked over and closed the mail room door. "How, why? You never told me that. Why would he do such a thing?" She leaned forward, waiting for an explanation.

"Yeah, see, I accidentally found out about some stuff he was doing that he didn't want nobody to know about." He'd begun busying himself with the mail again, obviously not eager to continue the conversation. "People are stupid enough to let personal mail come to their place of business, if you get my drift."

He was hinting at something but she didn't get it so she waited for further explanation. She folded her arms and leaned back on the counter. "Can't you be more specific?"

That determined look in her eye made him look away and continue to sort the mail. "Maybe some other time. Why are you so curious about all this?" John turned and looked at Kayla with a concerned look. He took her hand and said, "Don't go sticking that pretty nose of yours where it doesn't belong."

The concern in his voice caused Kayla's face to soften, causing him to soften again. "Look, Kayla, the less you know about that man, the better off you are. I don't know why you're interested in him, but trust me, you don't want to know all that man was into. Especially when you consider he's now dead probably because of some of those things." He turned and continued sorting the mail as a feeling of uneasiness came over her.

"I'll see you later, John." She leaned over and kissed him gently on the cheek, lightly stroking his back. "Take care."

She opened the door and began to leave when he said, "Trust me, Kayla, you don't want no part of Ed Oswell, dead or alive. Let sleeping dogs lie."

That night Kayla decided to call Michael. She had avoided him and had not returned his calls. "Hello, Michael."

"Hey. I'm glad you called. I've really missed you. You in the mood for company?"

"Depends."

"On what?"

"I still think you owe me an apology." It would be the last time she'd say it. If he didn't apologize this time she was determined to never call him again.

"Can I do it face-to-face? I think I owe you that."

His convincing tone made her heart soften and she replied, "Yes, I'm in the mood for company."

Michael wasn't sure what he'd say to Kayla when he rang her doorbell. They had barely spoken about anything other than Ed and he missed her terribly. It finally dawned on him that he would have to apologize for his behavior. He'd found it difficult to think about that night, let alone face the fact that he'd jeopardized their relationship because he was too stubborn to say "I'm sorry." He still had not addressed the underlying issue for his anger. He wasn't willing to admit that to himself or to Kayla. He'd told his brother about his previous relationship but he was too ashamed to tell anyone else.

As soon as Kayla opened the door Michael took one

look at her and knew he'd been a fool. "I'm so sorry, I don't know what came over me. I just saw you there with that man and couldn't deal with the thought of you being with another man. Please forgive me."

"I've missed you, Michael. Apology accepted." A minute of awkard silence passed before Kayla realized he was still standing on the other side of the door. "I'm sorry, come in. Let me take your coat." She shivered slightly. "It's getting chilly."

Michael stepped inside and wrapped his arms around her and kissed her lips gently. "Let's start a fire."

His eyes searched hers for a response. She felt herself softening and before long the coat was on the floor and the two were locked in a lovers' embrace.

Kayla visited with her family on Sunday after church. After a lunch with her family, Kayla helped her parents set up the new computer she'd bought them. They would be able to e-mail Terrance at school, send pictures, and surf the Net for their next vacation destination.

Janae and Alex shared the happy news of their upcoming addition to the family. George and Gail immediately started to make plans for their next grandchild. They wanted to set up a trust fund for the new baby like they'd done when Clark was born. The family spent time looking through old family albums. Gail had taken up the hobby of scrapbooking and had redone the albums beautifully. Kayla helped her father winterize the yard in preparation for the cold weather and by the end of the day she was exhausted.

When she got home she took a shower and passed

out on the sofa. She and Michael had plans to check out a jazz club later that evening.

The doorbell rang and woke her. She pulled her robe tightly around her and looked out to see Michael. She opened the door and immediately began apologizing. "I'm so sorry, Michael. I fell asleep. My folks wore me out. Just give me time to get dressed." She quickly appraised him and noted under his jacket he was wearing jeans and a polo shirt. He had a big, beautiful, invitingly warm, dimpled smile. He held a bag in one hand and fresh-cut flowers in the other. Stepping aside, she invited him in.

"I thought you might like these." He handed her the flowers and kissed her on the cheek.

"Thanks," she said and smelled the flowers. The scent of fresh-cut flowers always made her smile. These were an assortment of fall colors, yellow, brown, and purple. "They're lovely." She smiled and returned his kiss on the cheek. Her head flooded with all kinds of warm and good thoughts.

"I'll only take a minute to put these in a vase, then get dressed."

"The jazz club is casual dress. It's just a hole in the wall, but you'll enjoy the music."

She looked at the bag in his hand. He had been so preoccupied with looking at her he'd forgotten about the bag. He would have preferred that she just take off the robe. "Oh, here's a little something I picked up for you today. I spent the afternoon with a group of adolescent boys and one of our trips was to the bookstore. I'm trying to encourage them to read. I hope if they take ownership of a book they enjoy, it'll encourage them to read more. They all got library cards last month."

As he handed her the bag Kayla could hear that hum coming from her heart again. She paused briefly. Unsure what to expect, she slowly opened the bag and looked inside. It was an inspirational book by Iyanla Vanzant. "Oh, wow! This is really sweet. How'd you know I liked Iyanla?"

"I wasn't certain but you seem like the kind of woman who would. Do you already have it?"

The sincerity in his eyes made her blush. "No, I've heard that it's very good. Thank you so much."

"I'd better get dressed. Help yourself to a drink. There's plenty in the fridge. You can put on some music if you like or look at television. The remotes are all there on the table." She pointed to the table and gave a cursory look around. "Or you can read something from the bookcases."

She rushed into the bedroom and grabbed a pair of jeans and a casual silk blouse. She then selected sexy, matching underwear. Shaking her head at her naughty thoughts, she proceeded to the master bath for a quick shower. It took her less than thirty minutes to get ready.

"I hope I didn't keep you waiting too long."

Michael was sitting on the sofa with his eyes closed listening to Erykah Badu. He opened his eyes and looked at her.

"Not at all. You look amazing." The desire in his eyes was unmistakable. "I'm hungry, though you might like to eat dinner first."

Kayla took her purse from the kitchen table and asked, "Are you craving anything in particular?" She dumped her cosmetic bag in the purse and slung it over her shoulder.

"Actually, what I'm craving isn't on any menu."

Michael's voice was as mellow as a full-bodied, rare, expensive wine. Kayla immediately looked at him and the intense attraction between the two was hot enough to start a four-alarm fire.

"You didn't get enough last night and this morning?" Her lips formed a slight smirk.

"No, and never will." Michael hadn't meant for the words to come out. He had decided to slow things down. He sensed she thought they were moving too fast. For her sake he was willing to put the brakes on once in a while, but he knew he'd never get his fill of her.

"I'm in the mood for some good old soul food. How about Gladys's?"

"Let's roll, my mouth is starting to water." Michael rubbed his stomach. "You'd better get a jacket, it's a little chilly."

Kayla opened the hall closet on the way out and grabbed her jacket. He assisted her in putting it on. *Always the gentleman,* she thought.

"Thanks, Michael." She couldn't remember the last time she went on a date with a man where she dressed so casually. It felt good and natural. Their conversation and laughter in the car was light and familiar. Kayla was so comfortable she began to feel as though she were out with an old friend.

After settling down to dinner, Michael asked, "So tell me about your family?" Kayla told him about her parents, her siblings, her brother-in-law, Clark, and the fact that she was going to be an aunt again soon. All the while Michael listened attentively. He wanted to know everything about her.

She listened as he told her about his family. He and Trent were very close, did volunteering together, and had shared an apartment after college. His parents were divorced but were the best of friends. His father was a retired mailman and his mother continued to work as a nurse. They talked about work, goals, music, movies, and books. Both were avid readers.

Michael leaned forward when she spoke as if he was truly capturing all that she was saying. He often lifted a brow as if befuddled, and asked for clarification. *Finally,* she thought, *a man who listens as actively as he speaks.* He had convictions that he shared freely. He was definitely the total package, but Kayla couldn't get the notion of a fatal flaw and wondered what it was. She was convinced he had one, and as much as he had going for him, it had to be a seriously huge flaw.

After dinner they headed to the jazz club. Michael broke the silence in the car when he said, "It's just a hole in the wall, like I said before. Very informal, but they've got the best live music around. The sound system is great. Lots of artsy people hang around there."

"Sounds good to me."

He asked her about what she thought of the neo-soul movement in music. She loved the way he asked her about things like that. He asked her opinion about events and situations. She believed he knew more about her from the short time that they'd been together than Justin knew in all the three years they'd dated. She and Michael always had conversations that were animated and lively. Both definitely had strong opinions.

Michael was right about the club. For what the place lacked in decor, the music and atmosphere more than compensated. It was dimly lit with simple round wooden tables draped in white linen table-cloths with small wood chairs around them, denoting a certain intimacy not found in the new clubs. The band's featured singer was doing great justice to Rachelle Ferrell's "Welcome to My Love."

The patrons were very laid-back, a casually dressed crowd. No one passing out business cards or perpetrating like they were something they were not. It was an eclectic group of people, blacks, whites, Hispanics, and Asians, all sitting back, socializing, and enjoying the music.

They found an empty table, ordered drinks, and engaged in small talk. Kayla glanced around the crowd. "This is nice, Michael. I like the atmosphere in here. You can come and have a good time without getting all geeked up."

The waitress brought their drinks. Kayla thought the waitress was attractive in the way that men liked: tall, slender, long legs, long dark hair, almond-shaped eyes, with just enough makeup to accentuate her features. If Justin had been there, Kayla would have noticed him noticing the waitress, but not tonight. Michael only had eyes for her. She liked the way Michael made her feel. He was attentive and warm, always responsive to her.

Kayla swayed to the music, obviously having a good time. Michael took a sip of his drink and gently held her hand. "I'm glad you're having a good time. That's what having a good time is all about, being yourself. You don't have to get dressed up to enjoy yourself or listen to good music.

"I noticed when I was at your place that you had a picture of Justin on your bookcase," Michael said, abruptly changing subjects.

An alarm sounded in Kayla's head. She'd forgotten all about the picture. He'd had it taken for some local magazine that was doing an article about him and he gave her one of the extras.

Michael tried not to let it show, but he was disappointed to see the picture on the bookcase. They'd not gotten around to talking about their past lovers the night they had intended to, and he wanted to keep it that way. He did realize that before they progressed any further he wanted to be sure that Justin had not even a corner of Kayla's heart. He wanted that only for himself.

"To be honest, Michael, I didn't remember the picture was there. I've been so busy lately, all I've managed to do is work and sleep. Otherwise had I seen it, I would've torn it up and burned it." Kayla's mouth turned down at the corners as if tasting something bitter.

Michael laughed and said, "Ouch. Was the breakup that bad?"

"I didn't know how unhappy I was. I'd become complacent or lazy, whatever. At any rate it was over long before I told him good-bye."

Michael shook his head in understanding. He turned his attention to the singer and she could feel him tapping his feet under the table.

I guess that discussion is over, she thought. She continued to feel some tension, but decided to just enjoy her drink and the music.

After a few minutes she asked, "What are you thinking at this very moment, Michael?" Before he could answer a tall, beautiful young woman, dressed to the nines, was standing at the table. Kayla hadn't seen the woman approach and was somewhat startled by her sudden appearance.

Michael and the woman were locked in an intense

glare. The stranger finally spoke. "Hello, I'm surprised to see you here." The flirty, casual way she stood looking at Michael told Kayla the woman was definitely not a stranger to him. She gave Kayla a dismissive glance and continued, "Thought this was our place." She pouted her lips in mock disappointment.

Kayla cleared her throat and gave the woman a look that could have frozen the entire Pacific Ocean. Michael turned to Kayla and said, "Let's leave." He stood up.

"You not going to bother to introduce me?" The stranger continued her pout for just a second and then with a smile that dripped venom, extended her hand to Kayla. "Hi, I'm Sheila." Kayla reluctantly took the woman's hand and gave her such a firm handshake that she caused a wince.

"I'm Kayla. *And no, Ms. Thing, it's not good to meet you,* Kayla thought. Looking at Michael, Kayla said, "I'm not ready to go. The music is good and I'm having a good time. Now whatever is going on with you and Cynthia—"

Sheila snapped, "Sheila is the name." She glared at Kayla, who seemed unaffected by it all.

"*Whatever,* I suggest you take it outside because I'm staying." She casually leaned forward and took a sip of her drink. When her eyes met Michael's she couldn't read them. She didn't know what the look on his face meant.

"We can talk outside," he said to Sheila. Michael turned to Kayla. "I'll be right back." She responded with a look that indicated she couldn't care less whether he came back or not. Michael felt a knot form in his stomach.

He took Sheila by the elbow and escorted her outside. Over the past few months he'd seen many expressions on Kayla's face and he loved them all, until tonight. He loved the cadence her voice took on when she asked him how his day went, or when she described some event. Now she sounded cold and uncaring, like the kind of woman Sheila was.

"Why are you trying to start trouble, Sheila? You hate this place, told me not to ever bring you here again. Now that *we* are over, and have been over for months, it's suddenly 'our place.'" Michael could feel his entire body tense up. His jaw muscles flexed with tension. Sheila loved causing trouble.

When they dated she had constantly accused him of cheating, and played more games than a major league baseball team. She was driven by nothing but money. She always had to have the best. Sheila spent money before she could earn it.

Sheila stepped closer to Michael and purred, "Honey, I'm so sorry I didn't know what I had until it was gone. I miss you like crazy." She batted her eyes seductively and pursed her lips. "We can try again. It'll be better, I promise." Leaning over to kiss Michael on the lips, she made eye contact with Kayla but not before Michael held up his hand to block the kiss.

Kayla raced past the two and into a waiting cab. Michael tried to catch her, but Sheila grabbed and held on to him tighter than a size-six dress on a size-twelve body.

"Damn it, Sheila! Look what you've done." Michael pulled away from her and grabbed his head with both hands. "Have you forgotten why we broke up?" His voice was full of rage.

He looked at her with anger etched in his face and shouted, "You cheated, Sheila! No, not just cheated,

I forgot you *lied* and cheated." He tried to compose himself, but Michael couldn't let go of the anger.

"Maybe I didn't end it the way I should have, but you have no right to think that there's ever going to be a chance in hell that we'll be together again."

Sheila looked at him and laughed wickedly. "Sorry for spoiling your evening, Michael, but I was driving by and saw your car. When I saw you in there with that woman, I just thought I'd have a little fun at your expense." That's the kind of woman Sheila was, cold and calculating and vindictive. She didn't care about anyone but herself. She'd hurt him and now she'd hurt Kayla and that was unforgivable.

"You wretched—" he stopped short. "If you ever pull a stunt like that again you'll be sorry you ever met me."

Sheila gasped in shock. Michael was too much of a gentleman to speak to a woman in such a manner. She knew he'd never say it without meaning it. Michael pushed past her and walked to his car with one thing on his mind, Kayla.

When Michael got to Kayla's house, all the lights were off and it appeared as though she wasn't home. He rang the doorbell but got no answer. He stood there for several minutes, and then rang the bell again. Still no answer. He didn't want to let the night pass without an explanation and an apology. He should have introduced Kayla at first, but he was surprised by Sheila's appearance. He should never have left Kayla at the table to think the worst. All the things he shouldn't have done raced through his head and filled it with regret.

* * *

Sandy called Kayla almost as soon as she walked into the house. Sandy was enchanted by a man she'd met in New York whom she swore should have been named "luscious."

"That sounds like a name for an exotic dancer or something," Kayla responded dryly.

Sandy sensed Kayla's attitude but was too excited to let it dampen her spirit. "Girl, he's got it all, brains, looks, education, a good job, a body to die for, and he's passionate. Have mercy."

"Uh-uh, Sandy, don't tell me you gave it up to the man in a week," Kayla said in disbelief. Sandy was indeed the most sexually emancipated woman she knew.

"It felt right so I gave it to him the second night, third night—"

Kayla stopped her. "I get the message. You are way out there. You'll probably never hear from him again."

"Excuse you, Ms. Prude, but he's called me since I returned home and is coming for a visit in two weeks. Girl, when the thang is right, you can't put any time restraints on it. We were immediately attracted to each other and acted on it."

"Well, give me the skinny. How'd you two meet? What's his name?"

"Are you sure you want to hear the details, Ms. Prude? I mean violins weren't playing or anything, it was pure passion and unadulterated lust. This man is so good in all the right ways, Kay, I almost proposed to him."

"He must be special, I've never heard you talk about a man like this."

"Well, he's very special. But our meeting was a coincidence. I was checking into the hotel after a long grueling day of traveling and looking torn up. I really wasn't in the mood for anything but a hot bath, a cold drink, and a warm bed.

"All of a sudden the man behind me said, 'Excuse me, I couldn't help overhearing you say you're with Nubian Products. I'm Reginald Hillard and I work for the international division of Nubian out of Los Angeles.' Kayla, this man was like a piece of candy: deep chocolate, rich-looking, sweet, smooth, and irresistible. We talked for a few minutes on the ride up the elevator and agreed to meet later for dinner. He wanted to know about me, my job, everything. We spent most of the night just talking and we found we have a lot in common."

"I'll bet you do," Kayla said cynically.

"No, this is the real thing. Reginald is single and unattached. He says he travels a lot, and most women find his schedule intolerable."

"Sandy, he sounds wonderful, but how are you two going to manage a long-distance relationship?"

"This man is worth the effort and he's taking the first step. He's coming for a visit in two weeks."

"So I'll get to meet him if you two can tear yourselves away from the bedroom long enough?"

"Maybe."

Kayla awoke Sunday morning to a ringing doorbell. She refused to get out of bed to answer it because she knew Michael stood on the other side of her door. She wasn't ready to deal with him. Her mind was still processing the events of the previous evening. Sandy had been excited about her trip and the new man she'd met, so Kayla decided to keep the events of the previous evening to herself. She'd attend late services at church and then spend the day catching up on housework and pampering herself. She had thought about the situation with Sheila and decided she'd acted as badly as Michael did when he saw her out with John. She should have waited for an explanation, but she didn't like the fact that Michael escorted the woman out to talk to her. She didn't think there was anything going on between Michael and Sheila but she couldn't help wondering if Michael still had feelings for the woman.

By early afternoon Kayla was dancing around the house to old school jams and enjoying herself. She always felt like an old soul because she loved the music of the sixties and seventies, like the Isley Brothers, Rufus with Chaka Khan, and her all-time-favorite male group, the Temptations. She had a collection of soul classics on CDs that were her pride and joy. Most of the young people she knew liked hip-hop, which she occasionally enjoyed, but her favorite music was rhythm and blues. On occasions you might even hear Johnnie Taylor coming from her CD player.

She grew up listening to all kinds of music from Gershwin to Sarah Vaughan and everything in between. She loved the fact that new artists like Erykah Badu, Jill Scott, Angie Stone, and India.Arie were bringing back soul music. Even if they had renamed it neo-soul, it was all good.

By 4:00 in the afternoon, Kayla had completed housework, laundry, grocery shopping, and every other task on her list. She lit scented candles in the bathroom, turned the faucets on in the tub, and filled it with water and bubbles. She enjoyed a long soak in the tub all while she listened to Aretha Franklin's double CD and crooned to "Do Right Woman, Do Right Man." This was truly her time and she enjoyed every minute of it. It gave her time to think. When she finally emerged from the tub she gave herself a facial, manicure, and pedicure. Later that night she curled up with a book and some peace of mind.

"Kayla, girl, look at you!" Sandy sputtered.

"What? Is something on my face?" She'd begun to retrieve her compact from her purse to see what was on her face.

"I mean you look so happy. I've never seen you look like that. It must be Michael. Now you know I want all the details."

Kayla laughed at Sandy as she shook her head. "You are insane, you know."

"Girl, everybody knows I'm crazy, but I do know the look of love when I see it. I'm crazy, not stupid."

They enjoyed a long lunch with Kayla telling her about the date on Saturday.

Sandy's only comment about Sheila was, "I know the type. She wanted a confrontation. Old girl just wanted to create some drama. Although I would have paid money to see Michael block that kiss with his hand."

Sandy openly accepted she was in lust with Reginald and was completely clueless where it might end, but she was going to have a good time with this wonderful man. Meanwhile, she'd been on another date with her friend from the office. Admittedly, Sandy enjoyed how the man doted on her and spoiled her.

"But, honey, there's no lust connection. Besides, he's not the usual babe I enjoy dating."

All Kayla could do was shake her head at her friend's admission.

"Don't sit there judging me, Ms. Marshall. I'll bet if Michael didn't look like he does, you wouldn't have said two words to him at first."

"I'm not judging you, but you're shortchanging yourself if you allow looks to decide who to date and like. You limit the possibilities when you allow the exterior to dictate. I'll be the first to admit the outside is usually what attracts, but it's the inside that maintains the relationship. Besides, I told you before I don't like dating folks I work with."

Kayla allowed herself time to eat a few forkfuls of her spinach salad before continuing. "You mean to tell me you've never dated a man that you thought wasn't handsome on the outside, but had it going on in here?" Kayla asked as she pointed to her heart.

Sandy was stirring her iced tea. "Not since high school. Girl, I've had my share of mercy dates, but I know what it takes to make me happy and refuse to settle for less."

"Are you telling me that you believe only handsome men with money can make you happy?" The cynicism was creeping into Kayla's voice.

"No, it's just that I haven't seen an unattractive one with all the stuff I want."

"Listen to you. You haven't seen a handsome one with all of it either, but you date them. I'm confused, what exactly are you saying?" She took a sip from her drink and waited for an explanation.

"All I'm saying is that I have certain expectations and needs from a man, and there's no use wasting time on one that I know doesn't meet those expectations. Yes, one of them is attractiveness, and yes, one is money, but there are other things as well. I just start with the obvious two and work my way to the others."

As she folded her arms across her chest, giving the nonverbal clue that there would be no changing of opinion, the two friends just stared at each other for a moment. Kayla saw the firmness in her friend's eyes and knew a softer tactic would have to be employed.

"Are those the two most important ones?"

"No, they just happen to be the two I start with."

"Well, that's good to know because I was gonna suggest you hook up with that shallow Justin."

"No, thank you, I prefer to find my own scoundrels."

Sandy's comment brought a snicker from Kayla. "So what's so different about this man, that you gave in after all this time?"

A hint of a smile lit up Sandy's face as she told Kayla how persistent he'd been in asking her out. He refused to give up even with her best insults, and although he wasn't all that attractive, he was very nice and very attentive. She insisted that any man she dated had to have those two characteristics among the others she'd mentioned.

"Hmmm . . . interesting," Kayla replied with amusement in her voice.

"Don't even start that, Kay, trust me, this isn't going anywhere. I just like him 'cause he's a nice guy. Not everybody believes in all that violins and soft music stuff like you. Some of us just want hot, lusty loving, and don't you dare knock it until you've tried it."

"Well, how do you know that this man isn't capable of giving you that if you've never slept with him?"

"Hmmph, good point." Sandy grinned.

Before the two finished lunch, Sandy had one piece of advice for Kayla. "You know, I've seen the way Michael looks at you. I know that look, it's real, and you should stop avoiding his calls. Nobody knows more than I do about what you've been through, let it go."

"I don't know, Sandy, I'm just wondering if maybe this has all happened too fast. I'd barely stopped seeing Justin before I was with Michael. We got issues and it just seems like we can't get past them. We don't really discuss them."

Sandy looked inquisitively at her friend. "Maybe y'all should keep your clothes on long enough to discuss them."

Kayla laughed. "Seems like there's some underlying issues that we just can't seem to discuss. We are still getting to know each other's moods, likes, dislikes, and whatever but we can't seem to get to the difficult stuff. You know, the kind of stuff that people find painful. Something's bothering him and he won't tell me."

"Are you sure it's just him?"

"No, admittedly I've got issues too," Kayla said.

"Like?"

"Like the fact that I find it difficult to just give myself completely to him. I know you're tired of hearing this, but I just can't go down that road again. I was talking to John the other night—"

"Night! So you two are talking after work?"

"Yeah. Why not? We're friends." Kayla tried to play it down, but she knew the lecture was coming from Sandy. She'd had mixed feelings about John calling her at home, but it all seemed harmless.

"You're just asking for trouble. You know that man is a walking heartbreaker, right?"

"Sandy, please, I told you we're just friends. You of all people should understand that."

"No, I don't understand. I don't believe a man and a woman can be friends like that. Sex always, always gets in the way, or should I say the desire for sex? I have yet to meet a man who hasn't at some point thought about having sex with a woman he finds attractive whether they're friends or not. Men think differently, Kayla, more primal."

Kayla had to laugh as Sandy went on with her tirade. "Now correct me if I'm wrong, but isn't this the same John that has been asking you out since you started working there?"

"Yeah, he did in the past, but he doesn't ask me out now."

"Of course not, he's switched tactics. Now he's meeting you for drinks after work under the guise of your helping him with school and calling you in the evenings at home. Watch out, Kayla, the man has a plan. Besides, I've seen him and that man has sin written all over him." Sandy settled back into her chair with her arms folded. She couldn't believe how naive Kayla could be sometimes.

"I do believe you've lost your mind. Girl, where do you come up with this stuff? Men and women can be friends without sex getting in the way. I would have thought you'd be more progressive in that regard, Sandy, I'm surprised."

Kayla looked away and said, "Besides, we had a drawing at the office for free Bears tickets and I won a ticket and so did he. Am I not supposed to go just because he's going to be there? It's all harmless, we're coworkers and—"

"Friends, I know. I remember you telling Michael

that same line. You're talking to me now, Kayla. Just be careful." Sandy wanted to say more, but didn't want to continue lecturing her friend. She knew the kind of man John was and if he was interested in Kayla he would pursue her. Kayla was vunerable because of the situation that had occured on Saturday night with Michael and Sheila. Sandy knew nothing would happen unless Kayla wanted it to, but still her friend was playing with fire and didn't know it.

After lunch with Sandy, Kayla decided to ask Margaret if she would like her ticket to attend the Bears game on Sunday.

"No, I have plans for this Sunday. I thought you liked football."

"Oh, I do, it's just that I'm not sure if I want to go or not." Standing at Margaret's desk with the ticket in hand, Kayla tried to keep her apprehension at bay.

Margaret looked at her. "Is it because of that devilish John?"

Kayla asked, "How'd you know?"

"'Cause I know you. It's just a football game. If he gets too familar put him in his place. John's used to women making a fuss over him. He won't bother you if he thinks he's wasting his time. If he gets too fresh let me know. His mother attends my church and I know her well."

Kayla couldn't help laughing. "I'll keep that in mind."

The kickoff time was noon on Sunday. John had offered to pick Kayla up but she insisted on driving herself to Soldiers' Field. She had given thought to Sandy's advice and didn't want John to think that perhaps she was interested in him. When she got to the section where her company's seats were she looked for her seat number and found it, but not before John was waving her over.

Somehow her seat was next to his, or was it? she wondered. There were others there from Lancer and Newhouse. Kayla stopped and held a brief conversation with a few people from the art department. There were others from the legal department and she saw at least one other account manager. Everyone seemed to be relaxed and ready to enjoy the game. The company thought it was a nice way for coworkers to get to know each other better. If the workers brought dates, they'd spend time talking to whom they came with. It was an icebreaker of sorts. It allowed them to mingle socially outside the office.

She had brought a blanket because there was a chill in the air. She managed to get to her seat and was immediately greeted by John.

"Hey, Kayla, you're just in time. Kickoff's in three minutes." John rubbed his hands together excitedly. He wore a rust-colored jacket with a navy cable-knit sweater and jeans. He looked casual as he leaned forward ready to take in the action of the game. He helped her settle into her seat as he held her purse.

"You're a big football fan, huh?" Kayla smiled and nodded to the coworker sitting next to John. She didn't know his name. He acknowledged her with a nod and a smile in return.

"Big sports fan, period. But my favorite is football, I love it. I played some in high school and every chance I get now." John smile broadly. "What about you?"

"Picked up the love of football from my dad, he

loves it too. He brought us down to games when we were little. You know, when you're a kid a place like this is a big deal."

"It still is to me." John turned his attention back to the field.

Kayla began to feel bad about thinking that she had misjudged him. He was only there for the football game. The referees came out along with the captains on the field for the coin toss. The game started and the crowd came alive with anticipation.

It was only the third game of the season and despite the fact that the Bears had lost both previous games, the crowd was spirited. The Bears were playing their rivals the Minnesota Vikings. Randy Moss was still hot and the Bears were last in the league in offense and had the second worst record in defense. It was a highly anticipated game as the last-place Bears were starting to come alive.

The Chicago Cubs had swept a doubleheader from the Pittsburgh Pirates on Saturday, and now the Bears fans were looking for an upset in football too. Chicago natives love their sports and the crowd's energy vibrated through the stadium like the sound of ten trumpets in a glass room. Kayla was happy that she'd decided to come to the game. She hadn't thought about the times she'd spent at Soldiers' Field with her family in a long time. She'd been too busy to attend a game last season and had only gotten to watch a few on television.

Marty Booker intercepted a pass and ran thirty yards to score the first touchdown of the game. The crowd went wild, standing and cheering. John reached over in his excitement and hugged Kayla. She tried to pull away but he held her close and planted a steamy kiss on her lips. John smiled at her and said, "Sorry, I got carried away."

"Well, don't get so carried away, next time hug that guy sitting next to you over there." Kayla pointed to the nameless guy sitting next to John and they both looked over and smiled nervously. The extra point was successful and the Bears were leading seven to zero. After a few minutes the crowd calmed down. Kayla rubbed her hands together and searched her pockets for gloves.

"I didn't think I'd need these today, but I'm glad I have them." She put on the gloves and settled in her seat again.

John looked over at Kayla and asked if she was ready for a beer.

"No, thanks, I don't drink beer."

He recoiled in mock surprise. "That is sacrilegious here at the stadium, and lower your voice when you say that." Looking around, John didn't see any vendors so he decided to go to the refreshment stand. "You want anything?" he asked Kayla, who was concentrating on the game.

"No, I'm okay, thanks."

Just as Kayla was booing Randy Moss's ten-yard run she caught a glimpse of someone coming down the row. Thinking it was John, she was ready to give him the highlights of what he'd missed. Just as she turned her attention to him and was ready to speak, her words caught in her throat.

It wasn't John, it was Michael. "Kayla, I thought that was you. I didn't know you'd be here?"

She had avoided his calls and hadn't spoken to him since the incident with Sheila. Looking at him now, she felt her heart beginning to soften. He looked at her all wrapped up in her blanket and wished he was sitting there with her.

Absolutely dumbfounded, she searched for her voice. "Well, actually I won a ticket at work and tried to give it away, but everybody had plans. My company buys a block of seats."

Michael looked over to the empty seat. "I'm here with Trent and Barb. I'm sure they wouldn't mind if I joined you. Who's sitting there?"

Kayla cleared her throat before carefully thinking of her reply. "Someone from the company. I don't know how many seats in this section belong to our company, but are there any empty seats where you are?" Kayla was hoping to get Michael out of the area before John returned. They still were on shaky ground and she didn't want John's presence to upset the delicate balance they were trying to achieve in the relationship. She had been avoiding Michael's calls, but knew she still wanted to be with him. The way that he was looking at her made her know that he very much wanted to be with her as well.

"Can we go somewhere to talk?" she asked him as she held on to his hand.

"Sure."

Kayla gathered her blanket and purse. Michael turned to leave with Kayla right behind him.

Just as they got to the end of the row John walked up with a tray. Looking at Kayla, he said, "Hey, I brought a beer and nachos. Where you going?"

If she didn't know any better she'd swear John was trying to push Michael into an altercation. He'd completely dismissed Michael as if he weren't standing there.

She saw Michael's jaw muscle tighten as he looked at

her for an explanation. "I told you I don't drink beer, John," Kayla said a little louder than she'd planned.

He then turned his attention away from her and looked at Michael. "Well, you'll need something to wash down the nachos. They're nearly as good as—"

Michael was fuming as he turned to Kayla. "What the hell is he talking about?" Before Kayla could respond, Michael pulled his hand from her, pushed John to the side, and stormed away.

"Damn, what's that brother's problem now? Kayla, your man needs to get a grip, it's just beer and nachos."

John's false look of innocence didn't amuse Kayla. "I can't believe you did that, John." Kayla rushed away to find Michael. She called his name when she saw him. She knew he heard her, but he continued to walk rapidly. She tried to match his stride but he got away from her in the crowd.

"Damn!" she shouted to herself. This was not the fun day she thought she would have. Kayla decided to drive directly to Michael's house. There was too much friction between them and they needed to resolve it. She didn't understand how Michael could fly off the handle so quickly. He'd apologized and said he understood about her and John. Maybe they had too many unresolved issues for either one of them to be in another relationship, she began to think. Michael claimed to love her but the minute he saw her with another man he assumed the worst.

She was ready to discuss the situation that had happened on Saturday with Sheila, but now she wasn't sure if her first thought was more accurate. She wondered if Michael still had feelings for Sheila and that was why he left her sitting at the table. She didn't appreciate being left alone while he tried to reason with his ex-girlfriend. Kayla sat outside Michael's house for more than two hours and had begun to wonder if maybe he stayed for the rest of the game. She thought about all the tailgate parties she saw when she was leaving and thought maybe he'd stayed to party. She'd begun to feel foolish about showing up at his house, and then she saw his car turn the corner. She watched him pull into the garage and walk out to her car.

She got out and saw the look on his face. It almost frightened her enough to get back into her car, but she didn't back down. "Michael, what is wrong with you? Why did you blow up again? I explained to you that I was there with coworkers. John is a coworker! What is the problem? You've gone out with cowork-ers." It wasn't what she planned to say, but somehow it just spilled out of her mouth.

Michael was obviously still angry. "Look, Kayla, this isn't going to work. I don't know what kind of game you're playing, but I know John is more than a coworker. It's obvious there's something more be-tween you two."

She could feel her temperature start to rise as she said, "And what are you basing this amazing discovery on since you've seen us together a total of, what, two times for less than five minutes each time? Michael, you apologized, you told me—"

"Clearly I was wrong. I've been through this before, and I'm not going through it again." Michael turned and rushed into the garage, closing the door, leaving Kayla standing at the end of the driveway looking and feeling confused.

"Been through what, Michael? That's your problem, you won't talk to me about it. All you do is get angry," she yelled at the closed garage door. She walked to the front door, but stopped herself. She turned and ran to her car. She refused to be with a man who didn't trust her. Her heart was broken, but it would eventually mend, she believed. She had to believe that or she wouldn't have the energy to get to her car, or to drive home, go to work, or do anything else. Her hurt was so deep she had difficulty catching her breath.

Kayla was sitting at her desk Monday when a knock on her door caused her to look up. "Can I come in?"

Kayla looked at John and replied, "Yes."

She'd replayed the scenario over in her mind all weekend and wondered what John's intentions were. He walked in and closed the door. "I came to make sure you were okay. When you didn't come back to the seat, I figured you and your man had some making up to do. Everything cool?"

Kayla looked at him, trying to figure if he was asking out of an ulterior motive. His eyes revealed genuine concern. "No, everything's not cool. I can't believe you intentionally tried to incite Michael." Kayla was on the verge of tears but refused to cry. Michael was the one who'd broken her heart. He probably would have eventually broken it anyway, she'd convinced herself. Choking back tears, she sat and looked at John.

"Kayla, I swear I didn't pay attention to him until you looked at him. I'm the first to admit that I'm shortsighted when it comes to you. I've never tried to hide that and you have to admit that. I wasn't looking at him. My eyes were only on you."

Kayla crossed her legs and sat back in her chair.

"Are you sitting there telling me you weren't trying to deliberately make him angry?"

John casually said, "No, I'm telling you I didn't even see the man until I saw the look on your face. If you hadn't been there, he wouldn't have gotten away with pushing me. I only let that slide because of you. He would have gotten a beat-down under any other circumstances."

John leaned forward. "I promise, Kayla, I wouldn't intentionally do anything to cause harm or worry to you. I've been crazy about you for years. All I did was buy you a beer and some nachos 'cause I thought you'd enjoy them. It wasn't like they were an invitation to anything else. I know you better than that. The kiss was just an impulse." John felt his lips with his fingers as if he was reminiscing over their kiss.

John stood up. "If you thought otherwise, I'm sorry. Whatever happened between you and your man isn't my fault." His eyes surveyed her casually. "He's a damn fool if he lets that little gesture come between you two. If you were my woman, I'd expect other men to look at you the way I do. You got it like that. Later." John strolled confidently out the door.

Kayla couldn't help smiling. John was right, she wasn't going to allow Michael or any other man to make her feel bad because of something beyond her control. She knew that people continued to exhibit the same behavior and expected different results. She'd read somewhere that people often bring the same baggage from one relationship to another, and behaved the same way, but expected different results. She was determined not to allow herself to fall into that trap. She'd been there, done that, and if she couldn't move ahead she certainly wasn't going to step backward.

Kayla left work early that day. She was tired and wanted to get home. She stopped by the mail room to see John. He was running mail through the meter when he turned and saw her standing watching him. "Hey. What's up?" He looked at her briefcase and noted the time on the clock. "This has to be a first, you leaving this early."

"I'm going home to curl up with a good book."

"Want some company?"

She looked at him, trying to figure the best way to say what she had to say and thought direct was the best approach with John. "No, thank you. You know, John, you're a nice man, but you've got that same illness many men have."

He looked inquisitive. "What disease is that?"

"You don't listen. I told you Sunday I don't drink beer, but you decided to bring me one anyway. Learn to listen to what a woman says to you, John." Her voice was low but firm; she wasn't lecturing him.

He studied her for a minute. Kayla smiled and said, "Good night."

"What is wrong with you, man!" Trent was shouting at Michael. "Kayla is nothing like Sheila, you said that yourself! Why are you trying to punish her for what Sheila did to you!"

Trent had become frustrated trying to talk to his older brother. "Man, you said you love her, but how can you if you don't trust her? You have to get your temper and your trust under control."

Trent walked over to the refrigerator and took out

a beer. It felt good and cold as he pressed it to his head. "From what you've told me, Kayla loves you and only you. Why would she cheat? She's not that kind of woman. Don't make her suffer for what Sheila's done. You said yourself Kayla had trust issues after her last breakup. Sounds like the two of you have some serious talking to do. I think you should make the first move and go over there, drop to your knees, and beg that woman to forgive you."

Michael responded dryly, "I've already done that once. I don't know what else to tell her."

"Damn it, man! Tell her the truth, tell her what happened between you and Sheila. Tell her you were being an out-of-control jackass because you love her so much. Tell her you were jealous. Man, you gonna have to work it out and preferably before too much time passes and somebody else moves in."

Michael turned sharply to look at Trent.

"Yeah, man, you heard me right. Kayla is a quality woman and it's not going to be long before some man realizes that and—"

"Okay, okay, Trent, I get the point. I don't want to hear any more about Kayla and another man." Michael was visibly upset as he was pacing the floor and running his hands through his hair. He hadn't shaved and his five o'clock shadow was now reading ten o'clock.

"Don't let her get away, man, you'll regret it," Trent warned him again.

Michael looked at his brother and said, "What can I do? I closed the door in her face. You didn't see the way she looked at me. She was hurt." Michael looked wearily at Trent. "You don't know, man, Kayla has a lot of pride and she's very stubborn."

Trent let out a derisive laugh. "Man, I know you ain't calling *her* stubborn!" Michael softened as his brother continued to be amused. "You got a lot of nerve, big brother, a lot a nerve." His laughter continued as he looked at his brother and shook his head.

"That's enough, Trent, it's not funny. I don't know how I'm going to fix this. I love her so much, I can't image my life without her, but it may not be up to me."

"You'd better make it up to you and do it quickly."

All Michael could do was sit down and bring his hands to his head.

Michael called and left numerous messages for Kayla at home and at work. She hadn't returned any of his calls. He'd sent her flowers and cards filled with apologies, but he hadn't heard from her in over two weeks. Michael was losing hope each passing day; his heart burned at the thought of losing her. He wondered how he could have been so stupid. Trent was right, it was a mixture of jealousy and mistrust that had driven Kayla away. It had been two weeks and he missed her terribly. He'd gone by her office but she refused to see him.

He suffered knowing that he'd caused her pain. He hadn't been totally open with her from the start, he should have told her about Sheila and what had happened. He should have told her that he was so in love with her that the thought of her being with another man drove him to fits of jealous rage.

He'd never had much of a temper before, but where she was concerned he wanted no man to look at her with such longing as he'd seen John do. John was definitely after Kayla, and Michael felt he'd probably driven her into his arms. The thought made him drive directly to Kayla's house after work. If she wouldn't return his calls, maybe she would talk to him face-to-face. He was determined to try again and find her at home.

It wasn't in her nature to be cruel, he knew that. He'd felt the way she would sometimes melt into his arms as though it were the most natural thing in the world. She'd look up at him and smile. The thought of her warm smile made his desire to see her intensify. He would gladly give up his right arm for just one more of those warm smiles.

When he got to Kayla's house he was disappointed she wasn't home. He waited until just shortly after 11:00 that night but she didn't show up. He drove home with a heavy heart as he thought she was probably with John, smiling at him and warming his heart. Michael hit the steering wheel with such force it rattled. "How foolish can one man be?"

He decided to drive back to Kayla's. He would sit outside all night if necessary. When he got back to her house it was nearly 12:30. He knew it was too late for a visit but he had to talk to her. As he pulled into the parking space in front of her house, he saw the living room light on. He wasn't sure what to expect, but told himself that even if John was there, he'd make Kayla listen to him. If they were going to part, they would at least part with a better understanding of what happened between them. She meant too much to him for them to end the relationship badly. He'd apologize at the very least and beg her to take him back.

He nervously rang the doorbell. He tried to listen for voices inside, but all he could hear was music.

Kayla was startled to see Michael at her door. She saw him when he had come by earlier and she pretended not to be home. Seeing him looking so defeated had nipped at her heart, but she was determined not to keep making the same mistakes. After he'd left she thought she'd dodged him and perhaps he wouldn't come by anymore.

She casually opened the door. "Come on in." She didn't know why she was so quick to welcome him into her home after he'd left her standing at the end of his driveway with her heart on the ground. It was time for them to talk, end the relationship, or whatever was going to happen. It wouldn't be a yo-yo relationship, she decided. If they ended it, she wouldn't return to him despite the fact that she knew she loved him with all that she could.

She walked into the kitchen. "I was about to make myself a cup of tea, would you like one?"

Michael tried to gauge her casual demeanor.

She had her back to him at the sink, letting the water from the faucet pour into the teapot. When he didn't respond she turned off the faucet and faced him. "You want some tea?"

Michael surveyed her face closer and saw the sadness. He'd hurt her. "Uh—yeah, thanks." He took off his jacket and went to the foyer closet to hang it up. He was thankful she was alone, but wasn't sure what words were needed to make things right between them. He felt her aloofness as he did when they'd first met. It was awkward because they'd been so close. She wouldn't allow him to hurt her again and he understood that.

"What brings you to my door so late, Michael?" She continued to stand near the stove with her arms folded. She'd obviously been preparing for bed as she had on a bathrobe and her hair was slightly damp.

He had to fight the urge to hold her and stroke her hair. "I needed to see you and talk to you. You hadn't returned my calls. . . ."

"Why would you want to see and talk to someone you don't trust?"

The directness of her question and the edge in her voice startled him briefly. "Can we sit down?" He pulled out a kitchen chair for her. She looked at him wearily before sitting down. Kayla hadn't expected to see Michael and wasn't sure what his reason was for coming to see her. She thought maybe he'd formally end the relationship. That would be his style, to apologize and then tell her it was over.

That was probably why Sheila was still so upset with him, he never gave her the chance to work things out. Michael sat down and put both hands on the table and looked directly at her. "Kay, I swear to you the last thing in the world I want to do is hurt you. I'd rather have my heart ripped from my chest. As a matter of fact that's how I've felt the past few weeks. Not seeing or hearing from you, knowing that I hurt you the way I did. I should have been more honest and forthright about my past. I thought we could leave the past in the past but there's something I need to tell you."

Here comes that big flaw, Kayla's mind whispered.

"I don't know how to say this so I'm just gonna say it." He stared at her and she saw a slight flex in his jaw before he continued, "I caught Sheila in *our* bed with another man."

She gasped as her hands immediately covered her mouth. "Michael, I'm so sorry. I didn't know."

"Of course not, the only other person I've managed to tell this to is Trent, and even he had to drag it out of me. It was rough for a long time, I just had a hard time trying to trust women again. I know it sounds cliché but honestly trusting someone after something like that is difficult."

The teapot began to whistle and Kayla nervously got up to prepare the tea. Michael finally relaxed, almost as if talking to her was the most natural thing in the world. It became easier as he imagined her without the bathrobe. She was his woman and it didn't matter if they hadn't seen each other in weeks.

"The thing is, Kayla, I know you are nothing like Sheila. I never should have accused you of cheating, I shouldn't have flown off the handle the way I did. It made me so jealous and crazy when I saw you with John that I—I just lost it."

Kayla set the teapot down after pouring two cups of tea, and turned to look at him. "But why?"

Michael looked at her incredulously. "Baby, I want you for myself. I don't want any other man to ever have you. I love you, Kayla. I know it's selfish, but I'm not at the point where I feel mature enough to share you with another man." It was a difficult admission for him, but he was being honest. She saw the pleading in his eyes and felt her heart soften. She couldn't help walking over to him. He stood to meet her and they embraced.

"God, I've missed you," Michael murmured as he felt her head rest on his chest.

"I've missed you too," Kayla finally admitted. "But

I won't allow you to hurt me again." She looked up at him, and there was no smile this time.

"I know, sweetheart, I know."

Kayla pushed away a few inches and asked him, "What are you going to do the next time you see me with John?"

"Will there be a next time?" He'd thought about it and knew that the reason for his behavior was ungrounded. Kayla wasn't interested in John or any other man. She was honest with him and he knew he had all the reason in the world to trust her.

"Possibly, he's a friend."

Michael paused and thought about it. "Put my jealousy in check and try like hell not to get angry."

Kayla asked, "If you really trust me, does it matter if you see me with another man? Don't you understand that I'm the one who chooses, not the other man? Sheila chose that other man, he didn't make her do anything she didn't want to do. I don't want to hurt you, Michael, but you can't control a woman by insisting that she not have male friends."

He knew she was right, and he knew that his jealousy had nearly cost him her love. He knew she was a quality woman and John could do anything he wanted, but if Kayla didn't want him, there was no way he could have her.

"I understand that now. I understand that you are the kind of woman who is honest and loyal and demands the same from her man."

Finally, Kayla thought, *a man who understands it!*

"Are you just saying that because you think that's what I want to hear?" She wanted things to be clear, no mistaking this time, because she wouldn't allow him to hurt her again.

He looked down at her and said, "I can't risk not understanding it."

"So what's next?" she asked.

"I think we both need to be honest. I feel some hesitation from you sometimes."

She bit her lip, slightly unsure if she wanted to tell him what was on her mind. "I think, or thought, maybe you still had feelings for Sheila. I wasn't sure where I fit in."

Michael shook his head. "No, absolutely not. I don't have any feelings for Sheila, except maybe dislike. She hasn't had a place in my heart for a long time, and I'm not sure if she ever really did. I never felt for any woman the way I feel about you."

He tilted her chin upward with his finger. "You can take that to the bank." He cleared his throat and said, "I know that I didn't handle the situation with Sheila properly. I should have told you who she was and asked her to leave. It surprised me to even see her there because she hated the place. If I could . . . "

Michael looked away briefly and turned his attention back to her. "This isn't coming out like I planned. I shouldn't have left you sitting there to think the worst. You mean the world to me. I love you." He gently kissed her lips and asked, "Now what about you, do you have any residual feelings for the lawyer?"

"About the same ones you have for Sheila, and you can take that to the bank."

Michael felt relieved. He looked at his lady love and for the first time that night she smiled at him. He knew then they were on the right road. He promised himself that he'd keep his temper and jealousy in check.

Michael didn't care if he was moving too fast, he wanted her to know how he felt. "You have affected me in ways I never thought possible. Every thought I have has you in it. I'm willing to spend the rest of my life making you happy. I love everything about you. Everything. The mistakes I made nearly broke us apart. I'm sorry, Kayla."

It was going to be difficult for her, but she had to say it. "I apologize for my behavior that night and for keeping you at a distance since then. I should have waited for an explanation, or at least talked to you about it. I was wrong too, maybe even a little jealous." She put her thumb and index finger together, indicating what she thought was "a little." She smiled at Michael and pointed to the bookcase where Justin's picture was. "I need a picture of you to put there."

He glanced in the direction and a slow smile came to his face when he saw that the picture of Justin was gone. "How about a picture of us?"

"I'd like that even better." The two stood in their embrace long after their tea had cooled.

"I can't believe I let this time get away without calling you. I've been so busy job-hunting, and after the honeymoon and vacation I had a million things to do." Deb was apologizing for not calling Kayla sooner. "What's going on?"

"It's good to hear your voice, Deb. You're the one that's been to the white beaches, you tell me. I've seen Kit at work and I must admit marriage seems to agree with him. How was the honeymoon-slash-vacation?"

"Kay, I can't find words to describe it. Yes, I can, divine, celestial. Girl, it was simply *mahhhhhvelous*. We had a wonderful time. I've got pictures and videos."

"I'm glad you're back, I missed you at work. I don't know what I'm going to do without you there. Let's get together soon, I've got to see those pictures and videos."

"Well, that's partly the reason I'm calling. Kit and I are having a small get-together in a few weeks. Nothing formal, just a few friends, good food, drinks, and games. We'd love for you and Justin to come."

"That sounds like fun, but Justin won't be there."

"I could tell something was going on between you two when you showed up at the reception alone. You doing okay?"

Kayla chuckled. "I'm happier than a death row inmate who's been given a reprieve. That man's long gone and forgotten."

Chapter 11

After a few weeks passed, things were starting to return to normal at the office, but not for Kayla. Having taken over a few of Ed's clients, she felt there was something glaring at her, but she couldn't figure out what it was as she spent several nights reading and rereading his spreadsheets and activity reports. Working late, she was surprised to look up and see Kit Warson staring at her.

"Hey, you burning the late night oil again, Kay? You keep this up and you'll be running the place soon."

Kayla smiled as she stood up, arching her back and stretching. "I wish. Are you leaving?"

"Yeah, one more late night and Deb's gonna kick me out."

"Nah, I doubt that. Let me close out of my computer and I'll walk out with you."

She bent over and began exiting her programs. "Have you heard any more about the investigation into Ed's death?"

"Just the rumors that have run rampant since the funeral."

"Oh, what rumors have you heard?" Kayla wasn't going to mention the fact that Detective Civello had called her, sharing more information than she thought he ever would. He'd asked her to do a bit of internal investigative work for him.

"You know, the usual, that Ed killed himself because he was in over his head with a huge gambling debt."

Looking around as she turned off her computer, she tried to sound uninterested. "Hmm, I heard that too. Did you hear anything about him perhaps embezzling money from the company?"

Kit's face suddenly became serious and the half smile that graced his handsome face was gone. The corners of his mouth turned down as if he'd tasted something bitter. "To be quite honest with you, it's more than a rumor, unfortunately. Please don't share this information with anyone else, but we're being audited in an effort to determine how much money was taken."

Kayla eyes blinked uncontrollably for a few seconds as if she was trying to understand what Kit was saying. She'd gone over Ed's files with a fine-tooth comb and didn't find one inconsistency. She'd even given copies to Detective Civello in hopes of finding something that would shed light on any illegal activities. "That sounds very serious. Do they have any idea of how much money's missing?" She took her jacket from the coatrack and began slipping her arms through, but her attention was directed to Kit's anxiety as he shook his head from side to side.

"No, not at this point, but they're looking into all of his activities for the past several months."

"Hmm, that's interesting." The two rode silently down the elevator. Kit escorted her to the car and asked that when she worked late she get the newly appointed security guard to see her safely to her car. She agreed, knowing that whatever happened to Ed was closer than she was willing to admit. He also reinvited her to the gathering that had been postponed because he'd gone out of town unexpectantly on business. It was to be held a week from Friday.

Settling down for a night of late dinner and late television, she picked up two large envelopes that contained Ed's last few weeks of mail. Since she'd taken over his client list, she'd fallen so far behind that opening his mail was the last thing on her mind. Tonight seemed like a perfect time for going through it. She opened the first envelope and let the contents fall out, covering half of the table. Kayla hardly ever received this amount of mail in two months let alone a few weeks. Several of the envelopes were addressed from clients, several were junk mail, and a few were blind addresses, no company names on them.

She sorted the mail into various categories and stacked it neatly in each category according to the postmarked date. After taking a few bites of her dinner, which she decided wasn't worth eating, she began the task of opening the envelopes. The first few were letters from clients asking questions about their accounts and making inquiries regarding various other services the company could provide.

With the expediency of e-mail she wondered why clients bothered with snail mail when they could have answers to their inquiries in a matter of minutes. Upon her opening another of what she thought was a routine letter from a client, a check floated out and fell to the floor. She picked it up and looked at it. "What in—oh, my!" It was made payable to Edward

Oswell. She began hurriedly opening the other envelopes.

She picked up her cordless phone to call Margaret. "If you have no plans, let's do lunch. I've got something I'd like to discuss with you," she said into the receiver.

"Sure, Kayla."

Once seated and with the small talk out of the way, Kayla bluntly asked Margaret, "Have you heard any rumors about Ed stealing money from the company?"

Margaret shifted forward in her chair. "I'm glad we're having this conversation out of the office. You never know who's listening around there. You know the phones are monitored." Kalya looked up from her salad. "And yes, I knew about Ed stealing money, he'd been doing it for years. You know I used to be Mr. Newhouse's secretary several years ago. Before you came on board, Ed was direct-billing small accounts, and having them send their checks directly to him."

Kayla didn't want to believe what she was hearing even though she knew it was the truth.

"I've been at that place for fifteen years, I know where the bodies are buried." Margaret covered her mouth immediately, realizing the poor choice of words. "I'm sorry, but it's all true. He wouldn't go to legal to draw up the contracts, he did them himself. He was a slick one. His family got him out of the mess. How he kept his job I don't know."

Kayla sat with her mouth open, unable to say a word. She just sat and listened as Margaret told her more than she could bear to believe. Margaret's lips were moving, but the words seemed foreign to Kayla. She'd misjudged all involved, but she knew what needed to be done.

She'd spoken to Detective Civello several times over the past few weeks, and now sat across from him to give the latest information in an effort to determine where it was all going. "Margaret was Mr. Lancer's secretary and said that Ed was about to be fired, but somehow managed to keep his job. When Mr. Lancer retired a few years ago was when Ed started getting all the promotions."

The two sat and looked at each other as if trying to figure out the next move. "Do you think someone at Lancer and Newhouse is capable of murder?" she asked.

"Miss Marshall, we're all capable of murder, it's just that most of us don't act upon it." The comment almost made Kayla jump and run from his office, run from Lancer and Newhouse. It frightened her that violence could be so close and she not know from where it came. Nothing could affect her business life the way that this murder had. She wanted to feel the way she had felt before the murder.

Safety at work had never been a concern of hers. Even though the evening news was reporting more and more workplace violence, somehow it seemed to be unbelievable that someone she interacted with every day was capable of murder. It just wasn't fathomable, it happened other places, not where she worked. The denial blanketed her face, but in her heart she knew it could and did happen at Lancer and Newhouse, and she'd never feel the same about the place again. Sharks and barracudas were one thing, thieves and murderers were something totally different, something she wanted no part of.

Michael watched as Kayla left the police station. He followed her with caution, making sure he wouldn't be seen.

Frustrated with the idling cars and likening them to a parking lot, Kayla mumbled to herself, "This Chicago traffic, I swear it's getting worse." She turned on the CD player and India.Arie's voice soon filled the car. She thought back to the concert Michael had taken her to and immediately she began to relax.

When she got home Michael was there sitting on her front porch waiting for her. "Hey, baby," he greeted her and gave her a demanding kiss that made her blush. "I missed you today."

"It's getting harder for me to stay away from you. I didn't mean to show up here unannounced, but I had to see you."

Kayla smiled at the lame apology, but understood because she was feeling the same way. She moved closer to him and felt the stiffness between his legs. "I can feel how hard it is for you." She couldn't help being suggestive with Michael, she felt like butter in his arms, sweet and soft.

They hurried inside the house and into each other's arms. "It hasn't been all that long, Michael. We've both been busy." She hardly got the words out before he was smothering her face with kisses.

He pulled himself away. "No, I told myself I came here to talk to you." Looking at her intently, he groaned, "But it's so hard to talk to you without the urge to take you in my arms." He walked over to the sofa and took off his jacket. He couldn't be close to her and not touch her.

"Let me take your jacket." She took the jacket to the closet and hung it up, but not before she held it close and took in the faint scent of his distinguishable scent. She definitely could get lost in him if she allowed herself to be swept up in some kind of romantic ferror. She was more grounded now and wanted to make sure Michael was the man she thought he was.

"Can I get you something to drink?" Kayla walked over and turned the CD player on, causing Will Downing's sexy, melodic voice to fill the room.

"No, thank you. Please sit." He patted the space next to him on the sofa. He smiled at her stalling tactics.

Kayla sat down and when their eyes met she felt like melting. He gently took her hands and kissed them one at a time.

Kayla felt close to Michael, closer than she'd ever intended. Even when he wasn't with her, she smelled the citrus and sandalwood fragrance of his cologne, felt his warm hand on the small of her back. She longed for the kisses he'd frequently plant on her face, lips, and neck. She wanted to hear his voice, look into his eyes, feel his touch, and see his handsome face.

He pulled her to him and they shared a sensual, demanding kiss. She could feel her heart quicken, and her toes dug deep into her shoes. Michael fought hard for self-control as his manhood pulsated against his leg, just as his heart pulsated against his chest.

"Tell me, how was your day?" he asked as he tried to control himself. He didn't want her to think that their attraction was only physical. He had grown to need her more than even he was willing to admit.

"It was good, what about yours?"

"It was good too." Kayla noticed his hesitation but couldn't quite read it. "Is something wrong?"

"No, I just missed you. I wasn't sure about showing up unannounced. Thought maybe we could grab some dinner and watch a movie."

Kayla looked at him and knew there was more he wanted to say, but she'd wait and let him tell her what was on his mind. "Sure, let's order something, I'm dead tired. You feel like staying in?"

"Can't think of anything I'd rather do." Michael looked around and asked, "You want me to go out for a few movies?"

"How about we both go out for movies?" She looked at her watch. "Maybe one movie, it's getting late."

Michael walked over and took their jackets from the closet. He helped Kayla with hers and kissed her on the back of her neck. "Sounds good to me, we can pick up dinner on the way back."

"Hey, sleepyhead. How are you this morning?" Michael was smiling from ear to ear, looking like a mischievous little boy. She liked the fact that he could look manly and innocent all at the same time—it was natural for him.

"Good morning, I'm fine. What are you cooking, and more importantly why are you up so early?" Kayla asked, scratching her head.

He slid the eggs from the skillet and onto the plate. "Just in time. Come on, girl, cop a squat, and quit asking so many questions."

When she looked at the table, she couldn't believe her eyes. He'd cooked bacon, eggs, grits, and toast.

"I must say, I'm surprised. What's up?"

Michael scooped himself a small helping of grits and a single piece of dry wheat toast. Kayla looked at him suspiciously, wondering if he was at least going to put a little butter or jelly on the toast. When he broke a piece off and ate it, she had to blink. "Just dry wheat toast? Yuk!" she sputtered.

"I didn't really cook it for me. It's for you. I've had some cereal."

Michael smiled at her as he poured her a glass of orange juice. "Go ahead, eat up."

"I must say, no man has ever cooked me breakfast before." She took a bite of buttered toast and looked at him.

"Well, that's their loss. I hope to cook you many more, but right now I've got to get home so I can get ready for work. I didn't know I'd be here all night." He winked at her, which caused her to shake her head.

He could be so mannish, she thought, but she loved it.

Michael was putting on his jacket but stopped and asked, "Before I go, do you have plans for lunch?"

"No, why?"

"I'd like to meet you for lunch."

"Sure, name the place and time and I'll be there."

Michael suggested a deli near her job and said he'd meet her there at 12:30.

Kayla watched the clock the entire morning. Seemingly it took 12:30 forever to arrive so she could meet Michael.

When Kayla arrived at the deli, Michael was seated and sipping iced tea. "Hey, baby, I took the liberty of ordering lunch because I've got to get right back to the office. Hope you don't mind."

Kayla sat down and looked at the iced tea he'd ordered for her. Within a few minutes the waitress brought her a spinach salad and she smiled at Michael. She had told him months earlier how much she enjoyed spinach salad.

"No, not at all." She lifted her glass to take a sip. She'd walked briskly from her office and was a little winded. The tea felt cool and smooth going down her throat. Michael as always was dressed impeccably in a brown suit and a cream-colored turtleneck shirt. His black leather jacket was draped casually on the back of his chair. She'd almost forgotten how fine he was.

She noticed two ladies at a table to the right of them, checking him out as if he were a chocolate dessert and they'd been on Slim Fast for six months. They were obviously hungry, Kayla thought to herself as she arched her eyebrows and looked directly at the staring women. The two rolled their eyes and leaned forward in conspiratorial whispers.

"Kayla, I know we haven't been dating very long but I feel something very special for you, I just can't wait any longer. I get the impression sometimes that you think we're moving too fast, but I love you and it's time." Michael reached in his jacket pocket and pulled out a black velvet ring box. Kayla began hyperventilating. She couldn't believe it was happening this way. She always believed somehow she'd know when the time came. She could tell that something had been on Michael's mind the previous evening. He seemed to have held her closer, kissed her a little longer. He was close to her all night and she could feel his arms around her waist as she slept.

He took her left hand and gently kissed it. He got down on one knee and the other diners looked in their direction. People were openly staring and smiling. Kayla could hear them whispering, but her attention was all on Michael. He opened the ring box and took out a beautiful twin-diamond, pear-shaped engagement ring, the most exquisite she'd ever seen.

"Kayla, I love you dearly, and would very much like for you to become my wife." He then placed the ring on her finger, kissing her hand again.

Kayla's eyes had flooded with tears; she was speechless. She sat there looking from her hand to Michael, trying to speak, but it was as if a huge lump of straw were in her throat—there was no room for words, nothing would come out.

Michael smiled lovingly at her. "Now I know you're not at a loss for words, Kayla Marshall, soon to be Mrs. James. Just say yes."

Kayla returned his smile and nodded her head yes. Michael took both her hands and kissed them gingerly. "I love you, Kay. We can set a date anytime you want. I wanted to propose in a more romantic setting, but I looked at you last night as you slept and I couldn't wait any longer." Michael returned to his seat, holding her hand the entire time.

She smiled at him, finally able to speak. "I love you too, Michael."

"I'd like for you to meet my family. My mother's birthday is a week from Sunday and we're planning a party. I'd like to make the announcement then if that's okay with you." Kayla took a deep breath. Suddenly she felt like things were going too fast. She loved Michael, there was no doubt about that, but it seemed to overwhelm her, now that they were talking about meeting families and getting married.

"Wait, Michael, not so fast. Maybe your mother wants to enjoy her birthday celebration. Could we possibly wait until after the birthday party? Maybe the following week?" Michael looked at her suspiciously but agreed.

"That's fine, but can you come to the party? I'd like to introduce you to my family."

"Yes, I'd like that." She smiled nervously.

They hurriedly ate their salads in silence, but each time their eyes met they both would smile and giggle like two teenagers with a first case of puppy love. The two women that sat across from them who were so interested in Michael before Kayla sat down were occasionally staring at the two lovers. When Kayla would glance in their direction, they'd smile. Kayla speculated they were wondering why a catch like Michael would want to take himself out of circulation. He could probably have both of them if he wanted, she thought. Instead, he wanted her and only her.

Lunch was over almost as quickly as it began with Michael telling her he loved her and to have a good afternoon. Kayla wasn't sure how she made it back to the office building, her head was in such a befuddled state. She'd waited a lifetime for this and now she was having mixed feelings, unsure of what her next action should be. She took the ring off her finger and returned it gingerly to its box and into her purse as if it were some precious artifact requiring precision handling.

She was trying to decide how long to hold off sharing the good news with coworkers. She couldn't return from lunch wearing a rock that resembled the

Hope Diamond and not create some tongue wagging. For now she wanted it to be kept quiet. Before she made it to her office, however, Mr. Newhouse greeted her on the elevator. "You sure look deep in thought." He had a warm, friendly smile whenever she saw him. He'd told her he considered her to be one of the most talented people on his staff and had big plans for her.

"Hello, Mr. Newhouse, I'm sorry, I was just thinking about the Compaq campaign that I'm working on. My presentation is tomorrow and I want to be sure all my ducks are lined up." She knew it was a little white lie, but she wasn't about to tell him that she was elated about getting engaged, when she had a presentation in less than twenty-four hours that represented a huge potential of revenue for the company.

Sam Newhouse raised his brows as if impressed. "You know you can always count on me for assistance. Is there anything I can do?"

Bringing that silver-tongued devil into a presentation as insurance certainly couldn't hurt, she thought.

"Thanks, Mr. Newhouse, I certainly welcome any support you can provide. I've planned a special presentation for them that will spark their interest. If you could carve out some time in a few weeks for the second phase of the presentation I'd be grateful."

"No problem, have Margaret call Tess to block off some time."

Kayla knew that Mr. Newhouse was an eloquent and persuasive speaker. She could use him for backup later. As they got off the elevator and she exited right and he to the left, he said, "Be sure to keep me posted, Kayla. As a matter of fact I'll have Tess call Margaret and schedule us a lunch date in the next few weeks. I've got a few things I'd like to talk to you about."

"That sounds perfect, Mr. Newhouse, thanks." Kayla floated to her office on an engagement-induced high. She felt as if Ed McMahon had shown up on her doorstep with a huge check. Now she was being invited to lunch by the big boss, she was certain a promotion was in her future. All the hard work and long hours were finally going to pay off.

"Good afternoon, Margaret. Any messages for me?" She couldn't stop the huge smile that consumed her face.

"You've got quite a few, I put them on your desk. Nothing requiring immediate attention." Margaret did a double take as she looked from her computer to Kayla's face and back again.

"What did you have for lunch? You're glowing."

Kayla looked around the office as though on some covert operation and whispered, "Come in my office, I've got a secret to share with you."

Margaret leaped from behind her desk like a cat ready for action, eager to hear the news. As they entered the office Margaret settled on the burgundy leather chair and with a look of anticipation waited for Kayla to situate herself behind the desk in a matching swivel leather chair.

"Margaret, you know I told you about the guy I've been dating for the past few months, Michael. Well, I'm so excited, he asked me to marry him today, and I said yes. However, with so much going on here at work right now I don't want to make it public for another couple of weeks. I'd like to share the news with my family first, and land the Compaq deal in the bag.

So mum's the word for now," she said, finally exhaling. She'd said it all without taking a breath or pause.

Smiling broadly, Margaret walked around the desk. "Kayla, that's wonderful news, congratulations. I'm so happy for you. Did you two set a date?" She extended her arms and the two hugged.

"No, not yet, we're both so busy right now, but I've always thought June was a great time of year for a wedding. It gives me plenty of time to plan, although I don't know if I want a really big wedding. I've always wanted something small and intimate."

"I'm so happy for you, I feel like exploding." Margaret hugged her again. The two women talked for a few more minutes and worked hard at putting the finishing touches on the presentation. Kayla was determined to make it completely flawless. She went over every detail several times and even rehearsed in front of the mirror in her office. The slides had arrived from the art department and were impeccable. At the end of the day Kayla debated whether to call her sister, Janae, and tell her about the engagement. Not wanting anything to distract her from her presentation the next day, knowing Janae would want to go out and celebrate, she decided to wait until she could tell her entire family.

Michael called before she left her office. "I know you have an important presentation tomorrow, but I'd like to see you tonight."

"Yes, Michael, I want to see you tonight." Any other time Kayla would have insisted on going home for some quiet time, but felt Michael was so much a part of her that she wanted to see him as soon as she got home.

After dinner they cuddled up and listened to

music. "I've got some good news." Michael's voice was low and mellow.

Kayla softly asked, "What?"

"I've been promoted to vice president of marketing at Brooks and Walsh." He said it so matter-of-fact that at first Kayla thought maybe she misunderstood.

She unwrapped herself from his embrace and looked at him. "What?"

"I said I've been—"

"Promoted to vice president of marketing. I heard you, but why are you so calm? I can't believe you waited all day and half the night to tell me." Something close to aggravation clipped her words.

"I felt there were more important things going on with us." Michael's voice remained low and mellow. "Why aren't you wearing the ring?" He looked at her left hand.

Kayla had forgotten about placing the ring back on her finger when she got home. She explained to Michael that she didn't want her coworkers to know about the engagement before she announced it to her family and had removed the ring when she returned from lunch.

"I understand that, Kay, but why aren't you wearing it now?" She could hear the hurt in his voice. She looked into his eyes and said nothing.

"I noticed some hesitation today at the restaurant. Are you sure you want this, Kayla?"

He'd never looked so serious before, Kayla thought. "Yes, Michael. I'm sure about you and me. I've never been more sure about anything in my life." She then leaned over and gently kissed his bottom lip, then his top lip, and finally both lips.

She walked into the bedroom and retrieved the ring

from her purse. She brought the ring to Michael and said, "Please put it on my finger again. I like the way you do it." She smiled at him and his heart yielded. There was no doubt in his mind that this woman loved him and wanted to be his wife.

They sealed their promise to one another with a night of passion. Her last words to him as she drifted off to sleep were, "Good night, Mr. Vice President, I love you."

Kayla called Sandy as soon as she got to work in the morning. She wanted to invite her to lunch to share the good news about her engagement. Sandy was her dearest friend and she wanted her to know as soon as possible but Sandy couldn't make lunch. "Sorry, Kayla, maybe later. I've gotta go, I've got a meeting in half an hour."

"Me too, I have the Compaq people coming in for a presentation."

"Let me know how it works out, although I'm sure you'll dazzle them. Good luck. If you can pry yourself from Michael, maybe we can have dinner tonight." Sandy chuckled as she gathered her agenda for the meeting. "I want to hear what's going on with you two and the murder investigation."

"Sandy, you're not going to believe this but Detective Civello suspects someone close to Ed is responsible for his death, maybe someone at work." She filled her friend in on the weird twists and turns the investigation had taken and they both pondered what the final outcome would be.

Chapter 12

Kayla went to check the conference room where her presentation was to be held. It was set up exactly as requested. The long gray marble table with matching gray leather chairs always looked so elegant. The room was decorated with ceiling-to-floor windows accentuated with state-of-the-art blinds with a remote that allowed you to control how much sunlight you received. The art department had provided the room with wonderful abstract paintings in beautiful muted burgundy, pink, and gray tones that were always noticed by clients.

There were fresh-cut flowers in the room. Kayla had requested portfolios made up like small computers with highlights of her presentation done in pop-ups for the group. They were exquisite. The computer with the PowerPoint slides and screen were already set up. It was all perfect.

Although a little nervous, she was confident that the presentation was as well planned as any she'd ever done. The research time she'd put in on the Compaq company was so extensive she even knew the president's wife's and children's names. Like a Misawa warrior ready to do battle, and the conference room her battlefield, she stood firmly and nodded approvingly at the room.

When she returned to her office, her second-in-command, Margaret, was there.

"Good morning, Kayla. I was just about to check the conference room."

"Good morning, back at you. I've done a final check and it's perfect."

"Is there anything else you want me to do before the presentation?" Margaret was well dressed as usual whenever Kayla did office presentations. Her short tapered hair was groomed neatly in place. Her makeup was perfect and accentuated with red lipstick that was very attractive. She wore classic pearl earrings, and a navy pin-striped, tailored coatdress with turned-up white cuffs on each sleeve. Her low-heeled navy Aigner pumps completed the classy ensemble.

"No, Margaret, I think everything's good to go. I will need you to greet the group downstairs and bring them up to the conference room. I gave you their names and pictures last week, did you memorize them? Clients love it when you know who they are."

"Yes, Kayla, I know those faces and names almost as well as my own." They both smiled nervously.

"Margaret, you're the best. I wouldn't be surprised if Mr. Newhouse stuck his head in for an introduction, so be prepared."

"You have a lunch date with him next Wednesday, I scheduled a reminder in Lotus."

Kayla went into her office to get the materials for the presentation and carried them into the conference room. She'd spent hours researching her presentation and she was prepared.

After the clients were seated in the conference

room and queried about their flight and the usual courtesies were performed, the presentation went into full swing. It was flawless. The group was so impressed they agreed to sign contracts that day. They wanted to meet with the legal department to hash out a contract before their flight departed at 5:30 that evening.

Kayla left the group to discuss the merits of the presentation among themselves while she went to personally invite Mr. Newhouse to lunch with the group. She wanted to see the look on his face when she told him that they'd have a signed contract by the end of the business day.

As she approached his office she couldn't help noticing his secretary Tess coming from his office straightening her tight, short red skirt. She was an attractive woman with blond hair cascading past her shoulders. She had one of those Barbie doll figures that men loved and women envied, long legs, small waist, and flat stomach.

Her face was perfectly proportioned, making Kayla wonder if maybe a skilled plastic surgeon was responsible. She'd definitely had a nip and tuck here and there according to Margaret. "Hello, Tess, is Mr. Newhouse in?"

Once while Kayla had been in the bathroom two women from the art department came in, obviously unaware that Kayla was there, or not caring, talking about Tess.

"That silicone rehab slut actually had the nerve to think that sleeping with Evan was going to get her a job in the art department. That damn Tess is unbelievable."

Kayla had had to cover her mouth with both hands to keep the gasp in. The other lady responded.

"Well, she didn't fare too badly. She may not have gotten the job, but judging from that Infiniti she's driving and those expensive Lillie Rubin fashions she sports, her paycheck's a lot bigger than mine." She could hear the women suck their teeth in disgust.

When the two women had closed their respective stall doors, Kayla hurriedly flushed, washed, and dashed out. The place was such a gossip mill, she frequently called it hell with fluorescent lights.

Looking totally disinterested, Tess pressed the intercom button and announced, "Miss Marshall is here to see you." Tess never looked at Kayla, just instructed her to go on into Mr. Newhouse's office. Her red jacket was draped casually on the back of her chair, and from the way her neon-bright red lipstick was slightly smudged Kayla knew that the non–eye contact was from guilt.

"Thanks, Tess, that color suits you," and in her mind she continued with, *'Cause you a skank, scandalous hussy*. Kayla hated being catty, but she had to let the hussy know she wasn't a lightweight. She could feel the eyes boring into her back as she approached Mr. Newhouse's office.

Mr. Newhouse couldn't believe it when Kayla invited him to join the Compaq group for lunch while legal worked out the details of the contract. In his nearly twenty years in the business he'd only had one other major client sign after a pitch presentation. This was indeed a lofty gain for Kayla and the firm. Lunch was a celebration of sorts. Aaron Bishop, Compaq's creative marketing director, found Kayla so polished and persuasive he teasingly offered her a job with his company. There seemed to be a natural chemistry between the group and Kayla. She couldn't ever remember having felt such a sense of accomplishment as she looked over at Mr. Newhouse, who gave her a that-a-girl wink and smile.

By 5:30 Mr. Bishop and his group were on their way back to Denver with signed contracts and Kayla was seated at her computer detailing the meeting and lunch in her daily log. Margaret stuck her head in the door. "Congratulations again, Kayla. If there's nothing else you'd like for me to do, I'm going to head on home."

"As a matter of fact, Margaret, do you have about five more minutes?"

"Sure, what's up?"

"I just want to thank you for all the hard work you contributed to this successful venture and all the successes I've had since joining this firm. You've been outstanding."

Margaret flashed a smile.

"I'm almost certain that Mr. Newhouse has a promotion in mind for me in the next six months or so, and usually administrative assistants have the option of going with their managers or staying where they are. I would be very honored if you'd go with me, with a salary increase of course."

"I'm the honored one. It's been a pleasure working for you."

Kayla turned to her computer, finishing her daily log, when her phone rang. It was Sandy. "So how'd it go?"

"Sandy, you're not going to believe this, but they got on the plane with a signed contract."

"What! You're lying. Girl, you too fierce! What

are you doing after work, and why are you still there? Come on, let me take you out for a celebratory dinner."

The events of the day had suddenly zapped her energy, causing her voice to taper off. "Rain check, San, I am so wiped out I'm thinking about calling a cab to take me home. I'm not sure if I have enough energy to face the traffic."

"You do sound whipped. Well, you name the time and place for our celebration. Have you told Michael yet?"

"No, he's busy with that new beer marketing campaign for Anheuser Busch. I'm just going home to a hot bubble bath, and candles." Kayla let out a slight sigh before continuing, "Deb has invited us over on Friday night to look at their movies from the islands, some games, and eats. Why don't you join us?"

"Honey, I'd really love nothing better than to sit and look at their movies from the islands and play some boring cards, but I have other plans."

"Girl, please, what plans do you have for a Friday night, besides waiting for Reggie to call?"

"That shows what you know, my company is hosting another fund-raiser for the United Negro College Fund."

"Oh, so you'll be hobnobbing with the black aristocracy?"

"You got a lot of nerve teasing me with you dating one for three years."

"Don't remind me."

"I'll talk to you later."

"Bye, San, have a good time tomorrow. Let's go walking Saturday morning, I want to hear all the news from bourgieville."

Once Kayla stepped into the company garage, she saw a large shadowy figure near one of the cars and became frightened. She looked around for the new security guard, but of course he was nowhere to be found. Upon quiet, careful observation she noticed the figure wasn't threatening and as she continued to look and focus more, she saw that it was two people in a passionate embrace and one of them had on a tight, short red skirt.

Friday morning came too quickly for Kayla. She'd gone to bed early, but tossed and turned all night. She was still hyped from her successful presentation on Thursday, the engagement, and the revelation regarding the supposedly happily married Mr. Newhouse and his secretary. She had talked to Michael briefly and fallen into a fitful sleep.

When Kayla got to her office there was a huge colorful banner that read CONGRATULATIONS, KAYLA stretched over the entrance to her office. There was a large basket filled with champagne, cheese, crackers, and fruit on her desk. When she read the note it was from Mr. Newhouse congratulating her on an excellent job.

She called Deb to ask if any help was needed for the get-together, or if she needed her to bring a dish. Deb insisted she had everything under control. She wouldn't start a new job for two more weeks, which allowed her time to clean the house, cook, shop, and do all the things she never had time to do when working. They talked about the challenges of work and Deb congratulated her on landing the Compaq account. They continued with small talk for a few more minutes and were looking forward to seeing each other.

After Kayla finished dressing, she checked herself out in the mirror, deciding to wear her black leather pantsuit with a white, sheer, lace blouse. Her hair was parted on the right side and cascaded down the left side of her face and hung in big loose curls around her shoulders in a come-hither look. The look reminded her of the "bad girl" look of the fifties, à la Carmen Jones, sexy and alluring. She decided to accentuate the look with just enough red lipstick to look sexy, but not trashy. "Perfect," she said, turning from the foyer mirror and heading toward the kitchen to enter the garage. Kayla and Michael had agreed to meet at the party because he had a late meeting scheduled.

The gathering was in full swing when Deb greeted Kayla at the door. "Hey, Kayla. Ohh, you looking too good! I don't know if I'm going to let you in my house looking like that! Walking in here fashionably late and looking like every man's fantasy. You go, girl!" She grabbed her friend by the hand, twirling her around.

Kayla participated by happily going around with just enough dip in her step to look cute. "My ego needed a boost, so I gave it one." The two women exchanged a hug.

"Here, I know you said not to bring anything, but I brought some Moet. Maybe you and Kit will open it once everybody leaves," Kayla said and winked slyly at Deb.

"That sounds like an excellent idea, but, girl, I think he's still recuperating from the honeymoon."

As they walked through the foyer, laughter seemed

to permeate the house. "Come on in and let me introduce you to everybody, although I'm sure you know most of them."

Once they entered the living room, Kayla's eyes immediately met Michael's and the two seemed locked in a trance as if they were communicating telepathically. Deb made the introductions, and as she suspected Kayla knew just about everyone.

Larry Jarrett, who was in the art department of Lancer and Newhouse, was there with Pat Hughes, his on-again, off-again girlfriend, an elementary school teacher. Kit's sister Allison, a publishing representative, and her date, Malcolm, a sportswriter for a local African-American newspaper, were seated in the kitchen. Deb's brother Austin, who was "in-between" jobs and girlfriends, was selecting music for the group. Michael sat alone on the couch until Kayla walked into the room. They all exchanged pleasantries.

"What would you like to drink?" Deb asked Kayla.

"I'll have a rum and Coke, thanks, Deb."

Michael walked over to Kayla and greeted her with a kiss. "You look wonderful. I'm not sure if I want to share you right now." His eyes lavished praise on her entire body as he looked at her from head to toe.

Michael wore a black turtleneck with burgundy dress slacks, which Kayla swore were tailored for him. His shirt brought attention to his broad shoulders and slim waist. The black accented his dark eyes and made them even more alluring. The two stood eyeing each other for a few minutes. The heat and desire between them was unmistakable. The attraction was interrupted when the doorbell rang and Deb introduced the last of the guests. Barb and Trent walked in holding hands. "Hey, everybody." Barb smiled and waved at Kayla.

Kayla looked at Michael. "How did that happen?"

"I finally got the hint Barb kept dropping. She was interested in Trent and he kept asking me about her after they'd met at the company picnic. He's kinda shy when it comes to women. Trent took a lot of teasing as a kid because of his red hair and freckles. He's a bit insecure about them even now. I've never seen my little brother so wrapped up in a woman before." Michael smiled and leaned over to Kayla. He gave her a sweet kiss on her earlobe.

"He's probably saying the same thing about me," Michael uttered.

Kayla had to ponder the irony of this situation. Barb was deeply infatuated with Trent, and he was interested in her, but somehow fear of rejection had kept them apart. Then she wondered how a man that fine could be the least bit insecure. It wasn't like his hair was a flaming red, it really had just a hint of red in it. But she knew how it felt to be a little different from everybody else, be it red hair and freckles, or a few extra pounds in the wrong places. People loved pointing out and expounding on what they considered your deficiencies, regardless of how small or obvious they might be.

Barb walked over to Kayla as Trent was getting their drinks. Michael could see that the two women wanted to talk so he held up his glass and said, "Think I'll freshen this up. You want another drink, Kay?"

"Yes, please. Thanks."

Barb looked from one to the other and smiled. The two became giddy schoolgirls once Michael was out of ear range. "So what's up with you two?" Kayla asked.

"I've been so busy with work I haven't had a chance to call you. He is such a gentleman. Girl, the man gave me a warm bath, and well, let's just say he knows how to treat a woman. He's so sweet to me."

Kayla held her hand up and said, "Barb, wait a minute, I know you're not telling me you've fallen in love."

"I didn't say that I'm in love, but I'm in like big time, with a potential for love. All I'm saying is that the man treats me the way I want to be treated. He's warm, genuine, and considerate. And we're having a wonderful time together. He may or may not be Mr. Right, but he's surely Mr. Wonderful."

"Well, go on with your bad self. That sounds good to me." Kayla looked over at Michael, who was talking to Trent. "Trent is really fine. I think those two brothers were at the front of the line when good looks were being dished out."

Barb looked over at the two and said, "You gonna think I'm lying, but the first time I saw Trent, I swear I heard that song by Bridgette McWilliams, 'Morning,' in my head. I never paid that much attention to it before, I used to hear it on the radio during evening drive time. But for some reason when I saw Trent, the words and melody seemed to sound in my head. The next day I went to the music store like a fool singing the melody to the clerk. The man looked at me like I was crazy. I didn't know the artist, the name of the song, or anything. All I knew was I had to have this music that reminded me so much of this man I'd just met. This man that I wanted to be with in the morning, just like the song said. Well, luckily the guy at the record store finally figured what I was singing and found the CD. I wasn't leaving that store until I had that song."

They both chuckled, and Barb looked over at Trent again and said, "I don't know if it's love or not, but, girl, all I can say is, 'What a morning.'"

Kayla knew exactly the feeling her friend was describing. "You know, I thought I was going crazy. The first time I met Michael, the man made my heart hum. I'm glad to know that I'm not the only one in this predicament."

"You, me, and trillions of other folks! That's why people are willing to risk so much to find that right person, makes you do all kinds of foolish things like doubt your sanity. Make you sing them old Aretha Franklin I Ain't Never Loved A Man, Natural Woman, deep-down-in-your-soul love songs. It'll make you go out and make a complete fool of yourself at the music store." They both began laughing so hard neither could speak for a time. Barb went back to where Trent was standing and he handed her a drink. Kayla watched them for a few minutes and noticed how tenderly they looked at each other. Trent held her hand while they talked and Barb smiled lovingly at him.

Michael walked over and handed Kayla her drink. "They've got a heated game of bid whist going on in the kitchen. How about you and I go in there and whip the winners' butts?" he said.

"Hey, I almost majored in whist in college. I left undefeated and, as a matter of fact, my record is still etched in one of the tables in the student union."

"Well, you go on, girl. I like a woman with confidence."

"Now that's a rarity in a man."

"Baby, any man with an ounce of common sense can appreciate a woman with confidence. As a matter of fact, most brothers I know find it sexy and appealing."

Not as sexy or as appealing as those dimples, Kayla found herself thinking.

Deb walked over to Kayla. "I forgot you two met at the wedding. I told you to watch him though, he's quite gallant and chivalrous. He was always charming some girl back in the day."

Michael immediately blushed as he defended himself. "Deb, you know that's not true." He looked at Kayla and said, "In school, she was the one with the active social life. I spent all my time studying, trying to keep my scholarship."

Kayla nodded her head in agreement, as she sipped her drink. "That sounds like my college days too, I had to maintain a B average to keep my scholarship, and an A average to keep my parents off my behind." Kayla took a sip of her drink before continuing, "Plus I was too broke to do anything that cost money, so all I did was play cards and maybe go to a party every now and then."

Deb couldn't help but intervening. "Listen to you two poor, socially challenged individuals. Both of you have more ambition and drive than anybody in this room." She stood back and folded her arms. "As a matter of fact now that I think about it you two really have a lot in common."

Kayla and Michael looked at Deb and in unison asked, "Like what?" All three of them laughed heartily.

"I'm glad you two are dating." Deb didn't know the

full scope of the relationship because the two had not announced their engagement. Kayla and Michael both blushed at the comment because they knew they were doing more than "dating." As soon as they announced to their families that they were engaged, everybody else would know the full extent of their relationship.

Deb continued after a sip of her drink, "Although I'm not sure what will happen since you both are so competitive and stubborn." She looked from Kayla to Michael. "Hmm . . . you make a handsome couple too."

Kayla could feel the blood rushing to her face. Deb was embarrassing her in front of Michael, who seemed to be enjoying it all.

"Okay, come on in here, Michael, with your partner and take your butt-whipping like a man!" Larry shouted. Larry and Pat were gloating about beating Allison and John when Kayla and Michael walked over to the table.

"Watch them, they cheat," Malcolm said to Michael as he walked past.

Allison smiled at Kayla and denounced that with, "They got some kind of signal system worked out. Kick their butts, they're getting obnoxious."

"Nothing worse than a sore loser!" Pat shouted.

"Yes, there is!" Allison shouted back. "A poor winner!" The house reverberated with laughter. Kayla and Michael knew they had their work cut out for them, but they were up for the task.

There was a lot of good-natured teasing back and forth, but in the end Kayla and Michael's expertise and luck prevailed, giving Larry and Pat a well-deserved beating. And true to form they were poor losers, accusing their opponents of illegal tactics. The real surprise came later in the evening when the reigning Scrabble champion, Michael, challenged Kayla to a game. Kayla loved the written word and knew she was an expert Scrabble player so she was anxious to give Michael a good beating. When Michael came up with words she never heard of, Kayla had to challenge him, and to her amazement they were legitimate words. Michael was a formidable and zealous opponent who won by only a few points.

They enjoyed a competitive game and an even more stimulating conversation. Kayla swore he was just experiencing beginner's luck because he'd beaten her at their last three games of Scrabble. Barb and Trent left after only an hour. It was clear to everyone that they had other plans for the evening.

Michael was a Big Brother volunteer as well as a mentor with at-risk youths. He recruited both Malcolm and Larry to share the feeling one gets from helping others. Kayla listened with pride as he spoke of his achievements in both programs. She wanted to know how he found time for his volunteer work, as her own work schedule lately prohibited her from volunteering.

He explained that he budgeted two Saturdays a month to doing the work that nurtured his soul and commitment to the community. Kayla felt so attracted to him it frightened her.

As the evening wore on, Kayla and Michael spent more time talking. They had lively debates on everything from immigration laws to Jesse Jackson's adulterous affair. The food was scrumptious and the conversation invigorating. The videos and pictures taken in Nassau were beautiful. The white beaches, blue skies, and friendly smiles of the natives compelled Kayla to make Nassau her next vacation destination.

By 2:30 A.M. everyone was gone except Kayla and Michael, who had stayed to help Deb clean up, as Kit had passed out an hour before and was snoring loudly on the sofa. They were almost done with the cleanup when Deb said, "Thanks, you two, for helping me. I can sleep late in the morning and not feel guilty."

"It was a pleasure, Deb," Kayla said as she loaded the last platter into the dishwasher.

"Kayla, let me know when you're ready, I'll walk you to your car," Michael said as he finished clearing trash from the living room.

"Sure, I'll be ready in a minute."

Deb walked over to Kayla and whispered, "I can't believe how comfortable you two are with each other. It's like you've been dating for years." She patted her friend on the back. "I can tell the way Michael looks at you that he's really taken with you." Deb couldn't hide her pleasure as a smile as big as Wyoming spread across her face.

Kayla looked over at Michael, who was now seated on the sofa with Kit, who was sound asleep. "I know, it's happened rather quickly. I'm surprised some woman hasn't snatched him up."

Deb lowered her voice and took Kayla's hand. "His last girlfriend tried, but I guess he just wasn't ready. Plus she was a real-life gold digger."

Michael stood up and stretched. Kayla could see the firmness of his thighs, and his pecs were well developed, making her want to rest her head on his chest. Even just stretching seemed to put X-rated thoughts into her head. He walked over and gave Deb a hug and kiss on the cheek. "Thanks for the invite, I had a good time." Looking over at Kit on the couch, he pointed. "Tell party pooper I'll talk to him next week."

She found herself hopelessly attracted to Michael James; she'd love him the rest of her life. "I'm outta here too, thanks for a fun time." She gave Deb a hug and kiss. Looking at Michael, she said, "You ready, macho man? You can walk me to my car."

The cold December air nipped at Kayla and Michael as they left the house. "It really feels like winter out here." Kayla smiled and blew circles of cold air.

Michael laughed at Kayla as she shivered while opening her car door. "Here, wear my jacket until your car warms up. I'd like nothing better than to drive you home, Kayla, if you're too tired." Kayla allowed him to put the jacket around her shoulders as she got into the car and started it up.

"No, I'm fine, Michael. Why don't you hop in for a minute while my car warms up? It won't take long. Where'd you park?"

"Just a few spaces in front of you." Michael walked around the car and got into the passenger seat. "This is a nice car. It still has that new car smell. Sisters really are doing for themselves, huh?"

They both chuckled. Michael looked up at the stars. "It's really a beautiful night." Kayla looked up at the twinkling stars in the sky. There seemed to be millions of them peppering the purplish blue heavens. They both were enjoying this intimate quiet time.

> *"The stars*
> *That Nature hung in Heav'n and filled their lamps*
> *With everlasting oil, to give due light*
> *To the misled and lonely traveller."*

With closed eyes Kayla sat back and savored the splendor of the quote. "That's beautiful, Michael, who wrote that?" Opening her eyes, she looked at Michael. His intense eyes seemed to contain the passion and rapture of a man searching for love. She felt her heart softening and starting to hum, as it had done only when Michael was nearby.

He gingerly took her hand in his, as if it required special handling or it would crumble. "It's Milton." His voice was so low it was barely audible. "You know it's driving me crazy for you to sleep in one bed and me in another. I want to see you as soon as I get home. I want your face to be the last thing I see at night and the first thing I see in the morning." His lips were saying the words, but for the first time in her life she felt a kindred voice that told her the words were coming directly from his heart.

"I feel the same way too, but we both have a lot going on right now." She looked at Michael and continued, "We'll have plenty of time together soon. I promise." She leaned over and gave him a sensuous kiss on his lips. "But for now you've got twelve kids to pick up in the morning. Well, actually in about five hours. Hope you enjoy the trip to Mall of America. Call me when you get back."

"I've got tickets to next week's Bears game if you'd like to go." Michael remembered the last time they'd seen each other at a football game and was determined to make this experience a more pleasant one.

Kayla sensed his strategy and had to smile. "Sure, sounds like fun. They're having a bad season though."

Michael responded, "Don't remind me. But I figured you could bring your blanket and I could bring some hot chocolate."

She was trying to remember when she had told him that she loved drinking hot chocolate when she went to the football game with her family. It was early on, during one of their first dates. He listened and he remembered.

"Sounds like you've already got it planned."

"Have you given much thought to setting a date for the wedding?" Michael asked while he looked up at the stars.

"I haven't set a date, but I think June's a good time for a wedding. What do you think?"

"I think I'd like to marry you tomorrow if I could." He turned to her and smiled.

Kayla drove home in silence. She wanted to continue to hear the words that Michael had spoken to her, as they played over and over in her head and heart.

Chapter 13

Kayla patiently waited for Detective Civello, looking at the people being escorted around the police station. She decided then and there she hated police stations and had no desire to ever visit one again. The investigation into Ed's death had taken some weird twists and turns, and now that arrests would be imminent she felt more relaxed than she had in weeks.

The few leads she'd supplied Detective Civello were enough to put him on the track of the killer or killers and she felt good about that. He'd shared a lot with her, but wouldn't divulge the name of the suspect or suspects. He felt it was in her best interest not to have full access to that information. Unbeknownst to her, the detective had her followed by an undercover policeman to secure her safety. He promised her that she'd be one of the first to get the full particulars soon after an arrest was made.

"Ms. Marshall, come on in." Detective Civello appeared unshaven and rumpled, but the quickness of his eyes told her he was alert. Kayla settled into the same chair that she'd sat in only weeks before with all new respect for the detective. This was one person she'd seriously misjudged. Not only was he passionate about his work, he'd worked doggedly on the case.

He'd obviously missed many hours of sleep and she wondered if he'd even gone home to change clothes. His five o'clock shadow had taken on a life of its own as it masked his face like a bristly carpet. "I wanted to tell you in person how valuable you've been to this investigation. We couldn't have pursued the responsible party without your help. Thank you so much for putting yourself on the front line on this. You're a brave young woman." He obviously had a newfound respect for her as well.

"Thanks, but I think you may exaggerate a little. I just provided you with information that had fallen into my hands." She still wasn't totally relaxed in the police station, but he made her feel comfortable, protected.

"Yeah, and somehow I believe that the parties involved didn't believe you'd do that either. They didn't count on you getting involved."

Kayla looked down at her hands, unsure of what would happen once the information was made public.

"We of course won't let the press or general public know how we got access to this information, but sometimes they do get insider tips. We will be making an arrest later tonight. We've got a judge signing warrants as we speak."

"Well, I'm glad this is coming to a close," Kayla said nervously.

Detective Civello admired this young woman with so much fortitude that she'd put all that she had worked for at risk to expose a murderer. A lot of people would have ignored the clues she'd given the police, or would have tried to use it for personal gain. She was a special woman.

"You've gone above and beyond the call of duty.

You should be very proud of yourself. I wish we had more citizens like you."

Blushing slightly, she thanked him and said, "I owe you an apology for my rude behavior the first time I came to your office and accused you of lacking interest and passion in your job. The past few weeks have proven that to be very wrong. I should have been more respectful. I'm so sorry for assuming your demeanor was a lack of interest."

Detective Civello now blushed, putting his hands in his pockets. For an instant he appeared to be a ten-year-old being told what a good boy he'd been. Kayla had never noticed the deep dimples in his cheeks before. How she loved a man with dimples.

"The past few weeks have been a real learning experience for me. All the ideas and people I believed in haven't been what I thought they were at all." She'd begun rambling and she stopped herself. Straightening her shoulders, she smiled at the detective. "But I guess that's a part of learning. Thanks again for your help."

"Well, hopefully you'll never need the services of this office, but if you do, you know we're here for you."

Suddenly feeling lighter and more relaxed than she'd been in weeks, she asked, "I'm meeting my friend Sandy for dinner, would you like to join us? You look like you haven't eaten in a while."

Scratching his head, and bringing his hand down to his fierce five o'clock shadow, he replied, "No, maybe a rain check. I'm heading home to spend some time with my family for a change, perhaps get to bed at a decent hour."

Kayla stood. "Thanks again, Detective Civello, for everything."

"I'll call you in the morning once the arrest has been made. Have a nice dinner." They shook hands, and he watched as she exited his office and the squad room, making sure her tail knew to stay on her at least until the arrest was made. He wasn't sure if she was in danger or not, at this point, but wasn't willing to take any risk.

"So, Jessica Fletcher, how was the meeting with the detective?" Sandy was putting the menu on the table, her lips pursed together.

"Well, if you wanted to know, you should've come with me." Kayla was trying to sound perturbed.

Sandy wasn't buying it as she waved her hand dismissively. "Please, I've been to that police station more in the past few weeks than most of the people who work there. Uh-uh, no more playing girl detective for me." She looked carefully at her friend reading the menu in her hand. "And looks like no more for you either. They finally are closing this mess, aren't they?"

Kayla excitedly put the menu down. "Yes, finally, San, I can get some rest. Girl, I feel like I've been on a roller coaster for a month without stopping. So much has happened so quickly."

"Not to mention that *fiiiine* Michael and the fact that you've finally fallen in love."

"Well, actually, Sandy, it's more than that." Kayla's eyes grew with delight as she squealed, "He's asked me to marry him and I said yes!"

"Oh, my God! I am so happy for you." Sandy ran around the table and gave her friend a hug. "This is the best news I've heard all year." Sandy couldn't contain her happy tears as she looked into her friend's eyes.

"Sandy, are you crying?"

"Yes, I am, and if you tell anyone you'll never make it to the altar." They both laughed and continued their hug.

True to form, once Sandy gathered her composure she said, "Honey, Ray Charles could see you were in love with that man. I'm so glad you stopped hiding from him and put yourself and him out of your misery and consummated this union. You had me worried for a minute." Sandy called for the waiter. "We need champagne!"

Kayla awoke to a ringing telephone. At first she thought it was part of her dream, but realized her dream had nothing to do with a phone. She was having another dream about Michael. She rubbed her eyes and rolled over toward the nightstand, her eyes just barely adjusting and recognizing the time of 5:30. "Hello."

"Hello, Ms. Marshall, sorry if I woke you."

Formality at this hour irritated her. "Who is this?"

"It's Detective Civello, I just wanted you to know that we've arrested Samuel Newhouse for the murder of Edward Oswell."

"What?" The irritation left and was instantly replaced by disbelief.

"I said—"

"I heard what you said, and you told me you suspected someone close to Ed. I wasn't sure you meant within the company, let alone Mr. Newhouse. What—how—this is too much, I'm confused." She was sitting on the side of the bed now with her head down, trying to digest this bad news. This pill was much too bitter to swallow. Was anybody who they appeared to be? How could she be so totally wrong about this man too?

"Well, to make a long story short, Mr. Oswell was in fact way over his head in gambling debts. He was betting obsessively on college sports. He was not only placing money with a local bookie, but was also calling Antigua and other places doing some offshore gambling. The problem was that yes, he was directly billing clients and collecting the money to support his gambling debts, but he had a partner. Actually this partner was the one who started the scam, even before Mr. Oswell came to the company. That partner was Mr. Newhouse. When Mr. Oswell went to his family and told them about the gambling debt, they agreed to help him once more, but made him agree to get help. That's where he'd been the days just prior to his death. He'd also decided to come clean with regards to the theft from Lancer and Newhouse. He couldn't figure out how to do that without implicating Mr. Newhouse. Newhouse initially dangled a promise of a promotion. There was no way that could happen since Mr. Lancer had knowledge of the previous thefts by Mr. Oswell. Even though he's retired from the company, he wouldn't allow that to happen. Mr. Oswell's family had repaid all the money he'd stolen previously, which was why he was allowed to keep his job."

Kayla took a deep breath and listened attentively as the detective continued. It sounded like an episode of *Law & Order.*

"When he finally did confront Mr. Newhouse with

the fact that he was going to the police, we believe Mr. Newhouse then killed him, tried to make it look like a suicide. He didn't count on you bringing his paper trail to us. He thought you'd figure out Mr. Oswell was stealing from the company and that the company's audit would leave it at that. He didn't count on you going back to before Mr. Oswell started with the company and tracing the embezzling prior to that. It only took a few federal auditors to figure out the paper and money trail. Mr. Newhouse wasn't very creative with it either, he put the money in his wife's name at a local bank. Cheaters usually aren't as clever as they think they are. All we had to do was pull his secretary in for questioning and she sang like Barbra Streisand. Thanks again for that lead."

Kayla almost laughed at the thought of Tess being sweated by questioning policemen. She pictured the Barbie doll with her designer suit, makeup perfectly applied, every strand of hair in place, while being interrogated with a bright unflattering light shining directly on her. She'd be exposed for the scandalous, villainous witch that she was. Kayla had figured that Mr. Newhouse may have assisted with the embezzling scam. She'd even shared her suspicions with Michael, but never had she suspected Mr. Newhouse of murder.

"And all this is from stealing money that he already owned," she said slowly, as if trying desperately to comprehend.

"No, from stealing money that he would have to share, money needed to support a gambling habit that had been out of control for years, not to mention his very expensive secretary. Mr. Newhouse and Mr. Oswell played more than tennis and golf together, they both were into the bookies for large sums of money. From all accounts Mr. Newhouse had been scamming for years, pure greed."

She could hear him exhale a deep breath. He was tired and so was she, but the entire ugly business was exposed.

"God, how could I have been so wrong about someone? He was my mentor, he hired me right out of college. I trusted and believed in him." The disappointment was rooted so deep in her voice it seemed eternally planted.

"I think he was counting on that trust if you'd ever confronted him with knowledge of his duplicity in the theft. I don't believe you were in any danger, it appears that he and Mr. Oswell had a volatile relationship for many years. For what it's worth he's said he hadn't intended to kill Mr. Oswell, he did it in a moment of insanity. He saw no other way out at the time." After several minutes of quiet, he asked, "Are you there, Ms. Marshall? Are you okay?"

"Yes, yes, I'm fine. Just shaken, but I'll be okay." Her voice mirrored the dryness of her throat. It felt as if her vocal cords were made of sand, and one more word would make them disintegrate. She knew about the gambling debts, but somehow she figured he was murdered by some henchman for a bookie. She'd figured someone internally and in a position of power had to have knowledge of the direct billing. She remembered what Sandy had told her, "You never know what goes on behind closed doors." How many times had she heard that old expression? At least a hundred from her own mother. Margaret had provided her with the information regarding Mr. Newhouse's direct billing of clients.

"Thanks for keeping me informed, Detective Civello. I'm glad to hear that this is finally closed. Maybe I can move on with other things in my life now." She wasn't sure if she had a job anymore at Lancer and Newhouse. She did feel sorry for Ed, who at least tried in the end to do the right thing. Mr. Newhouse, on the other hand, who'd been stealing from the company for years, had succumbed to murder to keep his lies and deceit silent. It was all such a facade, how could she ever step foot in her office again? It was all too much for her to handle.

She lay in bed staring at the ceiling for almost an hour before getting up. It was almost 7:00 when she called Sandy.

"I'll be right over," Sandy said after Kayla filled her in.

Sandy arrived with coffee and croissants. She was barely in the door when she asked, "Do those people ever sleep? I guess they like to arrest people at a time when they won't be totally rested, makes it easier to get the truth out of them."

Kayla shook her head. "Now I know you've been watching way too much television. Did you figure Mr. Newhouse was the one?" She took a croissant from the bag and sat at the kitchen island.

"Not in a million years, he was so concerned the night he showed up with his driver, offering us a ride. He looked genuinely concerned about you. I thought for a second he had the hots for you. But you know what I always say—"

Kayla finished the sentence for her. "Yeah, yeah, you never know what goes on behind closed doors."

"Well, one thing's for sure, you are one brave and courageous sister to have made it through the stuff you've been dealing with. A lesser woman surely would have broken down by now." Sandy took a sip of her coffee and faked a shiver. "I know I would have run for the hills."

Kayla stood up and said, "I need a shower, maybe some more sleep. I'm gonna run a few errands and get some things done around the house." She suddenly felt exhausted.

"Great, so will I, we'll make it a day of shopping, maybe a movie."

"San, do you mind if I skip the shopping and just get some rest? I'm worn out, think I'll walk later and take a hot bath. Get some downtime."

Sandy walked over and rubbed her friend's back gently. "You know I'll take care of it for you. Are you sure you want to be alone? When is Michael coming back?"

"I'm sure. He'll be back tonight." She looked at her friend and saw the concern etched in her face. She smiled as she stood up. "I know you don't like being mushy, but you're the best friend anyone could have. I love you, Sandy." She hugged her friend.

"And I love you too, Kay, but don't ever tell anyone I got this mushy." As the two women parted, Sandy fluffed her hair and smoothed her skirt. "You know I do have a rep to maintain."

Kayla laughed. "Girl, please, get on out of here and enjoy yourself."

"All right, I'm gone, but I'll call you later, maybe we can do lunch or something."

Kayla returned to bed but had barely gotten comfortable when she heard her doorbell. She thought perhaps Sandy had forgotten something. When she opened the door she was surprised to see Michael wearing a baseball cap, an oversized sweatshirt, jeans, and a big, beautiful, invitingly warm, dimpled smile. "Hello, baby." It was all he needed to say. She fell into his arms and he hugged her tightly. "I got here as soon as I could. Detective Civello called me and told me what happened."

Kayla gently pushed away from Michael. "What? Why would he do that?"

"Because I asked him to. I thought you were in danger and went to him. He agreed and I helped him to make sure you were safe." Michael brought her back into his arms. "Do you think I'd stand idly by if I thought you were in harm's way? Whenever he couldn't provide man power to follow you, I did. He knew I couldn't be here the past couple of nights, so he made sure someone watched out for you. He called me first thing this morning and I drove straight back."

"But what about the boys' trip to—"

Michael put his index finger to her lips. "They're fine, I told the other Big Brothers I had to leave. Just let me hold you."

Kayla did just that. They stood and embraced for several minutes.

"I'm so sorry I missed your mother's birthday party."

"That couldn't be helped. You got sick, but we need to plan for our families to meet so we can announce our engagement." He looked at Kayla shyly and confessed, "I did tell Trent though. Well, actually he dragged it out of me."

"Yeah, I'm sure he did." She smiled. "I told Margaret and Sandy, I was too excited." They both laughed.

Kayla felt a knot forming in her stomach. She

wasn't sure if she'd gotten sick from the flu bug that was going around, or because she was going to meet her future her mother-in-law. The thought of Maudeen Kincaid had left her with no desire to have to put up with overbearing mothers. The one consolation was that she loved Michael with all her heart and soul. She smiled to herself and thought, *Janae and Mom will be there to help me.*

"What's that look about?" Michael was looking at her curiously.

"Oh, nothing, let's plan this shindig."

"So tell me, where do you want us to meet?" Kayla asked Sandy. Reginald was visiting and Sandy was eager for Kayla and Michael to meet him.

"I don't know, someplace where we can dance and have a good time. Maybe enjoy dinner before."

"They just opened that new supper club downtown near the Navy Pier. It's a restaurant and a dance club. Barb says the place was jamming last week when she and Trent were there."

"I can't believe those two are such an item."

"Believe it. They are so much in love, holding hands all the time. Looking soulfully into each other's eyes." Kayla sighed.

"Thought we were talking about Barb and Trent."

"We are."

"That sounds more like you and Michael to me."

"Okay, I can see you want to do jokes. Well, what time do you want to meet?"

Michael was volunteering that Saturday morning and told Kayla he'd be there to pick her up. She was to call or leave a voice mail for him regarding the time.

She'd returned from her Saturday morning walk and had just stepped into the foyer of her home when she heard a noise coming from the bedroom. "Hey, I thought you were volunteering today," she shouted while removing her jacket and walking to the refrigerator. "I'm getting a glass of juice, you want anything?"

"I don't want to hurt you, but I will."

Kayla turned quickly from the refrigerator and looked into the crazed eyes of Samuel Newhouse. Her gaze drifted from his eyes to the gun he had pointed at her.

"What are you doing here?" Her voice trembled and she knew fear had caused her to ask such a dumb question.

"I need money and a car. And you're going to get them for me." His voice wasn't the smooth one she'd grown accustomed to—it reminded her of gravel, rough.

Kayla swallowed hard and tried to inch her way to the front door.

"Don't be stupid, Kayla. I like you a lot and I don't plan to hurt you, but I will. I have nothing to lose at this point."

"You didn't plan to shoot Ed Oswell either and look how that turned out. You've got plenty to lose. You've got money, you can get the best lawyer around. Your wife and children are there for you." She didn't want him to feel hopeless. She thought maybe if he believed he had something to look forward to he'd give up and leave her alone. She was afraid of him but didn't want to show her fear.

"How'd you get out anyway?" Kayla tried to sound cavalier as if she'd conversed with an escaped alleged murder suspect in the past.

"Don't worry about me, just do as I say and you'll walk away without a scratch." He sneered. "I've got money in a safety deposit box and you and I are going there to get it. After that you can walk away as long as you don't try to pull anything."

"Why do I have to go? Just take my car, the keys are there on the board." She pointed toward the keys.

"You must be crazy, or you think I am. You'll call the police before I can start the car."

"Mr. Newhouse, please, I promise not to call anyone. Just leave me alone," she pleaded.

"*Shut up!* You think I don't know it was you that spilled the beans about what you found at *my* company? I thought you wanted to swim with the big fish. In the end you just turned out to be a sniveling, whiny female. A tadpole. You could have made a lot of money too. After I shut Ed up you started snooping too much. Why do you think I gave you access to all his information? You're smart, I knew you'd figure it out. Thought you'd come to me with an even better plan to make more money."

He was beginning to look and sound more unstable, Kayla thought.

"But instead you took the information to the cops. Come to think of it, who knows, if it weren't for you I could still be a free man. Nobody suspected me."

Kayla tried to remain calm. "Yes, they did. They suspected you from the start. The police came to me asking questions about you. There are those in the company that already suspected something was going on between you and Ed. It wasn't just me—"

"I'm not going to tell you again to shut up!" he snapped.

Kayla tried to hide the nausea that overwhelmed

her. Her eyes were widened with fear and she knew the situation would end badly for her if she tried anything while they were in the house.

"Just grab the keys and take me to the safety deposit box."

Obediently she took the keys from the board and put her jacket back on. They then headed out to the garage, where she hesitated.

"Don't try to be a hero. You're much too pretty to end up with a hole in your head like the last person who betrayed me. They say it's even easier the second time." He stroked her face, which sent a cold chill up her back.

He directed her and they ended up driving south on I-55. "How much farther?" she asked.

"A long ways, we're going to St. Louis."

"St. Louis? I thought you said we were going to a safety deposit box."

"What, they don't have safety deposit boxes in St. Louis?"

Kayla glanced over at him. He hadn't shaved and his hair had grown past his collar. He didn't look at all like the well-maintained man she'd last seen. He'd obviously stolen the ill-fitting clothes he wore, as they hung off of him.

She needed to soften him. Kayla thought if maybe she got him talking he'd relax. "When's the last time you saw your wife and kids?" she asked even though he continued to point the gun at her side. She saw him falter slightly. Kayla didn't want to appear as nervous as she was. She didn't want to upset him and cause him to harm her in any way.

"They came to see me today. I decided then I couldn't spend the rest of my life in prison. Like you said, I have money. You can buy almost anything in Chicago if you want it bad enough. Even a quick break out of jail."

"I guess you're right." She gauged his mood before continuing, "Your wife is a beautiful woman. Very classy. Whatever made you cheat on her with Tess?" She could feel him looking at her as she stared straight ahead, trying to appear as natural as possible. There was an accident on the other side of the highway and traffic had slowed down. She put on her signal and got into the passing lane. Although the accident was on the other side of the highway, people were slowing down to gawk. She noticed a trucker looking down at her from the other side of the highway and she winked at him, trying to get his attention. He ignored her and pulled ahead.

"Tess is also a beautiful woman. She's young too, full of vitality. Likes the finer things in life and knows how to get them. She actually came on to me several times, even before she became my secretary. I resisted for a while, but like I said, that woman knows how to get what she wants." Even now as he spoke of her, a nasty smile formed on his lips.

"Maybe you wouldn't have that gun pointed at me if you'd resisted her." Kayla knew she was pushing it but continued, "Don't go off, I'm just saying. Seems to me she's the one who encouraged you to steal to support her lifestyle. You live in a fabulous home, belong to an elite country club, you had it all before you met her. You didn't have to steal until she came into your life." She looked over to him for his acquiescence. The nasty smile had been replaced by another sneer.

"I think a jury would understand that. Your wife

and children have been coming to see you, evidently they've forgiven you."

"My wife has filed for divorce since I've been in jail. The only reason she brought the kids was that they wanted to see me. I'd refused to let them see me in jail before but I gave in, thinking maybe if I saw her I could talk some sense into her."

"You probably still can, but not if you're running away. She loves you. Women don't fall out of love just because something bad happens." Kayla couldn't believe what she was saying, but if it got her home safely she was willing to tell the crazed gunman anything.

He looked at her and guffawed. "You've never been married, have you, Kayla?"

"No, I haven't, but I've been in a long-term relationship. I can tell you I put up with all kinds of stuff, and stayed with him because I loved him." She felt a knot in her stomach forming as she tried to sound convincing.

"Was it the guy you brought to the Christmas party last year? He was a lawyer as I recall."

"Yeah."

"I liked him. How long had you two dated?"

Kayla mumbled, "You would."

"What?"

"Umm, three years."

"Not the same thing. Tess isn't the first woman I've cheated with. Hell, she's not even the second or third." He sneered that lecherous grin again and said, "I thought about having you at one time. Probably would have if things had gone a little differently."

Kayla couldn't help thinking, *Not in this lifetime, you twisted, sick fool.*

"Maybe, but I sure wouldn't have you stealing for

me. Especially to the extent that Tess was doing. Did you buy her that Infiniti?" She wanted to keep him talking and hopefully think perhaps Tess was the source of his predicament, not she.

"Yes."

"Did your wife find out about it?"

"How'd you know that?" He appeared startled as he turned quickly to look at her. Once he saw there was no change of expression on her face he relaxed again.

"I just guessed, but it's like I told you, I've been through some things. Women find out a lot before we confront you. Most of the time we know long before we tell you or you tell us. Sometimes we just let it go on. If we don't want to change the status quo, we'll let you continue sneaking around making a fool of yourselves and us." Kayla couldn't believe the stuff she was saying, but it was working. Sam was nodding his head and seemed more relaxed than he'd been. The gun was now pointed more toward her seat.

"I didn't get a chance to use the bathroom before we left, can we please stop at the next gas station? I'm about to bust."

"Yes, but don't try anything." When they got to the next exit there was a Quick Trip gas station.

"Just act natural," he instructed. He had her come across the seat and exit from the same side he did, all the time holding her arm firmly with one hand and pointing the gun with the other. She obeyed and went inside with him. Before entering, he threatened to shoot her at the hint of any sudden moves or if she tried to ask for help. She got the bathroom key from the attendant. Sam walked side by side with her to the bathroom with the gun pointed at her side. He tried to go in the bathroom with her, but she pleaded.

"Please don't do this. I can't get away, there's no window. I'll leave the door unlocked, just let me have some privacy."

"All right, but I'm warning you, don't try anything." His icy blue eyes sent a chill through her as he closed the door, leaving it open a crack.

Kayla immediately took out her cell phone that she had in the inside pocket of her jacket. She'd always told Sandy it would be there for any emergency whenever she went walking, and she knew there was no greater emergency than the situation she was in right now. She flipped open the phone and dialed 911 and left the phone on as she repositioned it in her pocket. She said a silent prayer that maybe enough of the conversation could be heard and recorded that would tell police where she was. She also knew that cell phones had towers that could track the location of a call. With the door ajar she knew if she tried talking, Sam would have shot her.

She flushed the toilet and washed her hands quickly.

"Are we getting back on 55 South?" she asked.

"Yeah, I'll let you know if there's a change of plans."

"Okay, well, St. Louis, here we come. How much farther is it? Where are we now?"

Sam answered before asking her to shut up again because he wanted to think.

Hours passed before either one said anything. Kayla thought the longer she could stay alive the better her chances were of escaping the madman. Every once in a while Sam would mumble something incoherently and she could tell he was getting tired. She knew people did crazy things when they became tired. She also knew their reflexes weren't as fast or accurate. She looked at the gun, which he now pointed lower.

"Do you know how much farther? Are we going to stop for something to eat?"

"No, just keep driving, I want to get there as soon as possible. The last sign said twenty-five miles."

Chapter 14

The car came to a crawl as it reached the Illinois-Missouri border. There were construction barrels along the Martin Luther King Bridge, making drivers cautious. Traffic was extremely heavy and she noticed a lot of cars that had flags with the St. Louis Rams' logo on them. "There must be a football game. I think Busch Stadium is nearby," she announced. She thought about Michael inviting her to the football game. She prayed silently that she would be there with him to enjoy the game even if the Bears lost.

"Well, we're going to the downtown area, so we're close." He looked over at her and said, "Oh, yeah, I forgot you've been down here a couple times on business. You did a good job, they applauded your hard work. Thought the rest of the group were screwups."

Kayla thought she could make her move if she jumped out of the car suddenly. She nixed the idea because by the time she unsecured the seat belt, Sam would have shot her. She decided the best place to attempt the escape was at the bank. In the meantime she'd become observant of everything and everyone around her.

The downtown bank was on Market Street in close proximity to Busch Stadium. Because of the football game at the stadium, the street buzzed with activity. After securing a parking space Kayla put the car in park and looked over at Sam. "I guess you want me to come with you?" she asked rhetorically.

Before, Sam had insisted that she scoot over and get out the same side he did, but he'd relaxed and thought it was okay to let her exit from the other side. He was closer to getting away, which made him relax and let his guard down. She unbuckled her seat belt as he began to exit from the car.

Sam looked around nervously, almost as though sensing some sort of danger. Kayla took that time to make her break. He looked disoriented. She bolted as fast as she could without looking back. She heard two gunshots but she continued to run. Then she heard her name and felt two strong but gentle arms grab her. She turned around and Michael had her in his arms.

Her heart raced as did her mind, trying to figure out what had happened. She pulled away slightly and looked toward the direction of the car and saw policemen huddled around the body of Samuel Newhouse. She gasped and looked at Michael, who pulled her to him and held her. She broke down and cried as she thought of what could have happened.

She spent hours talking to the police and FBI agents before she was allowed to leave.

Detective Civello was there and explained to her that Mrs. Newhouse had been called immediately after her husband had been discovered missing. She informed the police that he had a safety deposit box at a bank in St. Louis. It was there that he'd stashed money, a passport, and several other items that would aid him in an escape. She knew about the box and had gone there to see what was in it. It was also the place where he kept the title to the Infiniti that he'd bought his mistress. Kayla knew the woman was smart when they'd first met, but wondered why she would put up with such an abominable man.

A truck driver had called the local police and reported a man holding a gun on a woman while driving. He gave them the descriptions and the license plate of the car. Kayla insisted on getting the man's name and address because she had to thank him for saving her life.

Michael insisted that they spend the night in a St. Louis hotel because it had gotten late. He wanted Kayla to rest before the drive back to Chicago. She insisted on them going out to buy her new clothes to wear back home. She told him she wanted to trade her car in as soon as possible. When she and Justin had gone shopping for a car he insisted that she buy the Lexus; now the car had more bad memories associated with it than she wanted to live with.

Michael explained to her over dinner that the news of Sam's escape was all over the radio and television. Sandy had called him frantically when she tried to call Kayla but couldn't reach her.

Sandy had tried calling Kayla's cell but the message indicated she had either turned her cell off or that she was out of the calling area. Michael had called Detective Civello, who advised him that he suspected Sam Newhouse had sought out Kayla. The police had been to her home and found signs of forced entry, but she and her car were gone. When they got the information provided by the truck driver they flew to St. Louis and staked out the bank downtown. The FBI picked up their trail in Springfield, Missouri. They didn't want to risk something happening so they didn't attempt to stop the car. Michael had called Sandy to let her know that Kayla was safe. Sandy was to call Kayla's parents and let them know what had happened.

Kayla spent the night nestled in Michael's arms, but couldn't get out of her head the image of Sam Newhouse lying on the ground dead. He'd aimed his gun at her, but the police shot him before he could pull the trigger.

When Kayla and Michael were within a block of her home they saw there were local and national newspeople along with cameras staked across her front yard and on the street. Michael made a quick U-turn and announced, "You're coming home with me."

Kayla agreed; she wasn't in the mood to talk to anyone about the events of the prior day. She was exhausted and wanted to shut down for a while.

She'd send Sandy over later to get her some clothes and perhaps deal with the press. Sandy was good at handling people and didn't mind being the focus of attention. When Kayla called her parents they insisted that she stay with them until she was able to return home. She felt compelled to do as her parents asked. Michael didn't like it, but he understood her wanting to make her parents happy. He wanted her near to him.

When Kayla and Michael pulled up to the Marshall home, Janae immediately ran out the door and embraced her sister. She was shivering from the cold, but it didn't stop her from embracing her. The sisters hugged briefly before they heard Gail shout, "Hurry and get inside. It's too cold out there, Janae, without a jacket in your condition." Janae looked at Michael for the first time and smiled. "Thanks for being there for my sister and my family."

"Absolutely, my pleasure." He looked at his fiancée and said, "I'm never going to let anything bad happen to her again."

Janae believed him, she could tell by the way he looked at her sister and the tone of his voice that he would protect her. She felt bound to give him a hug and a quick peck on the cheek. Janae looped her arm through Michael's and the three walked quickly into the house.

"Kayla was right, Michael, you are quite a catch." Janae laughed as she watched Michael blush.

When they got inside Kayla was shocked to see her brother Terrance, Alex, Barb and Trent, Margaret, and an older couple. The older man looked like Michael and when he smiled she saw the dimples.

The woman had slightly reddish hair and freckles. George raced up to greet and welcome his daughter. "Girl, you tried to give your old man a heart attack." His embrace was an emotional one.

Her mother was next. As she hugged her daughter she broke down and starting crying. "I'm so glad you're safe. We have been out of our minds with worry. If Michael hadn't kept us informed through Sandy I don't know what we would have done." Mrs. Marshall then walked over and greeted Michael. "Thank you so much."

He bent down to hug her and she eagerly went into his arms. "It's good to finally meet you," Michael said. He shook Mr. Marshall's hand and the two exchanged a look of respect.

"I can't thank you enough for taking care of my daughter."

Michael looked over to the older couple and said, "Kayla, I'd like for you to meet my parents, Ivy and Vernon James."

Kayla smiled as she walked over and extended her hand.

"Oh, no, sugar. I want a hug. It's so good to meet you." Ivy James was petite and full of warmth. Her embrace relaxed Kayla. "I'm so sorry you've been through such a mess. We just wanted you to know we are all here for you, baby." Her eyes sparkled with sincerity. Kayla instantly liked her future mother-in-law and sighed in relief.

Mr. James stepped in for a hug. When he released her he said, "You are such a brave young lady. We are so proud to meet you." He then winked at Michael and said, "Son, you sure know how to pick 'em."

Terrance, Alex, and Margaret then greeted Kayla and Michael. "Sis, I tried to tell them not to worry because I knew you'd find a way to get back home safely. You've always been brave and smart." Terrance hugged his sister again and said, "I've missed you so much."

Barb and Trent hugged Kayla and added how happy they were to see her. Kayla had never felt more welcomed. "Where's Clark?" she asked.

Alex said, "We didn't want to excite her, so she's at home with the sitter."

"Come on to the dining room, we cooked dinner." Gail took Michael by the arm.

"Sure, Mrs. Marshall, but before we do, I'd like to ask you and Mr. Marshall something."

Gail smiled as her husband walked over and put

his arm around his wife's shoulder. "Sure, son, what's on your mind?"

"Well, sir, I've been in love with your daughter for some time now and I'd like to ask for her hand in marriage." There was a collective gasp in the room followed by lots of smiles and oohs.

"Michael, I can't imagine giving my daughter to anyone more deserving." He looked at his wife and they kissed. Michael's parents rushed over to Kayla and hugged her at the same time.

"I've always wanted a daughter and now it looks like I'm going to have two," Ivy exclaimed.

"Welcome to the family, Kayla." Mr. James held his future daughter-in-law's hand. Kayla looked over at Barb, who simply smiled and nodded.

They all crowded into the dining room and enjoyed the feast that the women had prepared. The dining room table looked like a smorgasbord at a restaurant, filled with various meats, vegetables, pasta dishes, and breads. After dinner they all settled into the family room for some good conversation. Ivy and Gail selected the music and before long there was dancing and lots of laughter.

The young people found pleasure in watching the older generation dance. Margaret grabbed Terrance and asked him to dance with her, setting the stage for the other young people to get on the floor. Kayla laughed at his shyness as he appeared self-conscious at first and then loosened up. Michael cut in and danced with Margaret.

Near the close of the evening Mr. Marshall and Michael disappeared together for a few minutes. When they returned Mr. Marshall told his wife, "Honey, I think Kayla would be more comfortable spending time with Michael. She's going to go home with him."

Mrs. Marshall smiled and agreed.

The drive home was quiet. Kayla was tired and slept most of the way. Every once in a while she opened her eyes and Michael would glance over at her. She felt loved and safe. As soon as they entered the house, Michael pulled her into his arms and kissed her lips feverishly. "I've wanted to do that all night." He held her close for some time.

She pulled away and looked up at Michael. "We still on for the Bears game next week?"

Michael gathered her in his arms again with a smile that made her shake her head and mumble, "Umm-mmm, mercy." At that moment she realized that regardless of what his and her shortcomings were, their love could overcome them all.

"Yep, we are." Then he gently put his lips to hers, engaging her in a kiss that was deep, lustful, and full of the promise of flawless love.

Dear Readers:

Thank you for purchasing my first novel. I sincerely hope you enjoyed reading it as much as I did writing it. I look forward to bringing you more romance and exciting reading in my next novel, which I am hard at work on. If you'd like to share your comments, or would like to hear more about my next novel, you may contact me at carolynj@nothnbut.net.

Peace and blessings,
Carolyn Neal

ABOUT THE AUTHOR

Carolyn Neal is a native of St. Louis, Missouri. The St. Louis University graduate is living happily with her husband and son just west of St. Louis in St. Peters. She learned very early on how *Flawless* love can be, and has parlayed that experience into her debut novel. Carolyn is currently working on her second novel.